MW01122177

Married

Married

AUGUST STRINDBERG

Translated and with an Introduction by
THOMAS SELTZER

ÆGYPAN PRESS

Special thanks to David Starner, Marc D'Hooghe, Charles Franks,
and the Online Distributed Proofreading Team (which can be found
at http://www.pgdp.net).

Married

A publication of

ÆGYPAN PRESS

www.aegypan.com

Table of Contents

Bibliography

Strindberg's works in English translation: Plays translated by Edwin Bjorkman; *Master Olof*, American Scandinavian Foundation, 1915; *The Dream Play, The Link, The Dance of Death,* New York, Charles Scribner's Sons, 1912; *Swanwhite, Simoon, Debit and Credit, Advent, The Thunderstorm, After the Fire,* the same, 1913; *There Are Crimes and Crimes, Miss Julia, The Stronger, Creditors, Pariah,* the same, 1913; *Bridal Crown, The Spook Sonata, The First Warning, Gustavus Vasa,* the same, 1916. Plays translated by Edith and Warner Oland, Boston Luce & Co., Vol. I (1912), *The Father, Countess Julie, The Stronger, The Outlaw*; Vol. II (1912), *Facing Death, Easter, Pariah, Comrades*; Vol. III (1914), *Swanwhite, Advent, The Storm, Lucky Pehr,* tr. by Velma Swanston Howard, Cincinnati, Stewart & Kidd Co., 1912. *The Red Room,* tr. by Ellie Schleussner, New York, Putnam's, 1913; *Confession of a Fool,* tr. by S. Swift, London, F. Palmer, 1912; *The German Lieutenant and Other Stories,* Chicago, A. C. McClurg & Co., 1915; *In Midsummer Days and Other Tales,* tr. by Ellie Schleussner, London, H. Latimer, 1913; *Motherlove,* tr. by Francis J. Ziegler, Philadelphia, Brown Bros., 2nd ed., 1916, *On the Seaboard,* tr. by Elizabeth Clarke Westergren, Cincinnati, Stewart & Kidd Co., 1913; *The Son of a Servant,* tr. by. Claud Field, introduction by Henry Vacher-Burch, New York, Putnam's, 1913; *The Growth of a Soul,* tr. by Claud Field, London, W. Rider & Co., 1913; *The Inferno,* tr. by Claud Field, New York, Putnam's, 1913; *Legends, Autobiographical Sketches,* London, A. Melrose, 1912; *Zones of the Spirit,* tr. by Claud Field, introduction by Arthur Babillotte, London, G. Allen & Co.

Introduction

These stories originally appeared in two volumes, the first in 1884, the second in 1886. The latter part of the present edition is thus separated from the first part by a lapse of two years.

Strindberg's views were continually undergoing changes. Constancy was never a trait of his. He himself tells us that opinions are but the reflection of a man's experiences, changing as his experiences change. In the two years following the publication of the first volume, Strindberg's experiences were such as to exercise a decisive influence on his views on the woman question and to transmute his early predisposition to woman-hating from a passive tendency to a positive, active force in his character and writing.

Strindberg's art in *Married* is of the propagandist, of the fighter for a cause. He has a lesson to convey and he makes frankly for his goal without attempting to conceal his purpose under the gloss of "pure" art. He chooses the story form in preference to the treatise as a more powerful medium to drive home his ideas. That the result has proved successful is due to the happy admixture in Strindberg of thinker and artist. His artist's sense never permitted him to distort or misrepresent the truth for the sake of proving his theories. In fact, he arrived at his theories not as a scholar through the study of books, but as an artist through the experience of life. When life had impressed upon him what seemed to him a truth, he then applied his intellect to it to bolster up that truth. Hence it is that, however opinionated Strindberg may at times seem, his writings carry that conviction which we receive only when the author reproduces' truths he has obtained first-hand from life. One-sided he may occasionally be in *Married*, especially in the later stories, but rarely unfaithful. His manner is often to throw such a glaring searchlight upon one spot of life that all the rest of it stays in darkness; but the places he does show up are never unimportant or trivial. They are well worth seeing with Strindberg's brilliant illumination thrown upon them.

August Strindberg has left a remarkably rich record of his life in various works, especially in his autobiographical series of novels. He was born in 1849 in Stockholm. His was a sad childhood passed in extreme poverty. He succeeded in entering the University of Upsala in 1867, but was forced for a time on account of lack of means to interrupt his studies. He tried his fortune as schoolmaster, actor, and journalist and made an attempt to study medicine. All the while he was active in a literary way, composing his first plays in 1869. In 1874 he obtained a position in the Royal Library, where he devoted himself to scientific studies, learned Chinese in order to catalogue the Chinese manuscripts, and wrote an erudite monograph which was read at the Academy of Inscriptions in Paris.

His first important literary productions were the drama *Master Olof* (1878) and the novel *The Red Room* (1879). Disheartened by the failure of *Master Olof*, he gave up literature for a long time. When he returned to it, he displayed an amazing productivity. Work followed work in quick succession — novels, short stories, dramas, histories, historical studies, and essays. *The Swedish People* is said to be the most popular book in Sweden next to the Bible. The mere enumeration of his writings would occupy more than two pages. His versatility led him to make researches in physics and chemistry and natural science and to write on those subjects.

Through works like *The Red Room, Married,* and the dramas *The Father* and *Miss Julia,* Strindberg attached himself to the naturalistic school of literature. Another period of literary inactivity followed, during which he passed through a mental crisis akin to insanity. When he returned to the writing of novels and dramas he was no longer a naturalist, but a symbolist and mystic. Among the plays he composed in this style are *To Damascus, The Dream Play,* and *The Great Highway.*

Strindberg married three times, divorced his first two wives, but separated amicably from the third. He died in 1913. The vast demonstration at his funeral, attended by the laboring classes as well as by the "upper" classes, proved that, in spite of the antagonisms he had aroused, Sweden unanimously awarded him the highest place in her literature.

THOMAS SELTZER

Asra

*H*e had just completed his thirteenth year when his mother died. He felt that he had lost a real friend, for during the twelve months of her illness he had come to know her personally, as it were, and established a relationship between them which is rare between parents and children. He was a clever boy and had developed early; he had read a great many books besides his schoolbooks, for his father, a professor of botany at the Academy of Science, possessed a very good library. His mother, on the other hand, was not a well-educated woman; she had merely been head housekeeper and children's nurse in her husband's house. Numerous births and countless vigils (she had not slept through a single night for the last sixteen years), had exhausted her strength, and when she became bedridden, at the age of thirty-nine, and was no longer able to look after her house, she made the acquaintance of her second son; her eldest boy was at a military school and only at home during the week ends. Now that her part as mother of the family was played to the end and nothing remained of her but a poor invalid, the old-fashioned relationship of strict discipline, that barrier between parents and children, was superseded. The thirteen-year-old son was almost constantly at her bedside, reading to her whenever he was not at school or doing home lessons. She had many questions to ask and he had a great deal to explain, and therefore all those distinguishing marks erected by age and position vanished, one after the other: if there was a superior at all, it was the son. But the mother, too, had much to teach, for she had learnt her lessons in the school of life; and so they were alternately teacher and pupil. They discussed all subjects. With the tact of a mother and the modesty of the other sex she told her son all he ought to know of the mystery of life. He was still innocent, but he had heard many things discussed by the boys at school which had shocked and disgusted him. The mother explained to him all she could explain; warned him of the greatest danger to a young man, and exacted a promise from him never to visit a house of ill-fame, not even out of curiosity, because, as she pointed out, in such a case no man could ever trust himself. And she implored him to live a temperate life, and turn to God in prayer whenever temptation assaulted him.

His father was entirely devoted to science, which was a sealed book to his wife. When the mother was already on the point of death, he made a discovery which he hoped would make his name immortal in the scientific world. He discovered, on a rubbish heap, outside the gates of Stockholm, a new kind of goose-foot with curved hairs on the usually straight-haired calyx. He was in communication with the Berlin Academy of Sciences, and the latter was even now considering the advisability of including the new variety in the "Flora Germanica"; he was daily expecting to hear whether or not the Academy had decided to immortalize his name by calling the plant Chenopodium Wennerstroemianium. At his wife's deathbed he was absentminded, almost unkind, for he had just received an answer in the affirmative, and he fretted because neither he nor his wife could enjoy the great news. She thought only of heaven and her children. He could not help realizing that to talk to her now of a calyx with curved hairs would be the height of absurdity; but, he justified himself, it was not so much a question of a calyx with straight or curved hairs, as of a scientific discovery; and, more than that, it was a question of his future and the future of his children, for their father's distinction meant bread for them.

When his wife died on the following evening, he cried bitterly; he had not shed a tear for many years. He was tortured by remorse, remembered even the tiniest wrong he had ever done her, for he had been, on the whole, an exemplary husband; his indifference, his absentmindedness of the previous day, filled him with shame and regret, and in a moment of blankness he realized all the pettishness and selfishness of his science which, he had imagined, was benefiting mankind. But these emotions were short-lived; if you open a door with a spring behind it, it will close again immediately. On the following morning, after he had drawn up an announcement of her death for the papers, he wrote a letter of thanks to the Berlin Academy of Sciences. After that he resumed his work.

When he came home to dinner, he longed for his wife, so that he might tell her of his success, for she had always been his truest friend, the only human being who had never been jealous or envious. Now he missed this loyal companion on whose approval he could count as a matter of course; never once had she contradicted him, for since he never told her more than the practical result of his researches, there was no room for argument. For a moment the thought occurred to him that he might make friends with his son; but they knew each other too little;

their relationship was that of officer and private soldier. His superior rank did not permit him to make advances; moreover, he regarded the boy with suspicion, because the latter possessed a keener intellect and had read a number of new books which were unknown to him; occasionally it even happened that the father, the professor, plainly revealed his ignorance to his son, the school-boy. In such cases the father was either compelled to dismiss the argument, with a few contemptuous remarks to "these new follies," or peremptorily order the school-boy to attend to his lessons. Once or twice, in self-defense, the son had produced one or other of his school-books; the professor had lost his temper and wished the new school-books to hell.

And so it came about that the father devoted himself to his collections of dried plants and the son went his own way.

They lived in a quiet street to the left of the Observatory, in a small, one-storey house, built of bricks, and surrounded by a large garden; the garden was once the property of the Horticultural Society, and had come into the professor's possession by inheritance. But since he studied descriptive botany, and took no interest in the much more interesting subjects of the physiology and morphology of plants, a science which was as good as unknown in his youth, he was practically a stranger to living nature. He allowed the garden with its many splendors to become a wilderness, and finally let it to a gardener on condition that he and his children should be allowed certain privileges. The son used the garden as a park and enjoyed its beauty as he found it, without taking the trouble to try and understand it scientifically.

One might compare the boy's character to an ill-proportioned compensation pendulum; it contained too much of the soft metal of the mother, not enough of the hard metal of the father. Friction and irregular oscillations were the natural consequences. Now he was full of sentiment, now hard and skeptical. His mother's death affected him beyond words. He mourned her deeply, and she always lived in his memory as the personification of all that was good and great and beautiful.

He wasted the summer following her death in brooding and novel-reading. Grief, and to no small extent idleness, had shaken his whole nervous system and quickened his imagination. His tears had been like warm April showers falling on fruit trees, wakening them to a precocious burgeoning: but alas! only too often the blossoms are doomed to wither and perish in a frosty May night, before the fruit has had time to set.

He was fifteen years old and had therefore arrived at the age when civilized man attains to manhood and is ripe to give life to a new generation, but is prevented from doing so by his inability to maintain a family. Consequently he was about to begin the ten years' martyrdom which a young man is called upon to endure in the struggle against an overwhelming force of nature, before he is in a position to fulfill her laws.

*I*t is a warm afternoon about Whitsuntide. The apple trees are gorgeous in their white splendor which nature has showered all over them with a profuse hand. The breeze shakes the crowns and fills the air with pollen; a part of it fulfils its destination and creates new life, a part sinks to the ground and dies. What is a handful of pollen more or less in the inexhaustible store-house of nature! The fertilized blossom casts off its delicate petals which flutter to the ground and wither; they decay in the rain and are ground to dust, to rise again through the sap and re-appear as blossoms, and this time, perhaps, to become fruit. But now the struggle begins: those which a kind fate has placed on the sunny side, thrive and prosper; the seed bud swells, and if no frost intervenes, the fruit, in due time, will set. But those which look towards the North, the poor things which grow in the shadow of the others and never see the sun, are predestined to fade and fall off; the gardener rakes them together and carts them to the pig-sty.

Behold the apple tree now, its branches laden with half-ripe fruit, little, round, golden apples with rosy cheeks. A fresh struggle begins: if all remain alive, the branches will not be able to bear their weight, the tree will perish. A gale shakes the branches. It requires firm stems to hold on. Woe to the weaklings! they are condemned to destruction.

A fresh danger! The apple-weevil appears upon the scene. It, too, has to maintain life and to fulfill a duty towards its progeny. The grub eats its way through the fruit to the stem and the apple falls to the ground. But the dainty beetle chooses the strongest and soundest for its brood, otherwise too many of the strong ones would be allowed to live, and competition would become overkeen.

The hour of twilight, the gathering dusk, arouses the passionate instincts of the beast-world. The night-crow crouches on the newly-dug flower-bed to lure its mate. Which of the eager males shall carry the prize? Let them decide the question!

The cat, sleek and warm, fresh from her evening milk, steals away from her corner by the hearth and picks her way carefully among daffodils and lilies, afraid lest the dew make her coat damp and ragged before her lover joins her. She sniffs at the young lavender and calls. Her call is answered by the black tom-cat which appears, broad-backed like a marten, on the neighbor's fence; but the gardener's tortoise-shell approaches from the cow-shed and the fight begins. Handfuls of the rich, black soil are flying about in all directions, and the newly-planted radishes and spinach plants are roughly awakened from their quiet sleep and dreams of the future. The stronger of the two remains in possession of the field, and the female awaits complacently the frenetic embraces of the victor. The vanquished flies to engage in a new struggle in which, perhaps, victory will smile on him.

Nature smiles, content, for she knows of no other sin than the sin against her law; she is on the side of the strong for her desire is for strong children, even though she should have to kill the "eternal ego" of the insignificant individual. And there is no prudery, no hesitation, no fear of consequences, for nature has plenty of food for all her children — except mankind.

*A*fter supper he went for a walk in the garden while his father sat down at his bedroom window to smoke a pipe and read the evening paper. He strolled along the paths, reveling in the delicious odors which a plant only exhales when it is in full bloom, and which is the finest and strongest extract of etheric oils, containing in a condensed form the full strength of the individual, destined to become the representative of the species. He listened to the nuptial song of the insects above the lime trees, which rings in our ears like a funeral dirge: he heard the purring call of the night-crow; the ardent mewing of the cat, which sounds as if death, and not life, were wooing; the humming note of the dung-beetle, the fluttering of the large moths, the thin peeping of the bats.

He stopped before a bed of narcissus, gathered one of the white, starry flowers, and inhaled its perfume until he felt the blood hammering in his temples. He had never examined this flower minutely. But during the last term they had read Ovid's story of Narcissus. He had not discovered a deeper meaning in the legend. What did it mean, this story of a youth who, from unrequited love, turned his ardor upon himself and was consumed by the flame when he fell in love with his own likeness seen in a well? As he stood, examining the white, cup-shaped petals, pale as the cheeks of an invalid with fine red lines such as one may see in the faces of consumptives when a pitiless cough forces the blood into the extremest and tiniest blood-vessels, he thought of a school-fellow, a young aristocrat, who was a midshipman now; he looked like that.

When he had inhaled the scent of the flower for some time, the strong odor of cloves disappeared and left but a disagreeable, soapy smell which made him feel sick.

He sauntered on to where the path turned to the right and finally lost itself in an avenue planted on both sides with elm trees whose branches had grown together and formed an arch overhead. In the semi-darkness, far down the perspective, he could see a large green swing, suspended by ropes, slowly moving backwards and forwards. A girl stood on the back board, gently swinging herself by bending her knees and throwing her body forward, while she clung, with arms raised high above her head, to the ropes at her side. He recognized the gardener's daughter, a girl who had been confirmed last Easter and had just begun to wear long skirts. Tonight, however, she was dressed in one of her old dresses which barely reached to her ankles.

The sight of the young man embarrassed her, for she remembered the shortness of her skirt, but she nevertheless remained on the swing. He advanced and looked at her.

"Go away, Mr. Theodore," said the girl, giving the swing a vigorous push.

"Why should I?" answered the youth, who felt the draft of her fluttering skirts on his throbbing temples.

"Because I want you to," said the girl.

"Let me come up, too, and I'll swing you, Gussie," pleaded Theodore, springing on to the board.

Now he was standing on the swing, facing her. And when they rose into the air, he felt her skirts flapping against his legs, and when they descended, he bent over her and looked into her eyes which were brilliant with fear and enjoyment. Her thin cotton blouse fitted tightly and showed every line of her young figure; her smiling lips were half-open, displaying two rows of sound white teeth, which looked as if they would like to bite or kiss him.

Higher and higher rose the swing, until it struck the topmost branches of the maple. The girl screamed and fell forward, into his arms; he was pushed over, on to the seat. The trembling of the soft warm body which nestled closely in his arms, sent an electric shock through his whole nervous system; a black veil descended before his eyes and he would have let her go if her left shoulder had not been tightly pressed against his right arm.

The speed of the swing slackened. She rose and sat on the seat facing him. And thus they remained with downcast eyes, not daring to look one another in the face.

When the swing stopped, the girl slipped off the seat and ran away as if she were answering a call. Theodore was left alone. He felt the blood surging in his veins. It seemed to him that his strength was redoubled. But he could not grasp what had happened. He vaguely conceived himself as an electrophor whose positive electricity, in discharging, had combined with the negative. It had happened during a quite ordinary, to all appearances chaste, contact with a young woman. He had never felt the same emotion in wrestling, for instance, with his school-fellows in the play-ground. He had come into contact with the opposite polarity of the female sex and now he knew what it meant to be a man. For he was a man, not a precocious boy, kicking over the traces; he was a strong, hardy, healthy youth.

As he strolled along, up and down the garden paths, new thoughts formed in his brain. Life looked at him with graver eyes, he felt conscious of a sense of duty. But he was only fifteen years old. He was not yet confirmed and many years would have to elapse before he would be considered an independent member of the community, before he would be able to earn a living for himself, let alone maintain a wife and family. He took life seriously, the thought of light adventures never occurred to him. Women were to him something sacred, his opposite pole, the supplement and completion of himself. He was mature now, bodily and mentally, fit to enter the arena of life and fight his way. What prevented him from doing so? His education, which had taught him nothing useful; his social position, which stood between him and a trade he might have learned. The Church, which had not yet received his vow of loyalty to her priests; the State, which was still waiting for his oath of allegiance to Bernadotte and Nassau; the School, which had not yet trained him sufficiently to consider him ripe for the University; the secret alliance of the upper against the lower classes. A whole mountain of follies lay on him and his young strength. Now that he knew himself to be a man, the whole system of education seemed to him an institution for the mutilation of body and soul. They must both be mutilated before he could be allowed to enter the harem of the world, where manhood is considered a danger; he could find no other excuse for it. And thus he sank back into his former state of immaturity. He compared himself to a celery plant, tied up and put under a flower-pot so as to make it as white and soft as possible, unable to put forth green leaves in the sunshine, flower, and bear seed.

Wrapped in these thoughts he remained in the garden until the clock on the nearest church tower struck ten. Then he turned towards the house, for it was bedtime. But the front door was locked. The house-maid, a petticoat thrown over her nightgown, let him in. A glimpse of her bare shoulders roused him from his sentimental reveries; he tried to put his arm round her and kiss her, for at the moment he was conscious of nothing but her sex. But the maid had already disappeared, shutting the door with a bang. Overwhelmed with shame he opened his window, cooled his head in a basin of cold water and lighted his lamp.

When he had got into bed, he took up a volume of Arndt's *Spiritual Voices of the Morning*, a book which had belonged to his mother; he read a chapter of it every evening to be on the safe side, for in the morning his time was short. The book reminded him of the promise of chastity given to his mother on her deathbed, and he felt a twinge of conscience. A fly which had singed its wings on his lamp, and was now buzzing round the little table by his bedside, turned his thoughts into another channel; he closed the book and lit a cigarette. He heard his father take off his boots in the room below, knock out his pipe against the stove, pour out a glass of water and get ready to go to bed. He thought how lonely he must be since he had become a widower. In days gone by he had often heard the subdued voices of his parents through the thin partition, in intimate conversation on matters on which they always agreed; but now no voice was audible, nothing but the dead sounds which a man makes in waiting upon himself, sounds which one must put side by side, like the figures in a rebus, before one can understand their meaning.

He finished his cigarette, blew out the lamp and said the Lord's Prayer in an undertone, but he got no farther than the fifth petition. Then he fell asleep.

He awoke from a dream in the middle of the night. He had dreamt that he held the gardener's daughter in his arms. He could not remember the circumstances, for he was quite dazed, and fell asleep again directly.

On the following morning he was depressed and had a headache. He brooded over the future which loomed before him threateningly and filled him with dread. He realized with a pang how quickly the summer was passing, for the end of the summer meant the degradation of school-life. Every thought of his own would be stifled by the thoughts of others; there was no advantage in being able to think independently; it required a fixed number of years before one could reach one's goal. It was like a journey on a good's train; the engine was bound to remain for a certain time in the stations, and when the pressure of the steam became too strong, from want of consumption of energy, a waste-pipe had to be opened. The Board had drawn up the time-table and the train was not permitted to arrive at the stations before its appointed time. That was the principal thing which mattered.

The father noticed the boy's pallor, but he put it down to grief over his mother's death.

Autumn came and with it the return to school. Theodore, by dint of much novel-reading during the summer, and coming in this way, as it were, in constant contact with grown-up people and their problems and struggles, had come to look upon himself as a grown-up member of society. Now the masters treated him with familiarity, the boys took liberties which compelled him to repay them in kind. And this educational institution, which was to ennoble him and make him fit to take his place in the community, what did it teach him? How did it ennoble him? The compendiums, one and all, were written under the control of the upper classes, for the sole purpose of forcing the lower classes to look up to their betters. The schoolmasters frequently reproached their pupils with ingratitude and impressed on them their utter inability to realize, even faintly, the advantage they enjoyed in receiving an education which so many of their poorer fellow-creatures would always lack. No, indeed, the boys were not sophisticated enough to see through the gigantic fraud and its advantages.

But did they ever find true joy, real pleasure in the subjects of their studies for their own sakes? Never! Therefore the teachers had to appeal incessantly to the lower passions of their pupils, to ambition, self-interest, material advantages.

What a miserable make-believe school was! Not one of the boys believed that he would reap any benefit from repeating the names and dates of hated kings in their proper sequence, from learning dead languages, proving axioms, defining "a matter of course," and counting the anthers of plants and the joints on the hindlegs of insects, to knowing the end no more about them than their Latin names. How many long hours were wasted in the vain attempt to divide an angle into three equal sections, a thing which can be done so easily in a minute in an *unscientific* (that is to say practical) way by using a graduator.

How they scorned everything practical! His sisters, who were taught French from Ollendorf's grammar, were able to speak the language after two years' study; but the college boys could not say a single sentence after six. Ollendorf was a name which they pronounced with pity and contempt. It was the essence of all that was stupid.

But when his sister asked for an explanation and enquired whether the purpose of spoken language was not the expression of human thought, the young sophist replied with a phrase picked up from one of the masters who in his turn had borrowed it from Talleyrand. Language was invented to hide one's thoughts. This, of course, was beyond the horizon of a young girl (how well men know how to hide their shortcomings), but henceforth she believed her brother to be tremendously learned, and stopped arguing with him.

And was there not even a worse stumbling-block in aesthetics, delusive and deceptive, casting a veil of borrowed splendor and sham beauty over everything? They sang of "The Knights' Vigil of Light." What knights' vigil? With patents of nobility and students' certificates; false testimonials, as they might have told themselves. Of light? That was to say of the upper classes who had the greatest interest in keeping the lower classes in darkness, a task in which they were ably assisted by church and school. "And onward, onward, on the path of light!"

Things were always called by the wrong name. And if it so happened that a light-bearer arose from the lower classes, everybody was ready and prepared to extinguish his torch. Oh! youthful, healthy host of fighters! How healthy they were, all these young men, enervated by idleness, unsatisfied desires and ambitions, who scorned every man who had not the means to pay for a University education! What splendid liars they were, the poets of the upper classes! Were they the deceivers or the deceived?

What was the usual subject of the young men's conversation? Their studies? Never! Once in a way, perhaps, they would talk of certificates. No, their conversation was of things obscene; of appointments with women; of billiards and drink; of certain diseases which they had heard discussed by their elder brothers. They lounged about in the afternoon and "held the reviews," and the best informed of them knew the name of the officer and could tell the others where his mistress lived.

Once two members of the "Knights' Vigil of Light," had dined in the company of two women on the terrace of a high-class restaurant in the Zoological Gardens. For this offence they were expelled from school. They were punished for their naïveté, not because their conduct was considered vicious, for a year after they passed their examinations and went to the University, gaining in this way a whole year; and when they had completed their studies at Upsala, they were attached to the Embassy in one of the capitals of Europe, to represent the United Kingdoms of Sweden and Norway.

In these surroundings Theodore spent the best part of his youth. He had seen through the fraud, but was compelled to acquiesce! Again and again he asked himself the question: What can I do? There was no answer. And so he became an accessory and learned to hold his tongue.

His confirmation appeared to him to be very much on a level with his school experience. A young minister, an ardent pietist, was to teach him in four months Luther's Catechism, regardless of the fact that he was well versed in theology, exegesis and dogmatics, besides having read the New Testament in Greek. Nevertheless the strict pietism, which demanded absolute truth in thought and action, could not fail to make a great impression on him.

When the catechumens were assembled for the first time, Theodore found himself quite unexpectedly surrounded by a totally different class of boys to whom he had been used at school. When he entered the assembly-room he was met by the stare of something like a hundred inimical eyes. There were tobacco binders, chimney sweeps, apprentices of all trades. They were on bad terms and freely abused one another, but this enmity between the different trades was only superficial; however much they quarreled, they yet held together. He seemed to breathe a strangely stifling atmosphere; the hatred with which they greeted him was not unmixed with contempt, the reverse of a certain respect or envy. He looked in vain for a friend, for a companion, like-minded, dressed as he was. There was not a single one. The parish was poor, the rich people sent their children to the German church which was then the fashion. It was in the company of the children of the people, the lower classes, that he was to approach the altar, as their equal. He asked himself what it was that separated him from these boys? Were they not, bodily, endowed with the same gifts as he? No doubt, for every one of them earned his living, and some of them helped to keep their parents. Were they less gifted, mentally? He did not think so, for their remarks gave evidence of keen powers of observation; he would have laughed at many of their witty remarks if he had not been conscious of his superior caste. There was no definite line of demarcation between him and the fools who were his school-fellows. But there was a line here Was it the shabby clothes, the plain faces, the coarse hands, which formed the barrier? Partly, he thought. Their plainness, especially, repulsed him. But were they worse than others because they were plain?

He was carrying a foil, as he had a fencing lesson later on. He put it in a corner of the room, hoping that it would escape attention. But it had been seen already. Nobody knew what kind of a thing it really was, but everybody recognized it as a weapon of some sort. Some of the boldest busied themselves about the corner, so as to have a look at it. They fingered the covering of the handle, scratched the guard with their nails, bent the blade, handled the small leather ball. They were like hares sniffing at a gun which had been lost in the wood. They did not understand its use, but they knew it for something inimical, something with a hidden meaning. Presently a belt-maker's apprentice, whose brother was in the Life Guards, joined the inquisitive throng and at once decided the question: "Can't you see that it is a sword, you fools?" he shouted, with a look at Theodore. It was a respectful look, but a look which also hinted at a secret understanding between them, which, correctly interpreted, meant: You and I understand these things! But a young rope-maker, who had once been a trumpeter in a military band, considered this giving of a verdict without consulting him a personal slight and declared that he "would be hanged if it wasn't a rapier!" The consequence was a fight which transformed the place into a bear-garden, dense with dust and re-echoing with screams and yells.

The door opened and the minister stood on the threshold. He was a pale young man, very thin, with watery blue eyes and a face disfigured by a rash. He shouted at the boys. The wild beasts ceased fighting. He began talking of the precious blood of Christ and the power of the Evil One over the human heart. After a little while he succeeded in inducing the hundred boys to sit down on the forms and chairs. But now he was quite out of breath and the atmosphere was thick with dust. He glanced at the window and said in a faint voice: "Open the sash!" This request re-awakened the only half-subdued passions. Twenty-five boys made a rush for the window and tried to seize the window cord.

"Go to your places at once!" screamed the minister, stretching out his hand for his cane.

There was a momentary silence during which the minister tried to think of a way of having the sash raised without a fight.

"You," he said at last to a timid little fellow, "go and open the window!"

The small boy went to the window and tried to disentangle the window cord. The others looked on in breathless silence, when suddenly a big lad, in sailor's clothes, who had just come home on the brig *Carl Johan*, lost patience.

"The devil take me if I don't show you what a lad can do," he shouted, throwing off his coat and jumping on the windowsill; there was a flash from his cutlass and the rope was cut.

"Cable's cut!" he laughed, as the minister with a hysterical cry, literally drove him to his seat.

"The rope was so entangled that there was nothing for it but to cut it," he assured him, as he sat down.

The minister was furious. He had come from a small town in the provinces and had never conceived the possibility of so much sin, so much wickedness and immorality. He had never come into contact with lads so far advanced on the road to damnation. And he talked at great length of the precious blood of Christ.

Not one of them understood what he said, for they did not realize that they had fallen, since they had never bee different. The boys received his words with coldness and indifference.

The minister rambled on and spoke of Christ's precious wounds, but not one of them took his words to heart, for not one of them was conscious of having wounded Christ. He changed the subject and spoke of the devil, but that was a topic so familiar to them that it made no impression. At last he hit on the right thing. He began to talk of their confirmation which was to take place in the coming spring. He reminded them of their parents, anxious that their children should play a part in the life of the community; when he went on to speak of employers who refused to employ lads who had not been confirmed, his listeners became deeply interested at once, and every one of them understood the great importance of the coming ceremony. Now he was sincere, and the young minds grasped what he was talking about; the noisiest among them became quiet.

The registration began. What a number of marriage certificates were missing! How could the children come to Christ when their parents had not been legally married? How could they approach the altar when their fathers had been in prison? Oh! what sinners they were!

Theodore was deeply moved by the exhibition of so much shame and disgrace. He longed to tear his thoughts away from the subject, but was unable to do so. Now it was his turn to hand in his certificates and the minister read out: son: Theodore, born on such and such a date; parents: professor and knight . . . a faint smile flickered like a feeble sunbeam over his face, he gave him a friendly nod and asked: "And how is your dear father?" But when he saw that the mother was dead (a fact of which he was perfectly well aware) his face clouded over. "She was a child of God," he said, as if he were talking to himself, in a gushing, sympathetic, whining voice, but the remark conveyed at the same time a certain reproach against the "dear father," who was only a professor and knight. After that Theodore could go.

When he left the assembly-room he felt that he had gone through an almost impossible experience. Were all those lads really depraved because they used oaths and coarse language, as his companions, his father, his uncle, and all the upper classes did at times? What did the minister mean when he talked of immorality? They were more savage than the spoilt children of the wealthy, but that was because they were more fully alive. It was unfair to blame them for missing marriage certificates. True, his father had never committed a theft, but there was no necessity for a man to steal if he had an income of six thousand crowns and could please himself. The act would be absurd or abnormal in such a case.

Theodore went back to school realizing what it meant "to have received an education"; here nobody was badgered for small faults. As little notice as possible was taken of one's own or one's parent's weaknesses, one was among equals and understood one another.

After school one "held the reviews," sneaked into a café and drank a liqueur, and finally went to the fencing-room. He looked at the young officers who treated him as their equal, observed all those young bloods with their supple limbs, pleasant manners and smiling faces, every one of them certain that a good dinner was awaiting him at home, and became conscious of the existence of two worlds: an upper and an underworld. He remembered the gloomy assembly-room and the wretched assembly he had just left with a pang; all their wounds and hidden defects were mercilessly exposed and examined through a magnifying- glass, so that the lower classes might acquire that true humility failing which the upper classes cannot enjoy their amiable weaknesses in peace. And for the first time something jarring had come into this life.

However much Theodore was tossed about between his natural yearning for the only half-realized temptations of the world, and his newly formed desire to turn his back on this world and his mind heavenwards, he did not break the promise given to his mother. The religious teaching which he and the other catechumens received from the minister in the church, did not fail to impress him deeply. He was often gloomy and wrapped in thought and felt that life was not what it ought to be. He had a dim notion that once upon a time a terrible crime had been committed, which it was now everybody's business to hide by practicing countless deceptions; he compared himself to a fly caught in a spider's web: the more it struggled to regain its freedom, the more it entangled itself, until at last it died miserably, strangled by the cruel threads.

One evening — the minister scorned no trick likely to produce an effect on his hard-headed pupils — they were having a lesson in the choir. It was in January. Two gas jets lighted up the choir, illuminating and distorting the marble figures on the altar. The whole of the large church with its two barrel-vaults, which crossed one another, lay in semi-darkness. In the background the shining organ pipes faintly reflected the gas flames; above it the angels blowing their trumpets to summon the sleepers before the judgment seat of their maker, looked merely like sinister, threatening human figures above life size; the cloisters were lost in complete darkness.

The minister had explained the seventh commandment. He had spoken of immorality between married and unmarried people. He could not explain to his pupils what immorality between husband and wife meant, although he was a married man himself; but on the subject of immorality in all its other aspects he was well-informed. He went on to the subject of self-abuse. As he pronounced the word a rustling sound passed through the rows of young men; they stared at him, with white cheeks and hollow eyes, as if a phantom had appeared in their midst. As long as he kept to the tortures of hell fire, they remained fairly indifferent, but when he took up a book and read to them accounts of youths who had died at the age of twenty-five of consumption of the spine, they collapsed in their seats, and felt as if the floor were giving way beneath them! He told them the story of a young boy who was committed to an asylum at the age of twelve, and died at the age of fourteen, having found peace in the faith of his Redeemer. They saw before their shrinking eyes a hundred corpses, washed and shrouded. "There is but one remedy against this evil," went on the minister, "the precious wounds of Christ." But how this remedy was to be used against sexual precocity, he did not tell them. He admonished them not to go to dances, to shun theaters and gaming-houses, and above all things, to avoid women; that is to say to act in exact contradiction to their inclinations. That this vice contradicts and utterly confounds he pronouncement of the community that a man is not mature until he is twenty-one, was passed over in silence. Whether it could be prevented by early marriages (supposing a means of providing food for all instead of banquets for a few could be found) remained an open question. The final issue was that one should throw oneself into the arms of Christ, that is to say, go to church, and leave the care of temporal things to the upper classes.

After this admonishment the minister requested the first five on the first form to stay behind. He wished to speak to them in private. The first five looked as if they had been sentenced to death. Their chests contracted; they breathed with difficulty, and a careful observer might have noticed that their hair had risen an inch at the roots and lay over their skulls in damp strands like the hair of a corpse. Their eyes stared from their blanched sockets like two round glass bullets set in leather, motionless, not knowing whether to face the question with a bold front, or hide behind an impudent lie.

After the prayer the hymn of Christ's wounds was sung; tonight it sounded like the singing of consumptives; every now and then it died away altogether, or was interrupted by a dry cough, like the cough of a man who is dying of thirst. Then they began to file out. One of the five attempted to steal away, but the minister called him back.

It was a terrible moment. Theodore who sat on the first form was one of the five. He felt sick at heart. Not because he was guilty of the offence indicated, but because in his heart he considered it an insult to a man thus to have to lay bare the most secret places of his soul.

The other four sat down, as far from each other as they could. The belt-maker's apprentice, who was one of them, tried to make a joke, but the words refused to come. They saw themselves confronted by the police-court, the prison, the hospital and, in the background, the asylum. They did not know what was going to happen, but they felt instinctively that a species of scourging awaited them. Their only comfort in their distressing situation was the fact that *he*, Mr. Theodore, was one of them. It was not clear to them why that fact should be a comfort, but they knew intuitively that no evil would happen to the son of a professor.

"Come along, Wennerstroem," said the minister, after he had lighted the gas in the vestry.

Wennerstroem went and the door closed behind him. The four remained seated on their forms, vainly trying to discover a comfortable position for their limbs.

After a while Wennerstroem returned, with red eyes, trembling with excitement; he immediately went down the corridor and out into the night.

When he stood in the churchyard which lay silent under a heavy cover of snow, he recapitulated all that had happened in the vestry. The minister had asked him whether he had sinned? No, he had not. Did he have dreams? Yes! He was told that dreams were equally sinful, because they proved that the heart was wicked, and God looked at the heart. "He trieth the heart and reins, and on the last day he will judge every one of us for every sinful thought, and dreams are thoughts. Christ has said: Give me your heart, my son! Go to Him! Pray, pray, pray! Whatsoever is chaste, whatsoever is pure, whatsoever is lovely — that is He. The alpha and the omega, life and happiness. Chasten the flesh and be strong in prayer. Go in the name of the Lord and sin no more!"

He felt indignant, but he was also crushed. In vain did he struggle to throw off his depression, he had not been taught sufficient common-sense at school to use it as a weapon against this Jesuitical sophistry. It was true, his knowledge of psychology enabled him to modify the statement that dreams are thoughts; dreams are fancies, he mused, creations of the imagination; but God has no regard for words! Logic taught him that there was something unnatural in his premature desires. He could not marry at the age of sixteen, since he was unable to support a wife; but why he was unable to support a wife, although he felt himself to be a man, was a problem which he could not solve. However anxious he might be to get married, the laws of society which are made by the upper classes and protected by bayonets, would prevent him. Consequently nature must have been sinned against in some way, for a man was mature long before he was able to earn a living. It must be degeneracy. His imagination must be degenerate; it was for him to purify it by prayer and sacrifice.

When he arrived home, he found his father and sisters at supper. He was ashamed to sit down with them, for he felt degraded. His father asked him, as usual, whether the date of the confirmation had been fixed. Theodore did not know. He touched no food, pretending that he was not well; the truth was that he did not dare to eat any supper. He went into his bedroom and read an essay by Schartau which the minister had lent him. The subject was the vanity of reason. And here, just here, where all his hopes of arriving at a clear understanding were centered, the light failed. Reason which he had dared to hope would some day guide him out of the darkness into the light, reason, too, was sin; the greatest of all sins, for it questioned God's very existence, tried to understand what was not meant to be understood. Why *it* was not meant to be understood, was not explained; probably it was because if *it* had been understood the fraud would have been discovered.

He rebelled no longer, but surrendered himself. Before going to bed he read two *Morning Voices* from Arndt, recited the Creed, the Lord's Prayer and the Blessing. He felt very hungry; a fact which he realized with a certain spiteful pleasure, for it seemed to him that his enemy was suffering.

With these thoughts he fell asleep. He awoke in the middle of the night. He had dreamt of a champagne supper in the company of a girl. And the whole terrible evening arose fresh in his memory.

He leapt out of bed with a bound, threw his sheets and blankets on the floor and lay down to sleep on the bare mattress, covering himself with nothing but a thin coverlet. He was cold and hungry, but he must subdue the devil. Again he repeated the Lord's Prayer, with additions of his own. By and by his thoughts grew confused, the strained expression of his features relaxed, a smile softened the expression of his mouth; lovely figures appeared before him, serene and smiling, he heard subdued voices, half-stifled laughter, a few bars from a waltz, saw sparkling glasses and frank and merry faces with candid eyes, which met his own unabashed; suddenly a curtain was parted in the middle; a charming little face peeped through the red silk draperies, with smiling lips and dancing eyes; the slender throat is bare, the beautiful sloping shoulders look as if they had been modeled by a caressing hand; she holds out her arms and he draws her to his thumping heart.

The clock was striking three. Again he had been worsted in the fight.

Determined to win, he picked up the mattress and threw it out of the bed. Then he knelt on the cold floor and fervently prayed to God for strength, for he felt that he was indeed wrestling with the devil. When he had finished his prayer he lay down on the bare frame, and with a feeling of satisfaction felt the ropes and belting cutting into his arms and shins.

He awoke in the morning in a high fever.

He was laid up for six weeks. When he arose from his bed of sickness, he felt better than he had ever felt before. The rest, the good food and the medicine had increased his strength, and the struggle was now twice as hard. But he continued to struggle.

His confirmation took place in the spring. The moving scene in which the lower classes promise on oath never to interfere with these things which the upper classes consider their privilege, made a lasting impression on him. It didn't trouble him that the minister offered him wine bought from the wine-merchant Högstedt at sixty-five öre the pint, and wafers from Lettstroem, the baker, at one crown a pound, as the flesh and blood of the great agitator Jesus of Nazareth, who was done to death nineteen hundred years ago. He didn't think about it, for one didn't think in those days, one had emotions.

A year after his confirmation he passed his final examination. The smart little college cap was a source of great pleasure to him; without being actually conscious of it, he felt that he, as a member of the upper classes, had received a charter. They were not a little proud of their knowledge, too, these young men, for the masters had pronounced them "mature." The conceited youths! If at least they had mastered all the nonsense of which they boasted! If anybody had listened to their conversation at the banquet given in their honor, it would have been a revelation to him. They declared openly that they had not acquired five percent of the knowledge which ought to have been in their possession; they assured everybody who had ears to listen that it was a miracle that they had passed; the uninitiated would not have believed a word of it. And some of the young masters, now that the barrier between pupil and teacher was removed, and simulation was no longer necessary, swore solemnly, with half-intoxicated gestures, that there was not a single master in the whole school who would not have been plucked. A sober person could not help drawing the conclusion that the examination was like a line which could be drawn at will between upper and lower classes; and then he saw in the miracle nothing but a gigantic fraud.

It was one of the masters who, sipping a glass of punch, maintained that only an idiot could imagine that a human brain could remember at the same time: the three thousand dates mentioned in history; the names of the five thousand towns situated in all parts of the world; the names of six hundred plants and seven hundred animals; the bones in the human body, the stones which form the crust of the earth, all theological disputes, one thousand French words, one thousand English, one thousand German, one thousand Latin, one thousand Greek, half a million rules and exceptions to the rules: five hundred mathematical, physical, geometrical, chemical formulas. He was willing to prove that in order to be capable of such a feat the brain would have to be as large as the cupola of the Observatory at Upsala. Humboldt, he went on to say, finally forgot his tables, and the professor of astronomy at Lund had been unable to divide two whole numbers of six figures each. The newly-fledged under-graduates imagined that they knew six languages, and yet they knew no more than five thousand words at most of the twenty thousand which composed their mother tongue. And hadn't he seen how they cheated? Oh! he knew all their tricks! He had seen the dates written on their finger nails; he had watched them consulting books under cover of their desks, he had heard them whispering to one another! But, he concluded, what is one to do? Unless one closes an eye to these things, the supply of students is bound to come to an end. During the summer Theodore remained at home, spending much of his time in the garden. He brooded over the problem of his future; what profession was he to choose? He had gained so much insight into the methods of the huge Jesuitical community which, under the name of the upper classes, constituted society, that he felt dissatisfied with the world and decided to enter the Church to save himself from despair. And yet the world beckoned to him. It lay before him, fair and bright, and his young, fermenting blood yearned for life. He spent himself in the struggle and his idleness added to his torments.

Theodore's increasing melancholy and waning health began to alarm his father. He had no doubt about the cause, but he could not bring himself to talk to his son on such a delicate subject.

One Sunday afternoon the Professor's brother who was an officer in the Pioneers, called. They were sitting in the garden, sipping their coffee.

"Have you noticed the change in Theodore?" asked the Professor.

"Yes, his time has come," answered the Captain.

"I believe it has come long ago."

"I wish you'd talk to him, I can't do it."

"If I were a bachelor, I should play the part of the uncle," said the Captain; "as it is, I'll ask Gustav to do it. The boy must see something of life, or he'll go wrong. Hot stuff these Wennerstroems, what?"

"Yes," said the Professor, "I was a man at fifteen, but I had a schoolfriend who was never confirmed because he was a father at thirteen."

"Look at Gustav! Isn't he a fine fellow? I'm hanged if he isn't as broad across the back as an old captain! He's a handful!"

"Yes," answered the Professor, "he costs me a lot, but after all, I'd rather pay than see the boy running any risks. I wish you'd ask Gustav to take Theodore about with him a little, just to rouse him."

"Oh! with pleasure!" answered the Captain.

And so the matter was settled.

One evening in July, when the summer is in its prime and all the blossoms which the spring has fertilized ripen into fruit, Theodore was sitting in his bedroom, waiting. He had pinned a text against his wall. "Come to Jesus," it said, and it was intended as a hint to the lieutenant not to argue with him when he occasionally came home from barracks for a few minutes. Gustav was of a lively disposition, "a handful," as his uncle had said. He wasted no time in brooding. He had promised to call for Theodore at seven o'clock; they were going to make arrangements for the celebration of the professor's birthday. Theodore's secret plan was to convert his brother, and Gustav's equally secret intention was to make his younger brother take a more reasonable view of life.

Punctually at seven o'clock, a cab stopped before the house, (the lieutenant invariably arrived in a cab) and immediately after Theodore heard the ringing of his spurs and the rattling of his sword on the stairs.

"Good evening, you old mole," said the elder brother with a laugh. He was the picture of health and youth. His highly-polished Hessian boots revealed a pair of fine legs, his tunic outlined the loins of a cart-horse; the golden bandolier of his cartridge box made his chest appear broader and his sword-belt showed off a pair of enormous thighs.

He glanced at the text and grinned, but said nothing.

"Come along, old man, let's be off to Bellevue! We'll call on the gardener there and make arrangements for the old man's birthday. Put on your hat, and come, old chap!"

Theodore tried to think of an excuse, but the brother took him by the arm, put a hat on his head, back to front, pushed a cigarette between his lips and opened the door. Theodore felt like a fish out of water, but he went with his brother.

"To Bellevue!" said the lieutenant to the cab-driver, "and mind you make your thoroughbreds fly!"

Theodore could not help being amused. It would never have occurred to him to address an elderly married man, like the cabman, with so much familiarity.

On the way the lieutenant talked of everything under the sun and stared at every pretty girl they passed.

They met a funeral procession on its return from the cemetery.

"Did you notice that devilish pretty girl in the last coach?" asked Gustav.

Theodore had not seen her and did not want to see her.

They passed an omnibus full of girls of the barmaid type. The lieutenant stood up, unconcernedly, in the public thoroughfare, and kissed his hands to them. He really behaved like a madman.

The business at Bellevue was soon settled. On their return the cab-driver drove them, without waiting for an order, to "The Equerry," a restaurant where Gustav was evidently well-known.

"Let's go and have something to eat," said the lieutenant, pushing his brother out of the cab.

Theodore was fascinated. He was no abstainer and saw nothing wrong in entering a public-house, although it never occurred to him to do so. He followed, though not without a slight feeling of uneasiness.

They were received in the hall by two girls. "Good evening, little doves," said the lieutenant, and kissed them both on the lips. "Let me introduce you to my learned brother; he's very young and innocent, not at all like me; what do you say, Jossa?"

The girls looked shyly at Theodore, who did not know which way to turn. His brother's language appeared to him unutterably impudent.

On their way upstairs they met a dark-haired little girl, who had evidently been crying; she looked quiet and modest and made a good impression on Theodore.

The lieutenant did not kiss her, but he pulled out his handkerchief and dried her eyes. Then he ordered an extravagant supper.

They were in a bright and pretty room, hung with mirrors and containing a piano, a perfect room for banqueting. The lieutenant opened the piano with his sword, and before Theodore knew where he was, he was sitting on the music-stool, and his hands were resting on the keyboard.

"Play us a waltz," commanded the lieutenant, and Theodore played a waltz. The lieutenant took off his sword and danced with Jossa; Theodore heard his spurs knocking against the legs of the chairs and tables. Then he threw himself on the sofa and shouted:

"Come here, ye slaves, and fan me!"

Theodore began to play softly and presently he was absorbed in the music of Gounod's *Faust*. He did not dare to turn round.

"Go and kiss him," whispered the brother.

But the girls felt shy. They were almost afraid of him and his melancholy music.

The boldest of them, however, went up to the piano.

"You are playing from the Freischütz, aren't you?" she asked.

"No," said Theodore, politely, "I'm playing Gounod's *Faust.*"

"Your brother looks frightfully respectable," said the little dark one, whose name was Rieke; "he's different to you, you old villain."

"Oh! well, he's going into the Church," whispered the lieutenant.

These words made a great impression on the girls, and henceforth they only kissed the lieutenant when Theodore's back was turned, and looked at Theodore shyly and apprehensively, like fowls at a chained mastiff.

Supper appeared, a great number of courses. There were eighteen dishes, not counting the hot ones.

Gustav poured out the liqueurs.

"Your health, you old hypocrite!" he laughed.

Theodore swallowed the liqueur. A delicious warmth ran through his limbs, a thin, warm veil fell over his eyes, he felt ravenous like a starving beast. What a banquet it was! The fresh salmon with its peculiar flavor, and the dill with its narcotic aroma; the radishes which seem to scrape the throat and call for beer; the small beef-steaks and sweet Portuguese onions, which made him think of dancing girls; the fried lobster which smelt of the sea; the chicken stuffed with parsley which reminded him of the gardener, and the first gerkins with their poisonous flavor of verdigris which made such a jolly, crackling sound between his crunching teeth. The porter flowed through his veins like hot streams of lava; they drank champagne after the strawberries; a waitress brought the foaming drink which bubbled in the glasses like a fountain. They poured out a glass for her. And then they talked of all sorts of things.

Theodore sat there like a tree in which the sap is rising. He had eaten a good supper and felt as if a whole volcano was seething in his inside. New thoughts, new emotions, new ideas, new points of view fluttered round his brow like butterflies. He went to the piano and played, he himself knew not what. The ivory keys under his hands were like a heap of bones from which his spirit drew life and melody.

He did not know how long he had been playing, but when he turned, round he saw his brother entering the room. He looked like a god, radiating life and strength. Behind him came Rieke with a bowl of punch, and immediately after all the girls came upstairs. The lieutenant drank to each one of them separately; Theodore found that everything was as it should be and finally became so bold that he kissed Rieke on the shoulder. But she looked annoyed and drew away from him, and he felt ashamed.

When Theodore found himself alone in his room, he had a feeling as if the whole world were turned upside down. He tore the text from the wall, not because he no longer believed in Jesus, but because its being pinned against the wall struck him as a species of bragging. He was amazed to find that religion sat on him as loosely as a Sunday suit, and he asked himself whether it was not unseemly to go about during the whole week in Sunday clothes. After all he was but an ordinary, commonplace person with whom he was well content, and he came to the conclusion that he had a better chance of living in peace with himself if he lived a simple, unpretentious, unassuming life.

He slept soundly during the night, undisturbed by dreams.

When he arose on the following morning, his pale cheeks looked fuller and there was a new gladness in his heart. He went out for a walk and suddenly found himself in the country. The thought struck him that he might go to the restaurant and look up the girls. He went into the large room; there he found Rieke and Jossa alone, in morning dresses, snubbing gooseberries. Before he knew what he was doing, he was sitting at the table beside them with a pair of scissors in his hand, helping them. They talked of Theodore's brother and the pleasant evening they had spent together. Not a single loose remark was made. They were just like a happy family; surely he had fallen in good hands, he was among friends.

When they had finished with the gooseberries, he ordered coffee and invited the girls to share it with him. Later on the proprietress came and read the paper to them. He felt at home.

He repeated his visit. One afternoon he went upstairs, to look for Rieke. She was sewing a seam. Theodore asked her whether he was in her way. "Not at all," she replied, "on the contrary." They talked of his brother who was away at camp, and would be away for another two months. Presently he ordered some punch and their intimacy grew.

On another occasion Theodore met her in the Park. She was gathering flowers. They both sat down in the grass. She was wearing a light summer dress, the material of which was so thin that it plainly revealed her slight girlish figure. He put his arms round her waist and kissed her. She returned his kisses and he drew her to him in a passionate embrace; but she tore herself away and told him gravely that if he did not behave himself she would never meet him again.

They went on meeting one another for two months. Theodore had fallen in love with her. He had long and serious conversations with her on the most sacred duties of life, on love, on religion, on everything, and between-whiles he spoke to her of his passion. But she invariably confounded him with his own arguments. Then he felt ashamed of having harbored base thoughts of so innocent a girl, and finally his passion was transformed into admiration for this poor little thing, who had managed to keep herself unspotted in the midst of temptation.

He had given up the idea of going into the Church; he determined to take the doctor's degree and — who knows — perhaps marry Rieke. He read poetry to her while she did needlework. She let him kiss her as much as he liked, she allowed him to fondle and caress her; but that was the limit.

At last his brother returned from camp. He immediately ordered a banquet at "The Equerry"; Theodore was invited. But he was made to play all the time. He was in the middle of a waltz, to which nobody danced, when he happened to look round; he was alone. He rose and went into the corridor, passed a long row of doors, and at last came to a bedroom. There he saw a sight which made him turn round, seize his hat and disappear into the darkness.

It was dawn when he reached his own bedroom, alone, annihilated, robbed of his faith in life, in love, and, of course, in women, for to him there was but one woman in the world, and that was Rieke from "The Equerry." On the fifteenth of September he went to Upsala to study theology.

*T*he years passed. His sound common-sense was slowly extinguished by all the nonsense with which he had to fill his brain daily and hourly. But at night he was powerless to resist. Nature burst her bonds and took by force what rebellious man denied her. He lost his health; all his skull bones were visible in his haggard face, his complexion was sallow and his skin looked damp and clammy; ugly pimples appeared between the scanty locks of his beard. His eyes were without luster, his hands so emaciated that the joints seemed to poke through the skin. He looked like the illustration to an essay on human vice, and yet he lived a perfectly pure life.

One day the professor of Christian Ethics, a married man with very strict ideas on morality, called on him and asked him pointblank whether he had anything on his conscience; if so, he advised him to make a clean breast of it. Theodore answered that he had nothing to confess, but that he was unhappy. Thereupon the professor exhorted him to watch and pray and be strong.

His brother had written him a long letter, begging him not to take a certain stupid matter too much to heart. He told him that it was absurd to take a girl seriously. His philosophy, and he had always found it answering admirably, was to pay debts incurred and go; to play while one was young, for the gravity of life made itself felt quite soon enough.

Marriage was nothing but a civil institution for the protection of the children. There was plenty of time for it.

Theodore replied at some length in a letter imbued with true Christian sentiment, which the lieutenant left unanswered.

After passing his first examination in the spring, Theodore was obliged to spend a summer at Sköfde, in order to undergo the cold water cure. In the autumn he returned to Upsala. His newly-regained strength was merely so much fresh fuel to the fire.

Matters grew worse and worse. His hair had grown so thin that the scalp was plainly visible. He walked with dragging footsteps and whenever his fellow students met him in the street, they cut him as if he were possessed of all the vices. He noticed it and shunned them in his turn. He only left his rooms in the evening. He did not dare to go to bed at night. The iron which he had taken to excess, had ruined his digestion, and in the following summer the doctors sent him to Karlsbad.

On his return to Upsala, in the autumn, a rumor got abroad, an ugly rumor, which hung over the town like a black cloud. It was as if a drain had been left open and men were suddenly reminded that the town, that splendid creation of civilization, was built over a sea of corruption, which might at any moment burst its bonds and poison the inhabitants. It was said that Theodore Wennerstroem, in a paroxysm of passion had assaulted one of his friends, and the rumor did not lie.

His father went to Upsala and had an interview with the Dean of the Theological Faculty. The professor of pathology was present. What was to be done? The doctor remained silent. They pressed him for his opinion.

"Since you ask me," he said, "I must give you an answer; but you know as well as I do that there is but one remedy."

"And that is?" asked the theologian.

"Need you ask?" replied the doctor.

"Yes," said the theologian, who was a married man. "Surely, nature does not require immorality from a man?"

The father said that he quite understood the case, but that he was afraid of making recommendations to his son, on account of the risks the latter would run.

"If he can't take care of himself he must be a fool," said the doctor.

The Dean requested them to continue such an agitating conversation in a more suitable place. . . . He himself had nothing more to add.

This ended the matter.

Since Theodore was a member of the upper classes the scandal was hushed up. A few years later he passed his final, and was sent by the doctor to Spa. The amount of quinine which he had taken had affected his knees and he walked with two sticks. At Spa he looked so ill that he was a conspicuous figure even in a crowd of invalids.

But an unmarried woman of thirty-five, a German, took compassion on the unhappy man. She spent many hours with him in a lonely summer arbor in the park, discussing the problems of life. She was a member of a big evangelical society, whose object was the raising of the moral standard. She showed him prospectuses for newspapers and magazines, the principal mission of which was the suppression of prostitution.

"Look at me," she said, "I am thirty-five years old and enjoy excellent health! What fools' talk it is to say that immorality is a necessary evil. I have watched and fought a good fight for Christ's sake."

The young clergyman silently compared her well-developed figure, her large hips, with his own wasted body.

"What a difference there is between human beings in this world," was his unspoken comment.

In the autumn the Rev. Theodore Wennerstroem and Sophia Leidschütz, spinster, were engaged to be married.

"Saved!" sighed the father, when the news reached him in his house at Stockholm.

"I wonder how it will end," thought the brother in his barracks. "I'm afraid that my poor Theodore is 'one of those Asra who die when they love.'"

Theodore Wennerstroem was married. Nine months after the wedding his wife presented him with a boy who suffered from rickets — another thirteen months and Theodore Wennerstroem had breathed his last.

The doctor who filled up the certificate of death, looked at the fine healthy woman, who stood weeping by the small coffin which contained the skeleton of her young husband of not much over twenty years.

"The plus was too great, the minus too small," he thought, "and therefore the plus devoured the minus."

But the father, who received the news of his son's death on a Sunday, sat down to read a sermon. When he had finished, he fell into a brown study.

"There must be something very wrong with a world where virtue is rewarded with death," he thought.

And the virtuous widow, *née* Leidschütz, had two more husbands and eight children, wrote pamphlets on overpopulation and immorality. But her brother-in-law called her a cursed woman who killed her husbands.

The anything but virtuous lieutenant married and was father of six children. He got promotion and lived happily to the end of his life.

Love and Bread

*T*he assistant had not thought of studying the price of wheat before he called on the major to ask him for the hand of his daughter; but the major had studied it.

"I love her," said the assistant.

"What's your salary?" said the old man.

"Well, twelve hundred crowns, at present; but we love one another. . . ."

"That has nothing to do with me; twelve hundred crowns is not enough."

"And then I make a little in addition to my salary, and Louisa knows that my heart. . . ."

"Don't talk nonsense! How much in addition to your salary?"

He seized paper and pencil.

"And my feelings. . . ."

"How much in addition to your salary?"

And he drew hieroglyphics on the blotting paper.

"Oh! We'll get on well enough, if only. . . ."

"Are you going to answer my question or not? How much in addition to your salary? Figures! figures, my boy! Facts!"

"I do translations at ten crowns a sheet; I give French lessons, I am promised proof-correcting. . . ."

"Promises aren't facts! Figures, my boy! Figures! Look here, now, I'll put it down. What are you translating?"

"What am I translating? I can't tell you straight off."

"You can't tell me straight off? You are engaged on a translation, you say; can't you tell me what it is? Don't talk such rubbish!"

"I am translating Guizot's *History of Civilization,* twenty-five sheets."

"At ten crowns a sheet makes two hundred and fifty crowns. And then?"

"And then? How can I tell beforehand?"

"Indeed, can't you tell beforehand? But you ought to know. You seem to imagine that being married simply means living together and amusing yourselves! No, my dear boy, there will be children, and children require feeding and clothing."

"There needn't be babies directly, if one loves *as we love* one another."

"How the dickens do you love one another?"

"*As we love* one another." He put his hand on his waistcoat.

"And won't there be any children if people love as you love? You must be mad! But you are a decent, respectable member of society, and therefore I'll give my consent; but make good use of the time, my boy, and increase your income, for hard times are coming. The price of wheat is rising."

The assistant grew red in the face when he heard the last words, but his joy at the old man's consent was so great that he seized his hand and kissed it. Heaven knew how happy he was! When he walked for the first time down the street with his future bride on his arm, they both radiated light; it seemed to them that the passers-by stood still and lined the road in honor of their triumphal march; and they walked along with proud eyes, squared shoulders and elastic steps.

In the evening he called at her house; they sat down in the center of the room and read proofs; she helped him. "He's a good sort," chuckled the old man. When they had finished, he took her in his arms and said: "Now we have earned three crowns," and then he kissed her. On the following evening they went to the theater and he took her home in a cab, and that cost twelve crowns.

Sometimes, when he ought to have given a lesson in the evening, he (is there anything a man will not do for love's sake?) canceled his lesson and took her out for a walk instead.

But the wedding-day approached. They were very busy. They had to choose the furniture. They began with the most important purchases. Louisa had not intended to be present when he bought the bedroom furniture, but when it came to the point she went with him. They bought two beds, which were, of course, to stand side by side. The furniture had to be walnut, every single piece real walnut. And they must have spring mattresses covered with red and white striped tick, and bolsters filled with down; and two eiderdown quilts, exactly alike. Louisa chose blue, because she was very fair.

They went to the best stores. They could not do without a red hanging-lamp and a Venus made of plaster of Paris. Then they bought a dinner-service; and six dozen differently shaped glasses with cut edges; and knives and forks, grooved and engraved with their initials. And then the kitchen utensils! Mama had to accompany them to see to those.

And what a lot he had to do besides! There were bills to accept, journeys to the banks and interviews with tradespeople and artisans; a flat had to be found and curtains had to be put up. He saw to everything. Of course he had to neglect his work; but once he was married, he would soon make up for it.

They were only going to take two rooms to begin with, for they were going to be frightfully economical. And as they were only going to have two rooms, they could afford to furnish them well. He rented two rooms and a kitchen on the first floor in Government Street, for six hundred crowns. When Louisa remarked that they might just as well have taken three rooms and a kitchen on the fourth floor for five hundred crowns, he was a little embarrassed; but what did it matter if only they loved one another? Yes, of course, Louisa agreed, but couldn't they have loved one another just as well in four rooms at a lower rent, as in three at a higher? Yes, he admitted that he had been foolish, but what *did* it matter so long as they loved one another?

The rooms were furnished. The bedroom looked like a little temple. The two beds stood side by side, like two carriages. The rays of the sun fell on the blue eiderdown quilt, the white, white sheets and the little pillow-slips which an elderly maiden aunt had embroidered with their monogram; the latter consisted of two huge letters, formed of flowers, joined together in one single embrace, and kissing here and there, wherever they touched, at the corners. The bride had her own little alcove, which was screened off by a Japanese screen. The drawing room, which was also dining room, study and morning-room, contained her piano, (which had cost twelve hundred crowns) his writing-table with twelve pigeon-holes, (every single piece of it real walnut) a pier-glass, armchairs; a sideboard and a dining-table. "It looks as if nice people lived here," they said, and they could not understand why people wanted a separate dining room, which always looked so cheerless with its cane chairs.

The wedding took place on a Saturday. Sunday dawned, the first day of their married life. Oh! what a life it was! Wasn't it lovely to be married! Wasn't marriage a splendid institution! One was allowed one's own way in everything, and parents and relations came and congratulated one into the bargain.

At nine o'clock in the morning their bedroom was still dark. He wouldn't open the shutters to let in daylight, but re-lighted the red lamp which threw its bewitching light on the blue eiderdown, the white sheets, a little crumpled now, and the Venus made of plaster of Paris, who stood there rosy-red and without shame. And the red light also fell on his little wife who nestled in her pillows with a look of contrition, and yet so refreshed as if she had never slept so well in all her life. There was no traffic in the street today for it was Sunday, and the church-bells were calling people to the morning service with exulting, eager voices, as if they wanted all the world to come to church and praise Him who had created men and women.

He whispered to his little bride to shut her eyes so that he might get up and order breakfast. She buried her head in the pillows, while he slipped on his dressing gown and went behind the screen to dress.

A broad radiant path of sunlight lay on the sitting room floor; he did not know whether it was spring or summer, autumn or winter; he only knew that it was Sunday!

His bachelor life was receding into the background like something ugly and dark; the sight of his little home stirred his heart with a faint recollection of the home of his childhood, and at the same time held out a glorious promise for the future.

How strong he felt! The future appeared to him like a mountain coming to meet him. He would breathe on it and the mountain would fall down at his feet like sand; he would fly away, far above gables and chimneys, holding his little wife in his arm.

He collected his clothes which were scattered all over the room; he found his white neck-tie hanging on a picture frame; it looked like a big white butterfly.

He went into the kitchen. How the new copper vessels sparkled, the new tin kettles shone! And all this belonged to him and to her! He called the maid who came out of her room in her petticoat. But he did not notice it, nor did he notice that her shoulders were bare. For him there was but one woman in all the world. He spoke to the girl as a father would to his daughter. He told her to go to the restaurant and order breakfast, at once, a first-rate breakfast. Porter and Burgundy! The manager knew his taste. She was to give him his regards.

He went out of the kitchen and knocked at the bedroom door.

"May I come in?"

There was a little startled scream.

"Oh, no, darling, wait a bit!"

He laid the breakfast table himself. When the breakfast was brought from the restaurant, he served it on her new breakfast set. He folded the dinner napkins according to all the rules of art. He wiped the wine-glasses, and finally took her bridal-bouquet and put it in a vase before her place.

When she emerged from her bedroom in her embroidered morning gown and stepped into the brilliant sunlight, she felt just a tiny bit faint;

he helped her into the armchair, made her drink a little liqueur out of a liqueur glass and eat a caviar sandwich.

What fun it all was! One could please oneself when one was married. What would Mama have said if she had seen her daughter drinking liqueurs at this hour of the morning!

He waited on her as if she were still his fiancée. What a breakfast they were having on the first morning after their wedding! And nobody had a right to say a word. Everything was perfectly right and proper, one could enjoy oneself with the very best of consciences, and that was the most delightful part of it all. It was not for the first time that he was eating such a breakfast, but what a difference between then and now! He had been restless and dissatisfied then; he could not bear to think of it, now. And as he drank a glass of genuine Swedish porter after the oysters, he felt the deepest contempt for all bachelors.

"How stupid of people not to get married! Such selfishness! They ought to be taxed like dogs."

"I'm sorry for those poor men who haven't the means to get married," replied his demure little wife kindly, "for I am sure, if they had the means they would all get married."

A little pang shot through the assistant's heart; for a moment he felt afraid, lest he had been a little too venturesome. All his happiness rested on the solution of a financial problem, and if, if. . . . Pooh! A glass of Burgundy! Now he would work! They should see!

"Game? With cranberries and cucumbers!" The young wife was a little startled, but it was really delicious.

"Lewis, darling," she put a trembling little hand on his arm, "can we afford it?"

Fortunately she said "we."

"Pooh! It doesn't matter for once! Later on we can dine on potatoes and herrings."

"Can you eat potatoes and herrings?"

"I should think so!"

"When you have been drinking more than is good for you, and expect a beefsteak after the herring?"

"Nonsense! Nothing of the kind! Your health, sweetheart! The game is excellent! So are these artichokes!"

"No, but you are mad, darling! Artichokes at this time of the year! What a bill you will have to pay!"

"Bill! Aren't they good? Don't you think that it is glorious to be alive? Oh! It's splendid, splendid!"

At six o'clock in the afternoon a carriage drove up to the front door. The young wife would have been angry if it had not been so pleasant to loll luxuriously on the soft cushions, while they were being slowly driven to the Deer Park.

"It's just like lying on a couch," whispered Lewis.

She playfully hit his fingers with her sunshade. Mutual acquaintances bowed to them from the footpath. Friends waved their hands to him as if they were saying:

"Hallo! you rascal, you have come into a fortune!"

How small the passers-by looked, how smooth the street was, how pleasant their ride on springs and cushions!

Life should always be like that.

It went on for a whole month. Balls, visits, dinners, theaters. Sometimes, of course, they remained at home. And at home it was more pleasant than anywhere else. How lovely, for instance, to carry off one's wife from her parents' house, after supper, without saying as much as "by your leave," put her into a closed carriage, slam the door, nod to her people and say: "Now we're off home, to our own four walls! And there we'll do exactly what we like!"

And then to have a little supper at home and sit over it, talking and gossiping until the small hours of the morning.

Lewis was always very sensible at home, at least in theory. One day his wife put him to the test by giving him salt salmon, potatoes boiled in milk and oatmeal soup for dinner. Oh! how he enjoyed it! He was sick of elaborate menus.

On the following Friday, when she again suggested salt salmon for dinner, Lewis came home, carrying two ptarmigans! He called to her from the threshold:

"Just imagine, Lou, a most extraordinary thing happened! A most extraordinary thing!"

"Well, what is it?"

"You'll hardly believe me when I tell you that I bought a brace of ptarmigans, bought them myself at the market for — guess!"

His little wife seemed more annoyed than curious.

"Just think! One crown the two!"

"I have bought ptarmigans at eightpence the brace; but —" she added in a more conciliatory tone, so as not to upset him altogether, "that was in a very cold winter."

"Well, but you must admit that I bought them very cheaply."

Was there anything she would not admit in order to see him happy?

She had ordered boiled groats for dinner, as an experiment. But after Lewis had eaten a ptarmigan, he regretted that he could not eat as much of the groats as he would have liked, in order to show her that he was really very fond of groats. He liked groats very much indeed — milk did not agree with him after his attack of ague. He couldn't take milk, but groats he would like to see on his table every evening, every blessed evening of his life, if only she wouldn't be angry with him.

And groats never again appeared on his table.

When they had been married for six weeks, the young wife fell ill. She suffered from headaches and sickness. It could not be anything serious, just a little cold. But this sickness? Had she eaten anything which had disagreed with her? Hadn't all the copper vessels new coatings of tin? He sent for the doctor. The doctor smiled and said it was all right.

"What was all right? Oh! Nonsense! It wasn't possible. How could it have been possible? No, surely, the bedroom paper was to blame. It must contain arsenic. Let us send a piece to the chemist's at once and have it tested."

"Entirely free from arsenic," reported the chemist.

"How strange! No arsenic in the wall papers?"

The young wife was still ill. He consulted a medical book and whispered a question in her ear. "There now! a hot bath!"

Four weeks later the midwife declared that everything was "as it should be."

"As it should be? Well, of course! Only it was somewhat premature!"

But as it could not, be helped, they were delighted. Fancy, a baby! They would be papa and mama! What should they call him? For, of course, it would be a boy. No doubt, it would. But now she had a serious conversation with her husband! There had been no translating or proof-correcting since their marriage. And his salary alone was not sufficient.

"Yes, they had given no thought to the morrow. But, dear me, one was young only once! Now, however, there would be a change."

On the following morning the assistant called on an old schoolfriend, a registrar, to ask him to stand security for a loan.

"You see, my dear fellow, when one is about to become a father, one has to consider how to meet increasing expenses."

"Quite so, old man," answered the registrar, "therefore I have been unable to get married. But you are fortunate in having the means."

The assistant hesitated to make his request. How could he have the audacity to ask this poor bachelor to help him to provide the expenses for the coming event? This bachelor, who had not the means to found a family of his own? He could not bring himself to do it.

When he came home to dinner, his wife told him that two gentlemen had called to see him.

"What did they look like? Were they young? Did they wear eye-glasses? Then there was no doubt, they were two lieutenants, old friends of his whom he had met at Vaxholm."

"No, they couldn't have been lieutenants; they were too old for that."

"Then he knew; they were old college friends from Upsala, probably P. who was a lecturer, and O. who was a curate, now. They had come to see how their old pal was shaping as a husband."

"No, they didn't come from Upsala, they came from Stockholm."

The maid was called in and cross-examined. She thought the callers had been shabbily dressed and had carried sticks.

"Sticks! I can't make out what sort of people they can have been. Well, we'll know soon enough, as they said they would call again. But to change the subject, I happened to see a basket of hothouse strawberries at a really ridiculous price; it really is absurd! Just imagine, hothouse strawberries at one and sixpence a basket! And at this time of the year!"

"But, my darling, what is this extravagance to lead to?"

"It'll be all right. I have got an order for a translation this very day."

"But you are in debt, Lewis?"

"Trifles! Mere nothings! It'll be all right when I take up a big loan, presently."

"A loan! But that'll be a new debt!"

"True! But there'll be easy terms! Don't let's talk business now! Aren't these strawberries delicious? What? A glass of sherry with them would be tip-top. Don't you think so? Lina, run round to the stores and fetch a bottle of sherry, the best they have."

After his afternoon nap, his wife insisted on a serious conversation.

"You won't be angry, dear, will you?"

"Angry? I! Good heavens, no! Is it about household expenses?"

"Yes! We owe money at the stores! The butcher is pressing for payment; the man from the livery stables has called for his money; it's most unpleasant."

"Is that all? I shall pay them to the last farthing tomorrow. How dare they worry you about such trifles? They shall be paid tomorrow, but they shall lose a customer. Now, don't let's talk about it anymore. Come out for a walk. No carriage! Well, we'll take the car to the Deer Park, it will cheer us up."

They went to the Deer Park. They asked for a private room at the restaurant, and people stared at them and whispered.

"They think we are out on a spree," he laughed. "What fun! What madness!"

But his wife did not like it.

They had a big bill to pay.

"If only we had stayed at home! We might have bought such a lot of things for the money."

Months elapsed. The great event was coming nearer and nearer. A cradle had to be bought and baby-clothes. A number of things were wanted. The young husband was out on business all day long. The price of wheat had risen. Hard times were at hand. He could get no translations, no proof-correcting. Men had become materialists. They didn't spend money on books, they bought food. What a prosaic period we were living in! Ideals were melting away, one after the other, and ptarmigans were not to be had under two crowns the brace. The livery stables would not provide carriages for nothing for the cab-proprietors had wives and families to support, just as everybody else; at the stores cash had to be paid for goods, Oh! what realists they all were!

The great day had come at last. It was evening. He must run for the midwife. And while his wife suffered all the pangs of childbirth, he had to go down into the hall and pacify the creditors.

At last he held a daughter in his arms. His tears fell on the baby, for now he realized his responsibility, a responsibility which he was unable to shoulder. He made new resolutions. But his nerves were unstrung. He was working at a translation which he seemed unable to finish, for he had to be constantly out on business.

He rushed to his father-in-law, who was staying in town, to bring him the glad news.

"We have a little daughter!"

"Well and good," replied his father-in-law; "can you support a child?"

"Not at present; for heaven's sake, help us, father!"

"I'll tide you over your present difficulties. I can't do more. My means are only sufficient to support my own family."

The patient required chickens which he bought himself at the market, and wine at six crowns the bottle. It had to be the very best.

The midwife expected a hundred crowns.

"Why should we pay her less than others? Hasn't she just received a check for a hundred crowns from the captain?"

Very soon the young wife was up again. She looked like a girl, as slender as a willow, a little pale, it was true, but the pallor suited her.

The old man called and had a private conversation with his son-in-law.

"No more children, for the present," he said, "or you'll be ruined."

"What language from a father! Aren't we married! Don't we love one another? Aren't we to have a family?"

"Yes, but not until you can provide for them. It's all very fine to love one another, but you mustn't forget that you have responsibilities."

His father-in-law, too, had become a materialist. Oh! what a miserable world it was! A world without ideals!

The home was undermined, but love survived, for love was strong, and the hearts of the young couple were soft. The bailiff, on the contrary, was anything but soft. Distraint was imminent, and bankruptcy threatened. Well, let them distrain then!

The father-in-law arrived with a large traveling coach to fetch his daughter and grand-child. He warned his son-in-law not to show his face at his house until he could pay his debts and make a home for his wife and child. He said nothing to his daughter, but it seemed to him that he was bringing home a girl who had been led astray. It was as if he had lent his innocent child to a casual admirer and now received her back "dishonored." She would have preferred to stay with her husband, but he had no home to offer her.

And so the husband of one year's standing was left behind to watch the pillaging of his home, if he could call it his home, for he had paid for nothing. The two men with spectacles carted away the beds and bedclothes; the copper kettles and tin vessels; the dinner set, the chandelier and the candlesticks; everything, everything!

He was left alone in the two empty, wretched rooms! If only *she* had been left to him! But what should she do here, in these empty rooms? No, she was better off where she was! She was being taken care of.

Now the struggle for a livelihood began in bitter earnest. He found work at a daily paper as a proof-corrector. He had to be at the office at midnight; at three in the morning his work was done. He did not lose his berth, for bankruptcy had been avoided, but he had lost all chance of promotion.

Later on he is permitted to visit wife and child once a week, but he is never allowed to see her alone. He spends Saturday night in a tiny room, close to his father-in-law's bedroom. On Sunday morning he has to return to town, for the paper appears on Monday morning. . . . He says good-bye to his wife and child who are allowed to accompany him as far as the garden gate, he waves his hand to them once more from the furthest hillock, and succumbs to his wretchedness, his misery, his humiliation. And she is no less unhappy.

He has calculated that it will take him twenty years to pay his debts. And then? Even then he cannot maintain a wife and child. And his prospects? He has none! If his father-in-law should die, his wife and child would be thrown on the street; he cannot venture to look forward to the death of their only support.

Oh! How cruel it is of nature to provide food for all her creatures, leaving the children of men alone to starve! Oh! How cruel, how cruel!

that life has not ptarmigans and strawberries to give to all men. How cruel! How cruel!

Compelled To

*P*unctually at half past nine on a winter evening he appears at the door leading to the glass-roofed verandah of the restaurant. While, with mathematical precision, he takes off his gloves, he peers over his dim spectacles, first to the right, then to the left, to find out whether any of his acquaintances are present. Then he hangs up his overcoat on its special hook, the one to the right of the fireplace. Gustav, the waiter, an old pupil of his, flies to his table and, without waiting for an order, brushes the crumbs off the tablecloth, stirs up the mustard, smooths the salt in the salt-cellar and turns over the dinner napkin. Then he fetches, still without any order, a bottle of Medhamra, opens half a bottle of Union beer and, merely for appearance sake, hands the schoolmaster the bill of fare.

"Crabs?" he asks, more as a matter of form than because there is any need of the question.

"Female crabs," answers the schoolmaster.

"Large, female crabs," repeats Gustav, walks to the speaking tube which communicates with the kitchen, and shouts: "Large female crabs for Mr. Blom, and plenty of dill."

He fetches butter and cheese, cuts two very thin slices of rye-bread, and places them on the schoolmaster's table. The latter has in the meantime searched the verandah for the evening papers, but has only found the official *Post*. To make up for this very poor success, he takes the *Daily Journal,* which he had not had time to finish at lunch, and after first opening and refolding the *Post,* and putting it on the top of the bread basket on his left, sits down to read it. He ornaments the rye-bread with geometrical butter hieroglyphics, cuts off a piece of cheese in the shape of a rectangle, fills his liqueur glass three quarters full and raises it to his lips, hesitates as if the little glass contained physic, throws back his head and says: Ugh!

He has done this for twelve years and will continue doing it until the day of his death.

As soon as the crabs, six of them, have been put before him, he examines them as to their sex, and everything being as it should be, makes ready to enjoy himself. He tucks a corner of his dinner napkin into his collar, places two slices of thin bread and cheese by the side of his plate and pours out a glass of beer and half a glass of liqueur. Then he takes the little crab-knife and business begins. He is the only man in Sweden who knows how to eat a crab, and whenever he sees anybody else engaged in the same pursuit, he tells him that he has no idea how to do it. He makes an incision all round the head, and a hole against which he presses his lips and begins to suck.

"This," he says, "is the best part of the whole animal."

He severs the thorax from the lower part, puts his teeth to the body and drinks deep drafts; he sucks the little legs as if they were asparagus, eats a bit of dill, and takes a drink of beer and a mouthful of rye-bread. When he has carefully taken the shell off the claws and sucked even the tiniest tubes, he eats the flesh; last of all he attacks the lower part of the body. When he has eaten three crabs, he drinks half a glass of liqueur and reads the promotions in the *Post.*

He has done this for twelve years and will continue doing it until he dies.

He was just twenty years old when he first began to patronize the restaurant, now he is thirty-two, and Gustav has been a waiter for ten years in the same place. Not one of its frequenters has known the restaurant longer than the school-master, not even the proprietor who took it over eight years ago. He has watched generations of diners come and go; some came for a year, some for two, some for five years; then they disappeared, went to another restaurant, left the town or got married. He feels very old, although he is only thirty-two! The restaurant is his home, for his furnished room is nothing but the place where he sleeps.

It is ten o'clock. He leaves his table and goes to the back room where his grog awaits him. This is the time when the bookseller arrives. They play a game of chess or talk about books. At half-past ten the second violin from the Dramatic Theater drops in. He is an old Pole who, after 1864, escaped to Sweden, and now makes a living by his former hobby. Both the Pole and the bookseller are over fifty, but they get on with the schoolmaster as if he were a contemporary.

The proprietor has his place behind the counter. He is an old sea captain who fell in love with the proprietress and married her. She rules in the kitchen, but the sliding panel is always open, so that she can keep an eye on the old man, lest he should take a glass too much before closing time. Not until the gas has been turned out, and the old man is ready to go to bed, is he allowed a nightcap in the shape of a stiff glass of rum and water.

At eleven o'clock the young bloods begin to arrive; they approach the counter diffidently and ask the proprietor in a whisper whether any of the private rooms upstairs are disengaged, and then there is a rustling of skirts in the hall and cautious footsteps are creeping upstairs.

"Well," says the bookseller, who has suddenly found a topic of conversation, "when are you going to be married, Blom, old man?"

"I haven't the means to get married," answered the school-master. "Why don't you take a wife to your bosom yourself?"

"No woman would have me, now that my head looks like an old, leather-covered trunk," says the bookseller. "And, moreover, there's my old Stafva, you know."

Stafva was a legendary person in whom nobody believed. She was the incarnation of the bookseller's unrealized dreams.

"But you, Mr. Potocki?" suggested the schoolmaster.

"He's been married once, that's enough," replies the bookseller.

The Pole nods his head like a metrometer.

"Yes, I was married very happily. Ugh!" he says and finishes his grog.

"Well," continues the schoolmaster, "if women weren't such fools, one might consider the matter; but they are infernal fools."

The Pole nods again and smiles; being a Pole, he doesn't understand what the word fool means.

"I have been married very happily, ugh!"

"And then there is the noise of the children, and children's clothes always drying near the stove; and servants, and all day long the smells from the kitchen. No, thank you! And, perhaps, sleepless nights into the bargain."

"Ugh!" added the Pole, completing the sentence.

"Mr. Potocki says 'ugh' with the malice of the bachelor who listens to the complaints of the married man," remarked the bookseller.

"What did I say?" asks the astonished widower. "Ugh!" says the bookseller, mimicking him, and the conversation degenerates into a universal grinning and a cloud of tobacco smoke.

It is midnight. The piano upstairs, which has accompanied a mixed choir of male and female voices, is silent. The waiter has finished his countless journeys from the speaking tube to the verandah; the proprietor enters into his daybook the last few bottles of champagne which have been ordered upstairs. The three friends rise from their chairs and go home, two to their "virgin couches," and the bookseller to his Stafva.

When schoolmaster Blom had reached his twentieth year, he was compelled to interrupt his studies at Upsala and accept a post as assistant teacher at Stockholm. As he, in addition, gave private lessons, he made quite a good income. He did not ask much of life. All he wanted was peace and cleanliness. An elderly lady let him a furnished room and there he found more than a bachelor finds as a rule. She looked after him and was kind to him; she gave him all the tenderness which nature had intended her to bestow on the new generation that was to spring from her. She mended his clothes and looked after him generally. He had lost his mother when he was a little boy and had never been accustomed to gratuitous kindness; therefore he was inclined to look upon her services as an interference with his liberty, but he accepted them nevertheless. But all the same the public house was his real home. There he paid for everything and ran up no bills.

He was born in a small town in the interior of Sweden; consequently he was a stranger in Stockholm. He knew nobody; was not on visiting terms with any of the families and met his acquaintances nowhere but at the public-house. He talked to them freely, but never gave them his confidence, in fact he had no confidence to give. At school he taught the third class and this gave him a feeling of having been stunted in his growth. A very long time ago he had been in the third class himself, had gradually crept up to the seventh, and had spent a few terms at the University; now he had returned to the third; he had been there for twelve years without being moved. He taught the second and third books of Euclid; this was the course of instruction for the whole year. He saw only a fragment of life; a fragment without beginning or end; the second and third books. In his spare time he read the newspapers and books on archaeology. Archaeology is a modern science, one might almost say a disease of the time. And there is danger in it, for it proves over and over again that human folly has pretty nearly always been the same.

Politics was to him nothing but an interesting game of chess — played for the king, for he was brought up like everybody else; it was an article of faith with him that nothing which happened in the world, concerned him, personally; let those look to it whom God had placed in a position of power. This way of looking at things filled his soul with peace and tranquility; he troubled nobody and nothing troubled him. When he found, as he did occasionally, that an unusually foolish event had occurred, he consoled himself with the conviction that it could not have been helped. His education had made him selfish, and the catechism had taught him that if everybody did his duty, all things would be well, whatever happened. He did his duty towards his pupils in an exemplary fashion; he was never late; never ill. In his private life, too, he was above reproach; he paid his rent on the day it fell due, never ran up bills at his restaurant, and spent only one evening a week on pleasure. His life glided along like a railway train to the second and, being a clever man, he managed to avoid collisions. He gave no thought to the future; a truly selfish man never does, for the simple reason that the future belongs to him for no longer than twenty or thirty years at the most.

And thus his days passed.

*M*idsummer morning dawned — radiant and sunny as mid-summer morning should be. The schoolmaster was still in bed, reading a book on the Art of Warfare in ancient Egypt, when Miss Augusta came into his room with his breakfast. She had put on his tray some slices of saffron bread, in honor of the festival, and on his dinner-napkin lay a spray of elder blossoms. On the previous night she had decorated his room with branches of the birch tree, put clean sand and some cowslips in the spittoon, and a bunch of lilies-of-the-valley on the dressing table.

"Aren't you going to make an excursion today, sir?" she asked, glancing at the decorations, anxious for a word of thanks or approval.

But Mr. Blom had not even noticed the decorations, and therefore he answered dryly:

"Haven't you realized yet that I never make excursions? I hate elbowing my way through a crowd, and the noise of the children gets on my nerves."

"But surely you won't stay in town on such a lovely day! You'll at least go to the Deer Park?"

"That would be the very last place I should go to, especially today, when it will be crowded. Oh! no, I'm better off in town, and I wish to goodness that this holiday nuisance would be stopped."

"There are plenty of people who say that there aren't half enough holidays these days when everybody has to work so hard," said the old woman in a conciliatory tone. "But is there anything else you wish, sir? My sister and I are making an excursion by steamer, and we shan't be back until ten o'clock tonight."

"I hope you'll enjoy yourselves, Miss Augusta. I want nothing, and am quite able to look after myself. The caretaker can do my room when I have gone out."

Miss Augusta left him alone with his breakfast. When he had eaten it, he lit a cigar and remained in bed with his *Egyptian Warfare*. The open window shook softly in the southern breeze. At eight o'clock the bells, large and small, of the nearest church began to ring, and those of the other churches of Stockholm, St. Catherine's, St. Mary's and St. Jacob's, joined in; they tinkled and jingled, enough to make a heathen tear his hair in despair. When the church bells stopped, a military band on the bridge of a steamer began to play a set of quadrilles from *The Weak Point*. The schoolmaster writhed between his sheets, and would have got out of bed and shut the window if it had not been so hot. Next there came a rolling of drums, which was interrupted by the strains of a brass quintet which played, on another steamer, the Hunter's Chorus from the *Freischütz*. But the cursed rolling of drums approached. They were marching at the head of the Riflemen on their way to camp. Now he was subjected to a medley of sounds: the Riflemen's march, the signals, the bells and the brass bands on the steamers, until at last the whole crash and din was drowned by the throbbing of the screw.

At ten o'clock he lit his spirit lamp and boiled his shaving water. His starched shirt lay on his chest of drawers, white and stiff as a board. It took him a quarter of an hour to push the studs through the button-holes. He spent half-an-hour in shaving himself. He brushed his hair as if it were a matter of the utmost importance. When he put on his trousers, he was careful that the lower ends should not touch the floor and become dusty.

His room was simply furnished, extremely plain and tidy. It was impersonal, neutral, like the room in a hotel. And yet he had spent in it twelve years of his life. Most people collect no end of trifles during such a period; presents, little superfluous nothings, ornaments. Not a single engraving, not a supplement to an illustrated magazine even, which at some time or other had appealed to him, hung on the walls; no antimacassar, no rug worked by a loving sister, lay on the chairs; no photograph of a beloved face stood on his writing-table, no embroidered pen-wiper lay by the side of the ink-stand. Everything had been bought as cheaply as possible with a view to avoiding unnecessary expense which might have hampered the owner's independence.

He leaned out of the window which gave him a view of the street and, across Artillery Place, of the harbor. In the house opposite a woman was dressing. He turned away as if something ugly had met his gaze, or something which might disturb his peace of mind. The harbor was gay with the fluttering flags on the steamers and sailing-ships, and the water glittered in the sunshine. A few old women, prayer-book in hand, passed his window on their way to church. A sentinel with drawn sword was walking up and down before the Artillery Barracks, glancing discontent-edly at the clock on the tower every now and then to see how much longer he would have to wait until the relieving guard arrived. Otherwise the street lay empty and grey in the hot sunshine. His eyes wandered back to the woman opposite. She was standing before her looking-glass, powder puff in hand, intent on powdering the corners of her nose, with

a grimace which made her look like a monkey. He left the window and
sat down in his rocking chair.

He made his program for the day, for he had a vague dread of solitude.
On week days he was surrounded by the school-boys, and although he
had no love for those wild beasts whose taming, or rather whose efficient
acquisition of the difficult art of dissembling, was his life task, yet he
felt a certain void when he was not with them. Now, during the long
summer vacations, he had established a holiday school, but even so he
had been compelled to give the boys short summer holidays, and, with
the exception of meal times when he could always count on the bookseller and the second violin, he had been alone for several days.

"At two o'clock," he mused, "when the guard has been relieved, and
the crowds have dispersed, I'll go to my restaurant to dine; then I'll
invite the bookseller to Strömsborg; there won't be a soul today; we can
have coffee there and punch, and stay till the evening when we'll return
to town and to Rejner's." (Rejner's was the name of his restaurant in
Berzelius Place.)

Punctually at two o'clock he took his hat, brushed himself carefully
and went out.

"I wonder whether there'll be stewed perch today," he thought. "And
mightn't one treat oneself to asparagus, as it's midsummer-day?"

He strolled past the high wall of the Government Bakery. In Berzelius
Park the seats which were usually occupied by the nursemaids of the
rich and their charges, were crowded with the families of the laborers
who had appeared in great numbers with their perambulators. He saw
a mother feeding her baby. She was a large, full-breasted woman, and
the baby's dimpled hand almost disappeared in her bosom. The schoolmaster turned away with a feeling of loathing. He was annoyed to see
these strangers in *his* park. It was very much like the servants using the
drawing room when their master and mistress had gone out; moreover,
he couldn't forgive them their plainness.

He arrived at the glass verandah, and put his hand on the door
handle, thinking once more of the stewed perch "with lots of parsley,"
when his eyes fell on a notice on the door. There was no necessity to
read it, he knew its purport: the restaurant was closed on midsummer-
day; he had forgotten it. He felt as if he had run with his head into a
lamp-post. He was furious; first of all with the proprietor for closing,
then with himself for having forgotten that the restaurant would be
closed. It seemed to him so monstrous that he could have forgotten an
incident of such importance, that he couldn't believe it and racked his
brain to find someone on whom he could lay the blame. Of course, it
was the fault of the proprietor. He had run off the lines, come into

collision. He was done. He sat down on the seat and almost shed tears of rage.

Thump! a ball hit him right in the middle of his starched shirt front. Like an infuriated wasp he rose from his seat to find the criminal; a plain little girl's face laughed into his; a laborer in his Sunday clothes and straw hat appeared, took her by the hand and smilingly expressed a hope that the child had not hurt him; a laughing crowd of soldiers and servant girls stared at him. He looked round for a constable for he felt that his rights as a human being had been encroached upon. But when he saw the constable in familiar conversation with the child's mother, he dropped the idea of making a scene, went straight to the nearest cab-stand, hired a cab, and told the driver to drive him to the bookseller's; he could not bear to be alone any longer.

In the safe shelter of the cab he took out his handkerchief and flicked the dust from his shirt front.

He dismissed the cab in Goten Street, for he felt sure that he would find his friend at home. But as he walked upstairs his assurance left him. Supposing he were out after all!

He was out. Not one of the tenants was at home. His knock sounded through an empty house; his footsteps re-echoed on the deserted stairs.

When he was again in the street he was at a loss to know what to do. He did not know Potocki's address, and where was he to find an address book on a day when all the shops were closed?

Without knowing where he was going, he went down the street, past the harbor, across the bridge. He did not meet a single man he knew. The presence of the crowd which occupied the town during the absence of their betters annoyed him, for, like the rest of us, the education which he had received at school had made an aristocrat of him.

In his first anger he had forgotten his hunger, but now it re-asserted itself. A new, terrible thought occurred to him, a thought which up to now he had put away from him out of sheer cowardice: Where was he to dine? He had started out with plenty of vouchers in his pocket, but only one crown and fifty öre in coin. The vouchers were only used at Rejner's, for convenience sake, and he had spent a crown on his cab fare.

He found himself again in Berzelius Park. Everywhere he met laborers and their families, eating what they had brought with them in baskets; hard-boiled eggs, crabs, pancakes. And the police did not interfere. On the contrary, he saw a policeman with a sandwich in one hand and a glass of beer in the other. But what irritated him more than anything else was the fact that these people whom he despised had the advantage of him. But why couldn't he go into a dairy and appease his hunger? Yes, why not? The very thought of it made him shudder.

After some little reflection he went down to the harbor, intending to cross over to the Deer Park. He was bound to find acquaintances there from whom he could borrow money (hateful thought!) for his dinner. And if so, he would dine at "Hazelmount," the best restaurant.

The steamer was so crowded that schoolmaster Blom had to stand close to the engine; the heat at his back was intolerable; his morning coat was being covered with grease spots, while he stood, with his gaze riveted on the untidy head of a servant girl and endured the rancid smell of the hair-oil. But he did not see a single face he knew.

When he entered the restaurant in the Deer Park, he squared his shoulders and tried to look as distinguished as possible.

The space before the restaurant was like the auditorium of a theater and seemed to serve the same purpose: that is to say, it was a place where one met one's friends and showed off. The verandah was occupied by officers, blue in the face with eating and drinking; with them were representatives of the foreign Powers, grown old and grey in their strenuous efforts to protect fellow-countrymen who had got mixed up with sailors and fishermen in drunken brawls, or assist at Gala perform-ances, christenings, weddings and funerals. So much for the aristocracy. In the center of a large space Mr. Blom suddenly discovered the chimney sweep of his quarter, the proprietor of a small inn, the chemist's assistant and others of the same standing. He watched the game-keeper in his green coat and silver lace, with his gilt staff, walking up and down and casting contemptuous glances at the assembled crowd, as if he were wondering why they were here? The schoolmaster felt self-conscious under the stare of all those eyes which seemed to say: "Look at him! there he goes, wondering how to get dinner!" But there was nothing else for it. He went on to the verandah where the people sat eating perch and asparagus, and drinking Sauternes and Champagne.

All of a sudden he felt the pressure of a friendly hand on his shoulder, and as he turned round, he found himself face to face with Gustav, the waiter, who seized his hand and exclaimed with undisguised pleasure:

"Is that really you, Mr. Blom? How are you?"

But Gustav, the waiter, who was so pleased to find himself for a few moments the equal of his master, held a piece of wood in his warm hand and met a pair of eyes which pierced his soul like gimlets. And yet this same hand had given him ten crowns only yesterday, and the owner of it had thanked him for six months' service and attention in the way one thanks a friend. The waiter went back to his companions and sat down amongst them, embarrassed and snubbed. But Mr. Blom left the verandah with bitter thoughts and pushed his way through the crowd; he fancied that he could hear a mocking: "He hasn't been able to get dinner, after all!"

He came to a large open space. There was a puppet-show, and Jasper was being beaten by his wife. A little further off a sailor was showing servant girls, soldiers and apprentices their future husband or wife in a wheel of fortune. They all had had dinner and were enjoying themselves; for a moment he believed himself their inferior, but only for a moment; then he remembered that they had not the vaguest idea of how an Egyptian camp was fortified. The thought gave him back his self-respect, and he wondered how it was possible that people could be so degraded as to find pleasure in such childishness.

In the meantime he had lost all inclination to try the other restaurants; he passed the Tivoli and went further into the heart of the park. Young men and women were dancing on the grass to the strains of a violin: a little further off a whole family was camping under an old oak; the head of the family was kneeling down, in his shirt sleeves, with bare head, a glass of beer in one hand, a sandwich in the other; his fat, jolly, clean-shaven face beamed with pleasure and good nature as he invited his guests, who were evidently his wife, parents-in-law, brothers, shop-assistants and servants, to eat, drink and be merry, for today was Midsummer day, all day long. And the jovial fellow made such droll remarks that the whole party writhed on the grass with amusement. After the pancake had been produced and eaten with the fingers, and the port bottle been round, the senior shop-assistant made a speech which was at once so moving and so witty that the ladies at one moment pressed their handkerchiefs to their eyes, while the head of the family bit his lips, and at the next interrupted the speaker with loud laughter and cheers.

The schoolmaster's mood became more and more morose, but instead of going away he sat down on a stone under a pine tree and watched "the animals."

When the speech was finished and father and mother had been toasted with cheers and a flourish of trumpets, executed on a concertina, accompanied by the rattling of all cups and saucers that happened to be empty, the party rose to play "Third Man," while mother and mother-in-law attended to the babies.

"Just like the beasts in the field," thought the schoolmaster, turning away, for all that was natural was ugly in his eyes, and only that which was unnatural could lay any claim to beauty in his opinion, except, of course, the paintings of "well-known" masters in the National Museum.

He watched the young men taking off their coats, the young girls slipping off their cuffs and hanging them on the blackthorn bushes; then they took up their positions and the game began.

The girls picked up their skirts and threw up their legs so that their garters, made of blue and red braid such as the grocers sell for tying up pots, were plainly visible, and whenever the cavalier caught his lady, he took her in his arms and swung her round so that her skirts flew; and young and old shrieked so with laughter that the park re-echoed.

"Is this innocence or corruption?" wondered the schoolmaster.

But evidently the party did not know what the learned word "corruption" meant, and that was the reason why they were so merry.

By the time they were tired of playing "Third Man" tea was ready. The schoolmaster was puzzled to know where the cavaliers had learnt their fine manners, for they moved about on all fours to offer the girls sugar and cake; and the straps of their waistcoats stood out like handles.

"The males showing off before the females!" thought the schoolmaster. "They don't know what they are in for."

He noticed how the head of the family, the jolly fellow, waited on father and mother-in-law, wife, shop-assistants and servant girls: and whenever one of them begged him to help himself first, he invariably answered that there was plenty of time for that.

He watched the father-in-law peeling a willow branch to make a flute for the little boy; he watched the mother-in-law wash up as if she had been one of the servants. And he thought that there was something strange about selfishness, since it could be so cleverly disguised that it looked as if no one gave more than he received; for it must be selfishness, it couldn't be anything else.

They played at forfeits and redeemed every forfeit with kisses, true, genuine, resounding kisses on the lips; and when the jolly book-keeper was made to kiss the old oak tree, his conduct was too absurd for anything; he embraced and caressed the gnarled trunk as if it had been a girl whom he had met secretly; everybody shouted with laughter, for all knew how to do it, although none of them would have liked to be caught doing it.

The schoolmaster who had begun by watching the spectacle with critical eyes, fell more and more under the spell of it; he almost believed himself to be one of the party. He smiled at the sallies of the shop-assistants, and before an hour was gone the head of the family had won his whole sympathy. No one could deny that the man was a comedian of the first rank. He could play "Skin-the-cat"; he could "walk backwards," "lie" on the tree-trunks, swallow coins, eat fire, and imitate all sorts of birds. And when he extracted a saffron cake from the dress of

one of the girls and made it disappear in his right ear, the schoolmaster
laughed until his empty inside ached.

Then the dancing began. The schoolmaster had read in Rabe's grammar: Nemo saltat sobrius, nisi forte insanit, and had always looked upon
dancing as a species of insanity. True, he had watched puppies and calves
dancing when they felt frisky, but he did not believe that Cicero's maxim
applied to the animal world, and he was in the habit of drawing a sharp
line between men and animals. Now, as he sat watching these young
people who were quite sober, and neither hungry nor thirsty, moving
round and round to the slow measures of the concertina, he felt as if
his soul were in a swing which was being kept going by his eyes and
ears, and his right foot beat time gently on the springy turf.

He spent three hours musing and watching, then he rose. He found
it almost difficult to tear himself away; it was just as if he were leaving
a merry party to which he had been invited; but his mood had changed;
he felt more reconciled. He was at peace with the world and pleasantly
tired, as if he had been enjoying himself.

It was evening. Smart carriages passed him, the lady-occupants lolling
on the back seats and looking in their long, white theater wraps like
corpses in their shrouds; it was fashionable then to look as if one had
been exhumed. The schoolmaster, whose thoughts were running in
another direction, was sure that the ladies must be bored to death and
felt no trace of envy. Below the dusty highroad, far out on the sea, the
steamers with their flags and brass bands were returning from their
pleasure trips; cheers, strains of music and snatches of song were wafted
by the sea breezes to the mountains and the Deer Park.

The schoolmaster had never felt so lonely in his life as he did this
evening in the moving throng. He fancied that everybody was looking
at him compassionately as he made his solitary way through the crowd,
and almost gave way to self-pity. He would have liked to talk to the first
comer, for the mere pleasure of hearing his voice, for in his loneliness
he felt as if he were walking by the side of a stranger. And now his
conscience smote him. He remembered the waiter Gustav, who had been
unable to hide his pleasure at meeting him. Now he had arrived at a
point when he would have given worlds if anybody had met him and
shown any pleasure at the fact. But nobody came.

Yes, somebody did, after all. As he was sitting by himself on the
steamer, a setter, who had lost his master, came to him and put its head
on his knee. The schoolmaster was not particularly fond of dogs, but
he allowed it to stay; he felt it pressing its soft warm body against his
leg, he saw the eyes of the forsaken brute looking at him in dumb appeal,
as if it were asking him to find its master.

But as soon as they landed, the setter ran away. "It needed me no longer," thought the schoolmaster, and he walked home and went to bed.

These trifling incidents of Midsummer day had robbed the schoolmaster of his assurance. They taught him that all foresight, all precautions, all the clever calculations in the world availed nothing. He felt a certain instability in his surroundings. Even the public house, his home, was not to be counted on. It might be closed any day. Moreover, a certain reserve on the part of Gustav troubled him. The waiter was as civil as before, more attentive even, but his friendship was gone; he had lost confidence. It afforded the schoolmaster food for thought, and whenever a tough piece of meat, or too small a dish of potatoes was set before him he thought:

"Haha! He's paying me out!"

It was a bad summer for the schoolmaster: the second violin was out of town and the book-seller frequented "Mosesheight," a garden restaurant in his own district, situated on a hill.

On an evening in autumn the bookseller and the second violin were sitting at their favorite table, drinking a glass of punch, when the schoolmaster entered, carrying under his arm a parcel which he carefully hid in an empty hamper in a cupboard used for all sorts of lumber. He was ill-tempered and unusually irritable.

"Well, old boy," the bookseller began for the hundredth time, "and when are you going to be married?"

"Confound your 'when are you going to be married!' As if a man hadn't enough trouble without it! Why don't you get married yourself?" growled the schoolmaster.

"Oh! because I have my old Stafva," answered the bookseller, who always had a number of stereotyped answers in readiness.

"I was married very happily," said the Pole, "but my wife is dead, now, ugh!"

"Is she?" mimicked the schoolmaster; "and the gentleman is a widower? How am I to reconcile these facts?"

The Pole nodded, for he did not in the least understand what the schoolmaster was driving at.

The latter felt bored by his friends; their topic of conversation was always the same; he knew their replies by heart.

Presently he went into the corridor for a few moments to fetch his cigar-case which he had left in the pocket of his overcoat. The bookseller instantly raided the cupboard and returned with the mysterious parcel. As it was not sealed, he opened it quickly; it contained a beautiful

American sleeping-suit; he hung it carefully over the back of the school-master's chair.

"Ugh!" said the Pole, grinning, as if he were looking at something unsightly.

The proprietor of the restaurant who loved a practical joke, bent over the counter, laughing loudly; the waiter stood rooted to the spot, and one of the cooks peeped through the door which communicated with the kitchen.

When the schoolmaster came back and realized the trick played on him, he grew pale with anger; he immediately suspected the bookseller; but when his eyes fell on Gustav who was standing in a corner of the room, laughing, his old obsession returned to him: "He's paying me out!" Without a word he seized his property, threw a few coins on the counter and left the restaurant.

Henceforth the schoolmaster avoided Rejner's. The bookseller had heard that he dined at a restaurant in his own district. This was true. But he was very discontented! The food was not actually bad, but it was not cooked to his liking. The waiters were not attentive. He often thought of returning to Rejner's, but his pride would not let him. He had been turned out of his home; in five minutes a bond of many years' standing had been severed.

A short time after fate struck him a fresh blow. Miss Augusta had inherited a little fortune in the provinces and had decided to leave Stockholm on the first of October. The schoolmaster had to look out for new lodgings.

But he had been spoilt, and there was no pleasing him. He changed his room every month. There was nothing wrong with the rooms, but they were not like his old room. It had become such a habit with him to walk through certain streets, that he often found himself before his old front door before he realized his mistake. He was like a lost child.

Eventually he went to live in a boarding house, a solution which he had always loathed and dreaded. And then his friends lost sight of him altogether.

One evening, as the Pole was sitting alone over his grog, smoking, drinking, and nodding with the capacity of the oriental to lapse into complete stupor, the bookseller burst in on him like a thunderstorm, flung his hat on the table, and shouted:

"Confound him! Has anybody ever heard anything like it?"

The Pole roused himself from his brandy-and-tobacco Nirvana, and rolled his eyes.

"I say, confound it! Has anybody ever heard anything like it? He's going to be married!"

"Who's going to be married?" asked the Pole, startled by the book-seller's violence and emphatic language.

"Schoolmaster Blom!"

The bookseller expected a glass of grog in exchange for his news. The proprietor left the counter and came to their table to listen.

"Has she any money?" he asked acutely.

"I don't think so," replied the bookseller, conscious of his temporary importance and selling his wares one by one.

"Is she beautiful?" asked the Pole. "My wife was very beautiful. Ugh!"

"No, she's not beautiful either," answered the bookseller, "but nice-looking."

"Have you seen her?" enquired the proprietor. "Is she old?" His eyes wandered towards the kitchen door.

"No, she's young!"

"And her parents?" continued the proprietor.

"I heard that her father was a brass founder in Orebro."

"The rascal! Well, I never!" said the proprietor.

"Haven't I always said so? The man is a born husband," said the bookseller.

"We all of us are," said the proprietor, "and take my word for it, no one escapes his fate!"

With this philosophical remark he closed the subject and returned to the counter.

When they had settled that the schoolmaster was not marrying for money, they discussed the problem of "what the young people were going to live on." The bookseller made a guess at the schoolmaster's salary and "what he might earn besides by giving private lessons." When that question, too, had been settled, the proprietor, who had returned to the table, asked for details.

"Where had he met her? Was she fair or dark? Was she in love with him?"

The last question was by no means out of the way; the bookseller "thought she was," for he had seen them together, arm in arm, looking into shop windows.

"But that he, who was such a stick, could fall in love! It was incredible!"

"And what a husband he would make!" The proprietor knew that he was *devilish particular* about his food, and that, he said, was a mistake when one was married.

"And he likes a glass of punch in the evening, and surely a married man can't drink punch every evening of his life. And he doesn't like children! It won't turn out well," he whispered. "Take my word for it, it won't turn out well. And, gentlemen, there's another thing," (he rose from his seat, looked round and continued in a whisper), "I believe, I'm hanged if I don't, that the old hypocrite has had a love affair of some sort. Do you remember that incident, gentlemen, with the — hihihi — sleeping suit? He's one of those whom you don't find where you leave them! Take care, Mrs. Blom! Mind what you are about! I'll say no more!"

It was certainly a fact that the schoolmaster was engaged to be married and that the wedding was to take place within two months.

What happened after, does not belong to this story, and, moreover, it is difficult to know what goes on behind the convent walls of domesticity when the vow of silence is being kept.

It was also a fact that the schoolmaster, after his marriage, was never again seen at a public house.

The bookseller, who met him by himself in the street one evening, had to listen to a long exhortation on getting married. The schoolmaster had inveighed against all bachelors; he had called them egotists, who refused to do their duty by the State; in his opinion they ought to be heavily taxed, for all indirect taxes weighed most cruelly on the father of a family. He went so far as to say that he wished to see bachelorhood punished by the law of the land as a "crime against nature."

The bookseller had a good memory. He said that he doubted the advisability of taking a *fool* into one's house, permanently. But the schoolmaster replied that *his* wife was the most intelligent woman he had ever met.

Two years after the wedding the Pole saw the schoolmaster and his wife in the theater; he thought that they looked happy; "ugh!"

Another three years went by. On a Midsummer day the proprietor of the restaurant made a pleasure trip on the Lake of Mälar to Mariafred. There, before Castle Cripsholm, he saw the schoolmaster, pushing a perambulator over a green field, and carrying in his disengaged hand a basket containing food, while a whole crowd of young men and women, "who looked like country folk," followed in the rear. After dinner the schoolmaster sang songs and turned somersaults with the youngsters. He looked ten years younger and had all the ways of a ladies' man.

The proprietor, who was quite close to the party while they were having dinner, overheard a little conversation between Mr. and Mrs. Blom. When the young wife took a dish of crabs from the basket, she apologized to Albert, because she had not been able to buy a single female crab in the whole market. Thereupon the schoolmaster put his arm round her, kissed her and said that it didn't matter in the least, because male or female crabs, it was all the same to him. And when one of the babies in the perambulator began to cry, the schoolmaster lifted it out and hushed it to sleep again.

Well, all these things are mere details, but how people can get married and bring up a family when they have not enough for themselves while they are bachelors, is a riddle to me. It almost looks as if babies brought their food with them when they come into this world; it really almost does look as if they did.

Compensation

He was considered a genius at College, and no one doubted that he would one day distinguish himself. But after passing his examinations, he was obliged to go to Stockholm and look out for a berth. His dissertation, which was to win him the doctor's degree, had to be postponed. As he was very ambitious, but had no private means, he resolved to marry money, and with this object in view, he visited only the very best families, both at Upsala where he studied for the bar, and later on at Stockholm. At Upsala he always fraternized with the new arrivals, that is to say, when they were members of aristocratic families, and the freshers felt flattered by the advances made by the older man. In this way he formed many useful ties, which meant invitations to his friends' country houses during the summer.

The country houses were his happy hunting ground. He possessed social talents, he could sing and play and amuse the ladies, and consequently he was a great favorite. He dressed beyond his means; but he never borrowed money from any of his friends or aristocratic acquaintances. He even went to the length of buying two worthless shares and mentioning on every possible occasion that he had to attend a General Meeting of the shareholders.

For two summers he had paid a great deal of attention to a titled lady who owned some property, and his prospects were the general topic, when he suddenly disappeared from high life and became engaged to a poor girl, the daughter of a cooper, who owned no property whatever.

His friends were puzzled and could not understand how he could thus stand in his own light. He had laid his plans so well, he "had but to stretch out his hand and success was in his grasp"; he had the morsel firmly stuck on his fork, it was only necessary for him to open his mouth and swallow it. He himself was at a loss to understand how it was that the face of a little girl whom he had met but once on a steamer could have upset all his plans of many years' standing. He was bewitched, obsessed.

He asked his friends whether they didn't think her beautiful?

Frankly speaking they didn't.

"But she is so clever! Just look into her eyes! What expressive eyes she has!"

His friends could see nothing and hear less, for the girl never opened her lips.

But he spent evening after evening with the cooper's family; to be sure, the cooper was a very intelligent man! On his knees before her (a trick often practiced at the country houses) he held her skeins of wool; he played and sang to her, talked about religion and the drama, and he always read acquiescence in her eyes. He wrote poetry about her, and sacrificed at her shrine his laurels, his ambitious dreams, even his dissertation.

And then he married her.

The cooper drank too much at the wedding and made an improper speech about girls in general. But the son-in-law found the old man so unsophisticated, so amiable, that he egged him on instead of shutting him up. He felt at his ease among these simple folk; in their midst he could be quite himself.

"That's being in love," said his friends. "Love is a wonderful thing."

And now they were married. One month — two months. He was unspeakably happy. Every evening they spent together and he sang a song to her about the Rose in the Wood, her favorite song. And he talked about religion and the drama, and she sat and listened eagerly. But she never expressed an opinion; she listened in silence and went on with her crochet work.

In the third month he relapsed into his old habit of taking an afternoon nap. His wife, who hated being by herself, insisted on sitting by him. It irritated him, for he felt an overwhelming need to be alone with his thoughts.

Sometimes she met him on his way home from his office, and her heart swelled with pride when he left his colleagues and crossed the street to join her. She took him home in triumph: he was *her* husband!

In the fourth month he grew tired of her favorite song. It was stale now! He took up a book and read, and neither of them spoke.

One evening he had to attend a meeting which was followed by a banquet. It was his first night away from home. He had persuaded his wife to invite a friend to spend the evening with her, and to go to bed early, for he did not expect to be home until late.

The friend came and stayed until nine o'clock. The young wife sat in the drawing room, waiting, for she was determined not to go to bed until her husband had returned. She felt too restless to go to sleep.

She sat alone in the drawing room. What could she do to make the time pass more quickly? The maid had gone to bed; the grandfather's clock ticked and ticked. But it was only ten o'clock when she put away her crochet work. She fidgeted, moved the furniture about and felt a little unstrung.

So that was what being married meant! One was torn from one's early surroundings, and shut up in three solitary rooms to wait until one's husband came home, half intoxicated. — Nonsense! he loved her, and he was out on business. She was a fool to forget that. But *did* he love her still? Hadn't he refused a day or two ago to hold a skein of wool for her? — a thing he loved to do before they were married. Didn't he look rather annoyed yesterday when she met him before lunch? And — after all — if he had to attend a business meeting tonight, there was no necessity for him to be present at the banquet.

It was half-past ten when her musing had reached this point. She was surprised that she hadn't thought of these things before. She relapsed into her dark mood and the dismal thoughts again passed through her mind, one by one. But now reinforcements had arrived. He never talked to her now! He never sang to her, never opened the piano! He had told her a lie when he had said that he couldn't do without his afternoon nap, for he was reading French novels all the time.

He had told her a lie!

It was only half-past eleven. The silence was oppressive. She opened the window and looked out into the street. Two men were standing down below, bargaining with two women. That was men's way! If he should ever do anything like that! She should drown herself if he did.

She shut the window and lighted the chandelier in the bedroom. "One ought to be able to see what one is about," he had once said to her on a certain occasion. — Everything was still so bright and new! The green coverlet looked like a mown lawn, and the little pillows reminded her of two white kittens curled up on the grass. The polish of her dressing-table reflected the light: the mirror had as yet none of those ugly stains which are made by the splashing of water. The silver on the back of her hair-brush, her powder-box, her tooth-brush, all shone and sparkled. Her bedroom slippers were still so new and pretty that it was impossible to picture them down-at-heel. Everything looked new, and yet everything seemed to have lost some of its freshness. She knew all his songs, all his drawing room pieces, all his words, all his thoughts. She knew before-hand what he would say when he sat down to lunch, what he would talk about when they were alone in the evening.

She was sick of it all. Had she been in love with him? Oh, yes! Certainly! But was this all then? Was she realizing all the dreams of her girlhood? Were things to go on like this until she died? Yes! But — but — but — surely they would have children! though there was no sign of it as yet. Then she would no longer be alone! Then he might go out as often as he liked, for she would always have somebody to talk to, to play with. Perhaps it was a baby which she wanted to make her happy. Perhaps matrimony really meant something more than being a man's legitimate mistress. That must be it! But then, he would have to love her, and he didn't do that. And she began to cry.

When her husband came home at one o'clock, he was quite sober. But he was almost angry with her when he found her still up.

"Why didn't you go to bed?" were the words with which he greeted her.

"How can I go to sleep when I am waiting for you?"

"A fine look out for me! Am I never to go out then? I believe you have been crying, too?"

"Yes, I have, and how can I help it if you — don't — love — me — any — more?"

"Do you mean to say I don't love you because I had to go out on business?"

"A banquet isn't business!"

"Good God! Am I not to be allowed to go out? How can women be so obtrusive?"

"Obtrusive? Yes, I noticed that yesterday, when I met you. I'll never meet you again."

"But, darling, I was with my chief —"

"Huhuhu!"

She burst into tears, her body moved convulsively.

He had to call the maid and ask her to fetch the hot-water bottle.

He, too, was weeping. Scalding tears! He wept over himself, his hardness of heart, his wickedness, his illusions over everything.

Surely his love for her wasn't an illusion? He did love her! Didn't he? And she said she loved him, too, as he was kneeling before her prostrate figure, kissing her eyes. Yes, they loved one another! It was merely a dark cloud which had passed, now. Ugly thoughts, born of solitude and loneliness. She would never, never again stay alone. They fell asleep in each other's arms, her face dimpled with smiles.

But she did not go to meet him on the following day. He asked no questions at lunch. He talked a lot, but more for the sake of talking than to amuse her; it seemed as if he were talking to himself.

In the evening he entertained her with long descriptions of the life at Castle Sjöstaholm; he mimicked the young ladies talking to the Baron, and told her the names of the Count's horses. And on the following day he mentioned his dissertation.

One afternoon he came home very tired. She was sitting in the drawing room, waiting for him. Her ball of cotton had fallen on the floor. In passing, his foot got entangled in the cotton; at his next step he pulled her crochet work out of her hand and dragged it along; then he lost his temper and kicked it aside.

She exclaimed at his rudeness.

He retorted that he had no time to bother about her rubbish, and advised her to spend her time more profitably. He had to think of his dissertation, if he was to have a career at all. And she ought to consider the question of how to limit their household expenses.

Things had gone far indeed!

On the next day the young wife, her eyes swollen with weeping, was knitting socks for her husband. He told her he could buy them cheaper ready-made. She burst into tears. What was she to do? The maid did all the work of the house, there was not enough work in the kitchen for two. She always dusted the rooms. Did he want her to send the maid away?

"No, no!"

"What did he want, then?"

He didn't know himself, but he was sure that something was wrong. Their expenses were too high. That was all. They couldn't go on living at their present rate, and then — somehow he could never find time to work at his dissertation.

Tears, kisses, and a grand reconciliation! But now he started staying away from home in the evening several times a week. Business! A man must show himself! If he stays at home, he will be overlooked and forgotten!

A year had passed; there were no signs of the arrival of a baby. "How like a little liaison I once had in the old days," he thought; "there is only one difference: this one is duller and costs more." There was no more conversation, now; they merely talked of household matters. "She has no brain," he thought. "I am listening to myself when I am talking to her, and the apparent depths of her eyes is a delusion, due to the size of her pupils — the unusual size of her pupils. —"

He talked openly about his former love for her as of something that was over and done with. And yet, whenever he did so, he felt a pain in his heart, an irritating, cruel pain, a remorseless pain that could never die.

"Everything on earth withers and dies," he mused, "why should her favorite song alone be an exception to this? When one has heard it three hundred and sixty-five times, it becomes stale; it can't be helped. But is my wife right when she says that our love, also, has died? No, and yet — perhaps she is. Our marriage is no better than a vulgar liaison, for we have no child."

One day he made up his mind to talk the matter over with a married friend, for were they not both members of the "Order of the Married?"

"How long have you been married?"

"Six years."

"And does matrimony bore you?"

"At first it did; but when the children came, matters improved."

"Was that so? It's strange that we have no child."

"Not your fault, old man! Tell your wife to go and see a doctor about it."

He had an intimate conversation with her and she went.

Six weeks after what a change!

What a bustle and commotion in the house! The drawing room table was littered with baby-clothes which were quickly hidden if anybody entered unexpectedly, and reappeared as quickly if it was only he who had come in. A name had to be thought of. It would surely be a boy. The midwife had to be interviewed, medical books had to be bought, and a cradle and a baby's outfit.

The baby arrived and it really was a boy! And when he saw the "little monkey that smelled of butter" clasped to her bosom, which until then had but been his plaything, he reverently discovered the mother in his little wife; and "when he saw the big pupils looking at the baby so intently that they seemed to be looking into the future," he realized that there were depths in her eyes after all; depths more profound than he could fathom for all his drama and religion. And now all his old love, his dear old love, burst into fresh flames, and there was something new added to it, which he had dimly divined, but never realized.

How beautiful she was when she busied herself about the house again! And how intelligent in all matters concerning the baby!

As for him, he felt a man. Instead of talking of the Baron's horses and the Count's cricket matches, he now talked, too much almost, of his son.

And when occasionally he was obliged to be out of an evening, he always longed for his own fireside; not because his wife sat there waiting for him, like an evil conscience, but because he knew that she was not alone. And when he came home, both mother and child were asleep. He was almost jealous of the baby, for there had been a certain charm in the thought that while he was out, somebody was sitting alone at home, eagerly awaiting his return.

Now he was allowed his afternoon nap. And as soon as he had gone back to town, the piano was opened and the favorite song of the *Rose in the Wood* was sung, for it was quite new to Harold, and had regained all its freshness for poor little Laura who hadn't heard it for so many days.

She had no time now for crochet work, but there were plenty of antimacassars in the house. He, on his part, could not spare the time for his dissertation.

"Harold shall write it," said the father, for he knew now that his life would not be over when he came to die.

Many an evening they sat together, as before, and gossiped, but now both took a share in the conversation, for now she understood what they were talking about.

She confessed that she was a silly girl who knew nothing about religion and the drama; but she said that she had always told him so, and that he had refused to believe it.

But now he believed it less than ever.

They sang the old favorite song, and Harold crowed, they danced to the tune and rocked the baby's cradle to it, and the song always retained its freshness and charm.

Frictions

*H*is eyes had been opened. He realized the perversity of the world, but he lacked the power to penetrate the darkness and discover the cause of this perversity; therefore he gave himself up to despair, a disillusioned man. Then he fell in love with a girl who married somebody else. He complained of her conduct to his friends, male and female, but they only laughed at him. For a little while longer he trod his solitary path alone and misunderstood. He belonged to "society," and joined in its pursuits, because it distracted him; but at the bottom of his heart he had nothing but contempt for its amusements, which he took no pains to conceal.

One evening he was present at a ball. He danced with a young woman of unusual beauty and animation. When the band ceased playing, he remained standing by her side. He knew he ought to talk to her but he did not know what to say. After a while the girl broke the silence.

"You are fond of dancing, Baron?" she said with a cold, smile.

"Oh no! not at all," he answered. "Are you?"

"I can't imagine anything more foolish," she replied.

He had met his man, or rather his woman.

"Why do you dance, then?" he asked.

"For the same reason that you do."

"Can you read my mind?"

"Easily enough; if two people think alike, the other always knows."

"H'm! You're a strange woman! Do you believe in love?"

"No!"

"Nor do I! You and I ought to get married."

"I'm beginning to think so myself."

"Would you marry me?"

"Why not? At any rate, we shouldn't fight."

"Horrible idea! But how can you be so sure?"

"Because we think alike."

"Yes, but that might become monotonous. We should have nothing to talk about, because the one would always know what the other is thinking."

"True; but wouldn't it be even more monotonous if we remained unmarried and misunderstood?"

"You are right! Would you like to think it over?"

"Yes, until the cotillion."

"No longer?"

"Why any longer?"

He took her back to the drawing room and left her there, drank several glasses of champagne and watched her during supper. She allowed two young members of the Diplomatic Corps to wait on her, but made fun of them all the time and treated them as if they were footmen.

As soon as the cotillion began, he went to her and offered her a bouquet.

"Do you accept me?" he asked.

"Yes," she replied.

And so they were engaged.

It's a splendid match, said the world. They are made for one another. They are equals as far as social position and money are concerned. They hold the same blasé views of life. By blasé the world meant that they cared very little for dances, theaters, bazaars, and other noble sports without which life is not really worth living.

They were like carefully wiped twin slates, exactly alike; but utterly unable to surmise whether or not life would write the same legend on both. They never asked one another during the tender moments of their engagement: Do you love me? They knew quite well that it was impossible, because they did not believe in love. They talked little, but they understood one another perfectly.

And they married.

He was always attentive, always polite, and they were good friends.

When the baby was born, it had but one effect on their relationship; they had something to talk about now.

But by-and-by the husband began to reveal a certain energy. He had a sense of duty, and moreover, he was sick of being idle. He had a private income, but was in no way connected with politics or the Government. Now he looked round for some occupation which would fill the void in his life. He had heard the first morning call of the awakening spirits and felt it his duty to do his share of the great work of research into the causes of human misery. He read much, made a careful study of politics and eventually wrote an article and sent it to a paper. The consequence was that he was elected a member of the Board of Education. This necessitated hard reading in future, for all questions were to be threshed out thoroughly.

The Baroness lay on the sofa and read Châteaubriand and Musset. She had no faith in the improvement of humanity, and this stirring up of the dust and mold which the centuries had deposited on human institutions irritated her. Yet she noticed that she did not keep pace with her husband. They were like two horses at a race. They had been weighed before the start and been found to be of the same weight; they had promised to keep side by side during the run; everything was calculated to make them finish the race and leave the course at the same time. But already the husband had gained by the length of a neck. Unless she hurried up, she was bound to be left behind.

And the latter really happened. In the following year he was made controller of the budget. He was away for two months. His absence made the Baroness realize that she loved him; a fact which was brought home to her by her fear of losing him.

When he returned home, she was all eagerness; but his mind was filled with the things he had seen and heard abroad. He realized that they had come to the parting of the ways, but he would have liked to delay it, prevent it, if possible. He showed her in great living pictures the functioning of the colossal gigantic machinery of the State, he tried to explain to her the working of the wheels, the multifarious transmissions, regulators and detents, unreliable pendulums and untrustworthy safety valves.

She was interested at first, but after a while her interest waned. Conscious of her mental inferiority, her insignificance, she devoted herself entirely to her baby, anxious to demonstrate to her husband that she yet had a value as a model mother. But her husband did not appreciate this value. He had married her for the sake of companionship, and he found in her an excellent nurse for his child. But how could it be helped now? Who could have foreseen such a thing?

The house was always full of members of Parliament, and politics was the subject of conversation at dinner. The hostess merely took care that no fault could be found with the cooking. The Baron never omitted to have one or two men amongst his guests who could talk to his wife about music and the drama, but the Baroness wanted to discuss nothing but the nursery and the bringing up of children. After dessert, as soon as the health of the hostess was drunk, there was a general stampede to the smoking-room where the political discussions were continued. The Baroness left her guests and went to the nursery with a feeling of bitterness in her heart; she realized that her husband had so far outdistanced her that she could never again hope to come up with him.

He worked much at home in the evening; frequently he was busy at his writing-table until the small hours of the morning, but always behind locked doors. When he noticed afterwards, as he sometimes did, that his wife went about with red eyes, he felt a pain in his heart; but they had nothing to say to each other.

Occasionally however, at those times when his work palled, when he realized that his inner life was growing poorer and poorer, he felt a void within him, a longing for warmth, for something intimate, something he had dreamed of long ago, in the early days of his youth. But every feeling of that sort he suppressed at once as unfaithfulness to his wife, for he had a very high conception of the duty of a husband.

To bring a little more variety into her daily life, he suggested one day that she should invite a cousin of whom she had often spoken, but whom he had never seen, to spend the winter with them in town.

This had always been a great wish of the Baroness's, but now that the realization of it was within her power, she changed her mind. She did not want her in the least now. Her husband pressed her for reasons, but she could not give him any. It roused his curiosity and finally she confessed that she was afraid of her cousin; afraid that she might win his heart, that he might fall in love with her.

"She must be a queer girl, we really must have her here!"

The Baroness wept and warned, but the Baron laughed and the cousin arrived.

One afternoon the Baron came home, tired as usual; he had forgotten all about the cousin and his curiosity in regard to her. They sat down to dinner. The Baron asked the cousin if she was fond of the theater. She replied that she was not. She preferred reality to make-believe. At home she had founded a school for black sheep and a society for the care of discharged prisoners. Indeed! The Baron was much interested in the administration of prisons. The cousin was able to give him a good deal of information, and during the rest of the dinner the conversation was exclusively about prisons. Eventually the cousin promised to treat the whole question in a paper which the Baron was going to read and work up.

What the Baroness had foreseen, happened. The Baron contracted a spiritual marriage with the cousin, and his wife was left out in the cold. But the cousin was also beautiful, and when she leaned over the Baron at his writing-desk, and he felt her soft arm on his shoulder and her warm breath against his cheek, he could not suppress a sensation of supreme well-being. Needless to say, their conversation was not always of prisons. They also discussed love. She believed in the love of the souls, and she stated as plainly as she could, that marriage without love was prostitution. The Baron had not taken much interest in the development of modern ideas on love, and found that her views on the subject were rather hard, but after all she was probably quite right.

But the cousin possessed other qualities, too, invaluable qualifications for a true spiritual marriage. She had no objection to tobacco smoke for instance, in fact, she was very fond of a cigarette herself. There was no reason, therefore, why she should not go into the smoking-room with the men after dinner and talk about politics. And then she was charming.

Tortured by little twinges of conscience, the Baron would every now and then disappear from the smoking-room, go into the nursery, kiss his wife and child, and ask her how she was getting on? The Baroness was grateful, but she was not happy. After these little journeys the Baron always returned to his friends in the best of tempers; one might have thought that he had faithfully performed a sacred duty. At other times it irritated and distressed him that his wife did not join the party in the smoking-room, too, as *his* wife; this thought was a burden which weighed quite heavily on him.

The cousin did not go home in the spring, but accompanied the couple to a watering-place. There she organized little performances for the benefit of the poor, in which she and the Baron played the parts of the lovers. This had the inevitable result that the fire burst into flames. But the flames were only spiritual flames; mutual interests, like views, and, perhaps, similar dispositions.

The Baroness had ample time to consider her position. The day arrived when she told her husband that since everything was over between them, the only decent thing to do was to part. But that was more than he had bargained for; he was miserable; the cousin had better return to her parents, and he would prove to his wife that he was a man of honor.

The cousin left. A correspondence between her and the Baron began. He made the Baroness read every letter, however much she hated doing it. After a while, however, he gave in and read the letters without showing them to his wife.

Finally the cousin returned. Then matters came to a crisis. The Baron discovered that he could not live without her.

What were they to do? Separate? It would be death. Go on as at present? Impossible! Annul the marriage which the Baron had come to look upon as legal prostitution and marry his beloved? However painful it might be, it was the only honest course to take.

But that was against the wishes of the cousin. She did not want it said of her that she had stolen another woman's husband. And then the scandal! the scandal!

"But it was dishonest not to tell his wife everything; it was dishonest to allow things to go on; one could never tell how the matter would end."

"What did he mean? How could it end?"

"Nobody could tell!"

"Oh! How dared he! What did he think of her?"

"That she was a woman!"

And he fell on his knees and worshipped her; he said that he did not care if the administration of prisons and the school for black sheep went to the devil; he did not know what manner of woman she was; he only knew that he loved her.

She replied that she had nothing but contempt for him, and went helter skelter to Paris. He followed at her heels. At Hamburg he wrote a letter to his wife in which he said that they had made a mistake and that it was immoral not to rectify it. He asked her to divorce him.

And she divorced him.

A year after these events the Baron and the cousin were married. They had a child. But that was a fact which did not interfere with their happiness. On the contrary! What a wealth of new ideas germinated in their minds in their voluntary exile! How strong were the winds which blew here!

He encouraged her to write a book on "young criminals." The press tore it to pieces. She was furious and swore that she would never write another book. He asked her whether she wrote for praise, whether she was ambitious? — She replied by a question: Why did he write? — A little quarrel arose. He said it was refreshing to hear her express views which did not echo his own — always his own. — Always his own? What did he mean? Didn't she have *views of her own?* She henceforth made it her business to prove to him on every occasion that she was capable of forming her own opinions; and to prevent any errors on his part she took good care that they always differed from his. He told her he did not care what views she held as long as she loved him. — Love? What about it? He was no better than other men and, moreover, he had betrayed her. He did not love her soul, but her body. — No, he loved both, he loved her, every bit of her! — Oh! How deceitful he had been! — No, he had not been deceitful, he had merely deceived himself when he believed that he loved her soul only.

They were tired of strolling up and down the boulevard, and sat down before a café. She lighted a cigarette. A waiter requested her rather uncivilly, not to smoke. The Baron demanded an explanation and the waiter said that the café was a first-class establishment and the management was anxious not to drive away respectable people by serving *these ladies*. They rose from their seats, paid and went away. The Baron was furious, the young Baroness had tears in her eyes.

"There they had a demonstration of the power of prejudice! Smoking was a foolish act as far as a man was concerned, but in a woman it was a crime! Let him who was able to do so, destroy this prejudice! Or, let us say, him who would care to do so! The Baron had no wish that his wife should be the first victim, even if it were to win for her the doubtful honor of having cast aside a prejudice. For it was nothing else. In Russia, ladies belonging to the best society smoked at the dinner-table during the courses. Customs changed with the latitudes. And yet those trifles were not without importance, for life consisted of trifles. If men and women shared bad habits, intercourse between them would be less stiff and formal: they would make friends more easily and keep pace with one another. If they had the same education, they would have the same interests, and cling together more closely during the whole of their lives."

The Baron was silent as if he had said something foolish. But she had not been listening to him; her thoughts had been far away.

"She had been insulted by a waiter, told that she was not fit to associate with respectable people. There was more behind that, than appeared on the surface. She had been recognized. Yes, she was sure of it, it was not the first time that she had noticed it."

"What had she noticed?"

"That she had been treated with little respect at the restaurants. The people evidently did not think that they were married; because they were affectionate and civil to one another. She had borne it in silence for a long time, but now she had come to the end of her tether. And yet this was nothing compared to what they were saying at home!"

"Well, what were they saying? And why had she never told him anything about it before?"

"Oh! horrible things! The letters she had received! Leaving the anonymous ones quite out of the question.

"Well, and what about him? Was he not being treated as if he were a criminal? And yet he had not committed a crime! He had acted according to all legal requirements, he had not broken his marriage vows. He had left the country in compliance with the dictates of the law; the Royal Consistory has granted his appeal for a divorce; the clergy, Holy Church, had given him his release from the bonds of his first marriage on stamped paper; therefore he had not broken them! When a country was conquered, a whole nation was absolved from its oath of loyalty to its monarch; why did society look askance at the release from a promise? Had it not conferred the right on the Consistory to dissolve a marriage? How could it dare to assume the character of a judge now and condemn its own laws? Society was at war with itself! He was being treated like a criminal! Hadn't the secretary of the Embassy, his old friend, on whom he had left his and his wife's cards, acknowledged them by simply returning one card only? And was he not overlooked at all public functions?"

"Oh! She had had to put up with worse things! One of her friends in Paris had closed her door to her, and several had cut her in the street."

"Only the wearer of a boot knew where it pinched. The boots which they were wearing now were real Spanish boots, and they were at war with society. The upper classes had cut them. The upper classes! This community of semi-imbeciles, who secretly lived like dogs, but showed one another respect as long as there was no public scandal; that was to say as long as one did not honestly revoke an agreement and wait until it had lapsed before one made use of one's newly-regained freedom! And these vicious upper classes were the awarders of social position and respect, according to a scale on which honesty ranked far below zero. Society was nothing but a tissue of lies! It was inexplicable that it hadn't been found out long ago! It was high time to examine this fine structure and inquire into the condition of its foundations."

They were on friendlier terms on arriving home than they had been for many years. The Baroness stayed at home with her baby, and was soon expecting a second one. This struggle against the tide was too hard for her, and she was already growing tired of it. She was tired of everything! To write in an elegantly furnished, well-heated room on the subject of discharged prisoners, offering them, at a proper distance, a well-gloved hand, was a proceeding society approved of; but to hold out the hand of friendship to a woman who had married a legally divorced man was quite another thing. Why should it be so? It was difficult to find an answer.

The Baron fought in the thick of the battle. He visited the Chamber of Deputies, was present at meetings, and everywhere he listened to passionate diatribes against society. He read papers and magazines, kept a keen eye on literature, studied the subject deeply. His wife was threatened by the same fate which had overtaken the first one; to be left behind! It was strange. She seemed unable to take in all the details of his investigations, she disapproved of much of the new doctrine, but she felt that he was right and fighting for a good cause. He knew that he could always count on her never-flagging sympathy; that he had a friend at home who would always stand by him. Their common fate drove them into each other's arms like frightened birds at the approach of a storm. All the womanliness in her, — however little it may be appreciated nowadays, — which is after all nothing but a memory of the great mother, the force of nature which is woman's endowment, was roused. It fell on the children like the warm glow of a fire at eventide; it fell on the husband like a ray of sunshine; it brought peace to the home. He often wondered how it was that he did not miss his old comrade, with whom he was wont to discuss everything; he discovered that his thoughts had gained force and vigor since he stopped pouring them out as soon as he conceived them; it seemed to him that he was profiting more by the silent approval, the kindly nod, the unwavering sympathy. He felt that his strength had increased, that his views were less under outside control; he was a solitary man, now, and yet he was less solitary than he had been in the past, for he was no longer constantly met by contradictions which merely filled his heart with misgivings.

It was Christmas Eve in Paris. A large Christmas tree, grown in the wood of St. Germain, stood in their little chalet on the Cours de la Reine. They were going out after breakfast to buy Christmas presents for the children. The Baron was preoccupied, for he had just published a little pamphlet, entitled: "Do the Upper Classes constitute Society?" They were sitting at breakfast in their cozy dining room, and the doors which led to the nursery stood wide open. They listened to the nurse playing with the children, and the Baroness smiled with contentment and happiness. She had grown very gentle and her happiness was a quiet one. One of the children suddenly screamed and she rose from the table to see what was the matter. At the same moment the footman came into the dining room with the morning post. The Baron opened two packets of printed matter. The first was a "big respectable" newspaper. He opened it and his eyes fell on a headline in fat type: "A Blasphemer!"

He began to read: "Christmas is upon us again! This festival dear to all pure hearts, this festival sacred to all Christian nations, which has brought a message of peace and good-will to all men, which makes even the murderer sheathe his knife, and the thief respect the sacred law of property; this festival, which is not only of very ancient origin, but which is also, especially in the countries of the North, surrounded by a host of historic associations, etc., etc. And then like foul fumes arising from a drain, an individual suddenly confronts us who does not scruple to tear asunder the most sacred bonds, who vomits malice on all respectable members of society; malice, dictated by the pettiest vengeance. . . ." He refolded the paper and put it into the pocket of his dressing gown. Then he opened the second parcel. It contained carica-

tures of himself and his wife. It went the same way as the first, but he
had to be quick, for his wife was reentering the dining room. He finished
his breakfast and went into his bedroom to get ready to go out. They
left the house together.

The sunlight fell on the frosted plane trees of the Champs Elysées,
and in the heart of the stony desert the Place de la Concorde opened
out like a large oasis. He felt her arm on his, and yet he had the feeling
as if she were supporting him. She talked of the presents which they
were going to buy for the children, and he tried to force himself to take
an interest in the subject. But all at once he interrupted her conversation
and asked her, à propos of nothing:

"Do you know the difference between vengeance and punishment?"

"No, I've never thought about it."

"I wonder whether it isn't this: When an anonymous journalist
revenges himself, it is punishment; but when a well-known writer, who
is not a pressman, fights with an open visor, meting out punishment,
then it is revenge! Let us join the new prophets!"

She begged him not to spoil Christmas by talking of the newspapers.

"This festival," he muttered, "on which peace and good-will. . . ."

They passed through the arcades of the Rue de Rivoli, turned into
the boulevards and made their purchases. They dined at the Grand
Hotel. She was in a sunny frame of mind and tried to cheer him up.
But he remained preoccupied. Suddenly he asked,

"How is it possible that one can have a bad conscience when one has
acted rightly?"

She did not know.

"Is it because the upper classes have so trained us, that our conscience
troubles us whenever we rebel against them? Probably it is so. Why
shouldn't he who has been hurt unjustly, have the right to attack
injustice? Because only he who has been hurt will attack, and the upper
classes hate being attacked. Why did I not strike at the upper classes in
the past, when I belonged to them? Because, of course, I didn't know
them then. One must look at a picture from a distance in order to find
the correct visual point!"

"One shouldn't talk about such things on Christmas Eve!"

"True, it is Christmas. This festival of. . . ."

They returned home. They lit the candles on the Christmas tree; it
radiated peace and happiness; but its dark branches smelt of a funeral
and looked sinister, like the Baron's face. The nurse came in with the
little ones. His face lighted up, for, he thought, when they are grown up
they will reap in joy what we have sown in tears; then their conscience
will only trouble them when they have sinned against the laws of nature;

they won't have to suffer from whims which have been caned into us at school, drummed into us by the parsons, invented by the upper classes for their own benefit.

The Baroness sat down at the piano when the maids and the footmen entered. She played melancholy old dances, dear to the heart of the people of the North, while the servants danced gravely with the children. It was very much like the penitential part of divine service.

After that the presents were distributed among the children, and the servants received their gifts. And then the children were put to bed.

The Baroness went into the drawing room and sat down in an armchair. The Baron threw himself on a footstool at her feet. He rested his head on her knees. It was so heavy — so heavy. She silently stroked his forehead. "What! was he weeping?"

"Yes!"

She had never before seen a man weep. It was a terrible sight. His big strong frame shook, but he made no sound.

"Why was he weeping?"

"Because he was unhappy."

"Unhappy with her?"

"No, no, not with her, but still, unhappy."

"Had anybody treated him badly?"

"Yes!"

"Couldn't he tell her all about it?"

"No, he only wanted to sit at her knees, as he used to sit long ago, at his mother's."

She talked to him as if he had been a child. She kissed his eyes and wiped his face with her handkerchief. She felt so proud, so strong, there were no tears in her eyes. The sight of her inspired him with new courage.

"How weak he had been! That he should have found the machine-made attacks of his opponents so hard to bear! Did his enemies really believe what they said?"

"Terrible thought! Probably they did. One often found stones firmly grown into pine trees, why should not opinions grow into the brain in the same way? But she believed in him, she knew that he was fighting for a good cause?"

"Yes, she believed it! But — he must not be angry with her for asking him such a question — but — did he not miss his child, the first one?"

"Yes, certainly, but it could not be helped. At least, not yet! But he and the others who were working for the future would have to find a remedy for that, too. He did not know, yet, what form that remedy would take, but stronger brains than his, and many together, would surely one day solve this problem which at present seemed insolvable."

"Yes, she hoped it would be so."

"But their marriage? Was it a marriage in the true sense of the word, seeing that he couldn't tell her what troubled him? Wasn't it, too, pro. . .?"

"No, it was a true marriage, for they loved one another. There had been no love between him and his first wife. But he and she did love one another, could she deny it?"

"She couldn't, he was her dear love." Then their marriage was a true marriage before God and before Nature.

Unnatural Selection

OR, THE ORIGIN OF RACE

*T*he Baron had read in *The Slaves of Life* with disgust and indignation that the children of the aristocracy were bound to perish unless they took the mothers' milk from the children of the lower classes. He had read Darwin and believed that the gist of his teaching was that through selection the children of the aristocracy had come to be more highly developed representatives of the genus "Man." But the doctrine of heredity made him look upon the employment of a foster-mother with aversion; for might not, with the blood of the lower classes, certain conceptions, ideas and desires be introduced and propagated in the aristocratic nursling? He was therefore determined that his wife should nurse her baby herself, and if she should prove incapable of doing so, the child should be brought up with the bottle. He had a right to the cows' milk, for they fed on his hay; without it they would starve, or would not have come into existence at all. The baby was born. It was a son! The father had been somewhat anxious before he became certain of his wife's condition, for he was, personally, a poor man; his wife, on the other hand, was very wealthy, but he had no claim to her fortune unless their union was blest with a legal heir, (in accordance with the law of entail chap. 00 par. 00). His joy was therefore great and genuine. The baby was a transparent little thoroughbred, with blue veins shining through his waxen skin. Nevertheless his blood was poor. His mother who possessed the figure of an angel, was brought up on choice food, protected by rich furs from all the eccentricities of the climate, and had that aristocratic pallor which denotes the woman of noble descent.

She nursed the baby herself. There was consequently no need to become indebted to peasant women for the privilege of enjoying life on this planet. Nothing but fables, all he had read about it! The baby sucked and screamed for a fortnight. But all babies scream. It meant nothing. But it lost flesh. It became terribly emaciated. The doctor was sent for.

He had a private conversation with the father, during which he declared that the baby would die if the Baroness continued to nurse him, because she was firstly too highly strung, and secondly had nothing with which to feed him. He took the trouble to make a quantitative analysis of the milk, and proved (by equations) that the child was bound to starve unless there was a change in the method of his feeding.

What was to be done? On no account could the baby be allowed to die.

Bottle or foster mother? The latter was out of the question. Let us try the bottle! The doctor, however, prescribed a foster mother.

The best Dutch cow, which had received the gold medal for the district, was isolated and fed with hay; with dry hay of the finest quality. The doctor analyzed the milk, everything was all right. How simple the system was! How strange that they had not thought of it before! After all, one need not engage a foster mother a tyrant before whom one had to cringe, a loafer one had to fatten; not to mention the fact that she might have an infectious disease.

But the baby continued to lose flesh and to scream. It screamed night and day. There was no doubt it suffered from colic. A new cow was procured and a fresh analysis made. The milk was mixed with Karlsbad water, genuine Sprudel, but the baby went on screaming.

"There's no remedy but to engage a foster mother," said the doctor.

"Oh! anything but that! One did not want to rob other children, it was against nature, and, moreover, what about heredity?"

When the Baron began to talk of things natural and unnatural, the doctor explained to him that if nature were allowed her own way, all noble families would die out and their estates fall to the crown. This was the wisdom of nature, and human civilization was nothing but a foolish struggle against nature, in which man was bound to be beaten. The Baron's race was doomed; this was proved by the fact that his wife was unable to feed the fruit of her womb; in order to live they were bound to buy or steal the milk of other women. Consequently the race lived on robbery, down to the smallest detail.

"Could the purchase of the milk be called robbery? The purchase of it!"

"Yes, because the money with which it was bought was produced by labor. Whose labor? The people's! For the aristocracy didn't work."

"The doctor was a socialist!"

"No, a follower of Darwin. However, he didn't care in the least if they called him a socialist. It made no difference to him."

"But surely, purchase was not robbery! That was too strong a word!"

"Well, but if one paid with money one hadn't earned!"

"That was to say, earned by manual labor?"

"Yes!"

"But in that case the doctor was a robber too!"

"Quite so! Nevertheless he would not hold back with the truth! Didn't the Baron remember the repenting thief who had spoken such true words?"

The conversation was interrupted; the Baron sent for a famous professor. The latter called him a murderer straight out, because he had not engaged a nurse long ago.

The Baron had to persuade his wife. He had to retract all his former arguments and emphasize the one simple fact, namely, the love for his child, (regulated by the law of entail).

But where was a foster mother to come from? It was no use thinking of looking for one in town, for there all people were corrupt. No, it would have to be a country girl. But the Baroness objected to a girl because, she argued, a girl with a baby was an immoral person; and her son might contract a hereditary tendency.

The doctor retorted that all foster mothers were unmarried women and that if the young Baron inherited from her a preference for the other sex, he would grow into a good fellow; tendencies of that sort ought to be encouraged. It was not likely that any of the farmers' wives would accept the position, because a farmer who owned land, would certainly prefer to keep his wife and children with him.

"But supposing they married a girl to a farm laborer?"

"It would mean a delay of nine months."

"But supposing they found a husband for a girl who had a baby?"

"That wasn't a bad idea!"

The Baron knew a girl who had a baby just three months old. He knew her only too well, for he had been engaged for three years and had been unfaithful to his fiancée by "doctor's orders." He went to her himself and made his suggestion. She should have a farm of her own if she would consent to marry Anders, a farm laborer, and come to the Manor as foster mother to the young Baron. Well, was it strange that she should accept the proffered settlement in preference to her bearing her disgrace alone? It was arranged there and then that on the following Sunday the banns should be read for the first, second and third time, and that Anders should go home to his own village for two months.

The Baron looked at her baby with a strange feeling of envy. He was a big, strong boy. He was not beautiful, but he looked like a guarantee of many generations to come. The child was born to live but it was not his fate to fulfill his destination.

Anna wept when he was taken to the orphanage, but the good food at the Manor (her dinner was sent up to her from the dining room, and she had as much porter and wine as she wanted) consoled her. She was also allowed to go out driving in the big carriage, with a footman by the side of the coachman. And she read *A Thousand and One Nights*. Never in all her life had she been so well off.

After an absence of two months Anders returned. He had done nothing but eat, drink, and rest. He took possession of the farm, but he also wanted his Anna. Couldn't she, at least, come and see him sometimes? No, the Baroness objected. No nonsense of that sort!

Anna lost flesh and the little Baron screamed. The doctor was consulted.

"Let her go and see her husband," he said.

"But supposing it did the baby harm?"

"It won't!"

But Anders must be "analyzed" first. Anders objected.

Anders received a present of a few sheep and was "analyzed."

The little Baron stopped screaming.

But now news came from the orphanage that Anna's boy had died of diphtheria.

Anna fretted, and the little Baron screamed louder than ever. She was discharged and sent back to Anders and a new foster mother was engaged.

Anders was glad to have his wife with him at last, but she had contracted expensive habits. She couldn't drink Brazilian coffee, for instance, it had to be Java. And her health did not permit her to eat fish six times a week, nor could she work in the fields. Food at the farm grew scarce.

Anders would have been obliged to give up the farm after twelve months, but the Baron had a kindly feeling for him and allowed him to stay on as a tenant.

Anna worked daily at the Manor and frequently saw the little Baron; but he did not recognize her and it was just as well that he did not. And yet he had lain at her breast! And she had saved his life by sacrificing the life of her own child. But she was prolific and had several sons, who grew up and were laborers and railway men; one of them was a convict.

But the old Baron looked forward with anxiety to the day on which his son should marry and have children in his turn. He did not look strong! He would have been far more reassured if the other little Baron, the one who had died at the orphanage, had been the heir to the estates. And when he read *The Slaves of Life* a second time, he had to admit that the upper classes live at the mercy of the lower classes, and when he read

Darwin again he could not deny that natural selection, in our time, was anything but natural. But facts were facts and remained unalterable, in spite of all the doctor and the socialists might say to the contrary.

An Attempt at Reform

She had noticed with indignation that girls were solely brought up to be housekeepers for their future husbands. Therefore she had learnt a trade which would enable her to keep herself in all circumstances of life. She made artificial flowers.

He had noticed with regret that girls simply waited for a husband who should keep them; he resolved to marry a free and independent woman who could earn her own living; such a woman would be his equal and a companion for life, not a housekeeper.

Fate ordained that they should meet. He was an artist and she, as I already mentioned, made flowers; they were both living in Paris at the time when they conceived these ideas.

There was style in their marriage. They took three rooms at Passy. In the center was the studio, to the right of it his room, to the left hers. This did away with the common bedroom and double bed, that abomination which has no counterpart in nature and is responsible for a great deal of dissipation and immorality. It moreover did away with the inconvenience of having to dress and undress in the same room. It was far better that each of them should have a separate room and that the studio should be a neutral, common meeting place.

They required no servant; they were going to do the cooking themselves and employ an old charwoman in the mornings and evenings. It was all very well thought out and excellent in theory.

"But supposing you had children?" asked the skeptics.

"Nonsense, there won't be any!"

It worked splendidly. He went to the market in the morning and did the catering. Then he made the coffee. She made the beds and put the rooms in order. And then they sat down and worked.

When they were tired of working they gossiped, gave one another good advice, laughed and were very jolly.

At twelve o'clock he lit the kitchen fire and she prepared the vegetables. He cooked the beef, while she ran across the street to the grocer's; then she laid the table and he dished up the dinner.

Of course, they loved one another as husbands and wives do. They said good-night to each other and went into their own rooms, but there was no lock to keep him out when he knocked at her door; but the accommodation was small and the morning found them in their own quarters. Then he knocked at the wall:

"Good morning, little girlie, how are you today?"

"Very well, darling, and you?"

Their meeting at breakfast was always like a new experience which never grew stale.

They often went out together in the evening and frequently met their countrymen. She had no objection to the smell of tobacco, and was never in the way. Everybody said that it was an ideal marriage; no one had ever known a happier couple.

But the young wife's parents, who lived a long way off, were always writing and asking all sorts of indelicate questions; they were longing to have a grandchild. Louisa ought to remember that the institution of marriage existed for the benefit of the children, not the parents. Louisa held that this view was an old-fashioned one. Mama asked her whether she did not think that the result of the new ideas would be the complete extirpation of mankind? Louisa had never looked at it in that light, and moreover the question did not interest her. Both she and her husband were happy; at last the spectacle of a happy married couple was presented to the world, and the world was envious.

Life was very pleasant. Neither of them was master and they shared expenses. Now he earned more, now she did, but in the end their contributions to the common fund amounted to the same figure.

Then she had a birthday! She was awakened in the morning by the entrance of the charwoman with a bunch of flowers and a letter painted all over with flowers, and containing the following words:

> "To the lady flower-bud from her dauber, who wishes her many happy returns of the day and begs her to honor him with her company at an excellent little breakfast — at once."

She knocked at his door — come in!

And they breakfasted, sitting on the bed — his bed; and the charwoman was kept the whole day to do all the work. It was a lovely birthday!

Their happiness never palled. It lasted two years. All the prophets had prophesied falsely.

It was a model marriage!

But when two years had passed, the young wife fell ill. She put it down to some poison contained in the wall-paper; he suggested germs of some sort. Yes, certainly, germs. But something was wrong. Something was not as it should be. She must have caught cold. Then she grew stout. Was she suffering from tumor? Yes, they were afraid she was.

She consulted a doctor — and came home crying. It was indeed a growth, but one which would one day see daylight, grow into a flower and bear fruit.

The husband did anything but cry. He found style in it, and then the wretch went to his club and boasted about it to his friends. But the wife still wept. What would her position be now? She would soon not be able to earn money with her work and then she would have to live on him. And they would have to have a servant! Ugh! those servants!

All their care, their caution, their wariness had been wrecked on the rock of the inevitable.

But the mother-in-law wrote enthusiastic letters and repeated over and over again that marriage was instituted by God for the protection of the children; the parents' pleasure counted for very little.

Hugo implored her to forget the fact that she would not be able to earn anything in future. Didn't she do her full share of the work by mothering the baby? Wasn't that as good as money? Money was, rightly understood, nothing but work. Therefore she paid her share in full.

It took her a long time to get over the fact that he had to keep her. But when the baby came, she forgot all about it. She remained his wife and companion as before in addition to being the mother of his child, and he found that this was worth more than anything else.

A Natural Obstacle

*H*er father had insisted on her learning book-keeping, so that she might escape the common lot of young womanhood; to sit there and wait for a husband.

She was now employed as book-keeper in the goods department of the Railways, and was universally looked upon as a very capable young woman. She had a way of getting on with people, and her prospects were excellent.

Then she met the green forester from the School of Forestry and married him. They had made up their minds not to have any children; theirs was to be a true, spiritual marriage, and the world was to be made to realize that a woman, too, has a soul, and is not merely sex. Husband and wife met at dinner in the evening. It really was a true marriage, the union of two souls; it was, of course, also the union of two bodies, but this is a point one does not discuss.

One day the wife came home and told her husband that her office hours had been changed. The directors had decided to run a new night train to Malmo, and in future she would have to be at her office from six to nine in the evening. It was a nuisance, for he could not come home before six. That was quite impossible.

Henceforth they had to dine separately and meet only at night. He was dissatisfied. He hated the long evenings.

He fell into the habit of calling for her. But he found it dull to sit on a chair in the goods department and have the porters knocking against him. He was always in the way. And when he tried to talk to her as she sat at her desk with the penholder behind her ear, she interrupted him with a curt:

"Oh! do be quiet until I've done!"

Then the porters turned away their faces and he could see by their backs that they were laughing.

Sometimes one or the other of her colleagues announced him with a:

"Your husband is waiting for you, Mrs. X."

"Your husband!" There was something scornful in the very way in which they pronounced the word.

But what irritated him more than anything else was the fact that the desk nearest to her was occupied by a "young ass" who was always gazing into her eyes and everlastingly consulting the ledger, bending over her shoulders so that he almost touched her with his chin. And they talked of invoices and certificates, of things which might have meant anything for all he knew. And they compared papers and figures and seemed to be on more familiar terms with one another than husband and wife were. And that was quite natural, for she saw more of the young ass than of her husband. It struck him that their marriage was not a true spiritual marriage after all; in order to be that he, too, would have had to be employed in the goods department. But as it happened he was at the School of Forestry.

One day, or rather one night, she told him that on the following Saturday a meeting of railway employés, which was to conclude with a dinner, would be held, and that she would have to be present. Her husband received the communication with a little air of constraint.

"Do you want to go?" he asked naïvely.

"Of course, I do!"

"But you will be the only woman amongst so many men, and when men have had too much to drink, they are apt to become coarse."

"Don't you attend the meetings of the School of Forestry without me?"

"Certainly, but I am not the only man amongst a lot of women."

"Men and women were equals, she was amazed that he, who had always preached the emancipation of women could have any objection to her attending the meeting."

"He admitted that it was nothing but prejudice on his part. He admitted that she was right and that he was wrong, but all the same he begged her not to go; he hated the idea. He couldn't get over the fact."

"He was inconsequent."

"He admitted that he was inconsequent, but it would take ten generations to get used to the new conditions."

"Then he must not go to meetings either?"

"That was quite a different matter, for his meetings were attended by men only. He didn't mind her going out without him; what he didn't like was that she went out alone with so many men."

"She wouldn't be alone, for the cashier's wife would be present as —"

"As what?"

"As the cashier's wife."

"Then couldn't he be present as her husband?"

"Why did he want to make himself so cheap by being in the way?"

"He didn't mind making himself cheap."

"Was he jealous?"

"Yes! Why not? He was afraid that something might come between them."

"What a shame to be jealous! What an insult! What distrust! What did he think of her?"

"That she was perfect. He would prove it. She could go alone!" "Could she really? How condescending of him!"

She went. She did not come home until the early hours of the morning. She awakened her husband and told him how well it had all gone off. He was delighted to hear it. Somebody had made a speech about her; they had sung quartets and ended with a dance.

"And how had she come home?"

"The young ass had accompanied her to the front door."

"Supposing anybody who knew them had seen her at three o'clock in the morning in the company of the young ass?"

"Well, and what then? She was a respectable woman."

"Yes, but she might easily lose her reputation."

"Ah! He was jealous, and what was even worse, he was envious. He grudged her every little bit of fun. That was what being married meant! To be scolded if one dared to go out and enjoy oneself a little. What a stupid institution marriage was! But was their union a true marriage? They met one another at night, just as other married couples did. Men were all alike. Civil enough until they were married, but afterwards, oh! Afterwards. . . . Her husband was no better than other men: he looked upon her as his property, he thought he had a right to order her about."

"It was true. There was a time when he had believed that they belonged to one another, but he had made a mistake. He belonged to her as a dog belonged to its master. What was he but her footman, who called for her at night to see her home? He was 'her husband.' But did she want to be 'his wife'? Were they equals?"

"She hadn't come home to quarrel with him. She wanted to be nothing but his wife, and she did not want him to be anything but her husband."

The effect of the champagne, he thought, and turned to the wall.

She cried and begged him not to be unjust, but to — forgive her.

He pulled the blankets over his ears.

She asked him again if he — if he didn't want her to be his wife anymore?

"Yes, of course, he wanted her! But he had been so dreadfully bored all the evening, he could never live through another evening like it."

"Let them forget all about it then!"

And they forgot all about it and continued loving one another.

On the following evening, when the green forester came for his wife, he was told that she had gone to the store rooms. He was alone in the counting-house and sat down on a chair. Presently a glass door was opened and the young ass put in his head: "Are you here, Annie?"

No, it was only her husband!

He rose and went away. The young ass called his wife Annie, and was evidently on very familiar terms with her. It was more than he could bear.

When she came home they had a scene. She reproached him with the fact that he did not take his views on the emancipation of women seriously, otherwise he could not be annoyed at her being on familiar terms with her fellow-clerks. He made matters worse by admitting that his views were not to be taken seriously.

"Surely he didn't mean what he was saying! Had he changed his mind? How could he!"

"Yes, he had changed his mind. One could not help modifying one's views almost daily, because one had to adapt them to the conditions of life which were always changing. And if he had believed in spiritual marriages in the days gone by, he had now come to lose faith in marriages of any sort whatever. That was progress in the direction of radicalism. And as to the spiritual, she was spiritually married to the young ass rather than to him, for they exchanged views on the management of the goods department daily and hourly, while she took no interest at all in the cultivation of forests. Was there anything spiritual in their marriage? Was there?"

"No, not any longer! Her love was dead! He had killed it when he renounced his splendid faith in — the emancipation of women."

Matters became more and more unbearable. The green forester began to look to his fellow-foresters for companionship and gave up thinking of the goods department and its way of conducting business, matters which he never understood.

"You don't understand me," she kept on saying over and over again.

"No, I don't understand the goods department," he said.

One night, or rather one morning, he told her that he was going botanizing with a girls' class. He was teaching botany in a girls' school.

"Oh! indeed! Why had he never mentioned it before? Big girls?"

"Oh! very big ones. From sixteen to twenty."

"H'm! In the morning?"

"No! In the afternoon! And they would have supper in one of the outlying little villages."

"Would they? The head-mistress would be there of course?"

"Oh! no, she had every confidence in him, since he was a married man. It was an advantage, sometimes, to be married."

On the next day she was ill.

"Surely he hadn't the heart to leave her!"

"He must consider his work before anything else. Was she very ill?"

"Oh! terribly ill!"

In spite of her objections he sent for a doctor. The doctor declared that there was nothing much the matter; it was quite unnecessary for the husband to stay at home. The green forester returned towards morning. He was in high spirits. He had enjoyed himself immensely! He had not had such a day for a long, long time.

The storm burst. Huhuhu! This struggle was too much for her! He must swear a solemn oath never to love any woman but her. Never!

She had convulsions; he ran for the smelling salts.

He was too generous to give her details of the supper with the schoolgirls, but he could not forego the pleasure of mentioning his former simile anent dogs and possession, and he took the occasion to draw her attention to the fact that love without the conception of a right to possession — on both sides — was not thinkable. What was making her cry? The same thing which had made him swear, when she went out with twenty men. The fear of losing him! But one can lose only that which one possesses! Possesses!

Thus the rent was repaired. But goods department and girls' school were ready with their scissors to undo the laborious mending.

The harmony was disturbed.

The wife fell ill. She was sure that she had hurt herself in lifting a case which was too heavy for her. She was so keen on her work that she could not bear to wait while the porters stood about and did nothing. She was compelled to lend a hand. Now she must have ruptured herself.

Yes, indeed, there was something the matter!

How angry she was! Angry with her husband who alone was to blame. What were they going to do with the baby? It would have to be boarded out! Rousseau had done that. It was true, he was a fool, but on this particular point he was right.

She was full of fads and fancies. The forester had to resign his lessons at the girls' school at once.

She chafed and fretted because she was no longer able to go into the store rooms, but compelled to stay in the counting-house all day long and make entries. But the worst blow which befell her was the arrival of an assistant whose secret mission it was to take her place when she would be laid up.

The manner of her colleagues had changed, too. The porters grinned. She felt ashamed and longed to hide herself. It would be better to stay at home and cook her husband's dinner than sit here and be stared at. Oh! What black chasms of prejudice lay concealed in the deceitful hearts of men!

She stayed at home for the last month, for the walk to and from her office four times a day was too much for her. And she was always so hungry! She had to send out for sandwiches in the morning. And every now and then she felt faint and had to take a rest. What a life! A woman's lot was indeed a miserable one.

The baby was born.

"Shall we board it out?" asked the father.

"Had he no heart?"

"Oh! yes, of course he had!"

And the baby remained at home.

Then a very polite letter arrived from the head office, enquiring after the young mother's health.

"She was very well and would be back at the office on the day after tomorrow."

She was still a little weak and had to take a cab; but she soon picked up her strength. However, a new difficulty now presented itself. She must be kept informed of the baby's condition; a messenger boy was dispatched to her home, at first twice a day, then every two hours.

And when she was told that the baby had been crying, she put on her hat and rushed home at once. But the assistant was there, ready to take her place. The head clerk was very civil and made no comment.

One day the young mother discovered accidentally that the nurse was unable to feed the baby, but had concealed the fact for fear of losing her place. She had to take a day off in order to find a new foster mother. But they were all alike; brutal egoists every one of them, who took no interest in the children of strangers. No one could ever depend on them.

"No," agreed the husband, "in a case of this sort one can only depend on oneself."

"Do you mean to insinuate that I ought to give up my work?"

"Oh! You must do as you like about that!"

"And become your slave!"

"No, I don't mean that at all!"

The little one was not at all well; all children are ill occasionally. He was teething! One day's leave after another! The poor baby suffered from toothache. She had to soothe him at night, work at the office during the day, sleepy, tired, anxious, and again take a day off.

The green forester did his best and carried the baby about in his arms half the night, but he never said a word about his wife's work at the goods department.

Nevertheless she knew what was in his mind. He was waiting for her to give in; but he was deceitful and so he said nothing! How treacherous men were! She hated him; she would sooner kill herself than throw up her work and "be his slave."

The forester saw quite clearly now that it was impossible for any woman to emancipate herself from the laws of nature; *under present circumstances,* he was shrewd enough to add.

When the baby was five months old, it was plainly evident that the whole thing would before very long repeat itself.

What a catastrophe!

But when that sort of thing once begins. . . .

The forester was obliged to resume his lessons at the girls' school to augment their income, and now — she laid down her arms.

"I am your slave, now," she groaned, when she came home with her discharge.

Nevertheless she is the head of the house, and he gives her every penny he earns. When he wants to buy a cigar he makes a long speech before he ventures to ask for the money. She never refuses it to him, but all the same he finds the asking for it unpleasant. He is allowed to attend meetings, but no dinners, and all botanizing with girls is strictly forbidden. He does not miss it much, for he prefers playing with his children.

His colleagues call him henpecked; but he smiles, and tells them that he is happy in spite of it, because he has in his wife a very sweet and sensible companion.

She, on her part, obstinately maintains that she is nothing but his slave, whatever he might say to the contrary. It is her one comfort, poor, little woman!

A Doll's House

They had been married for six years, but they were still more like lovers than husband and wife. He was a captain in the navy, and every summer he was obliged to leave her for a few months; twice he had been away on a long voyage. But his short absences were a blessing in disguise, for if their relations had grown a little stale during the winter, the summer trip invariably restored them to their former freshness and delightfulness.

During the first summer he wrote veritable love-letters to her and never passed a sailing ship without signaling: "Will you take letters?" And when he came in sight of the landmarks of the Stockholm Archipelago, he did not know how to get to her quickly enough. But she found a way. She wired him to Landsort that she would meet him at Dalarö. When he anchored, he saw a little blue scarf fluttering on the verandah of the hotel: then he knew that it was she. But there was so much to do aboard that it was evening before he could go ashore. He saw her from his gig on the landing-stage as the bow held out his oar to fend off; she was every bit as young, as pretty and as strong as she had been when he left her; it was exactly as if they were re-living the first spring days of their love. A delicious little supper waited for him in the two little rooms she had engaged. What a lot they had to talk about! The voyage, the children, the future! The wine sparkled in the glasses and his kisses brought the blood to her cheeks.

Tattoo went on the ship, but he took no notice of it, for he did not intend to leave her before one o'clock.

"What? He was going?"

"Yes; he must get back aboard, but it would do if he was there for the morning watch."

"When did the morning watch begin?"

"At five o'clock."

"Oh!. . . As early as that!"

"But where was she going to stay the night?"

"That was her business!"

He guessed it and wanted to have a look at her room; but she planted herself firmly on the threshold. He covered her face with kisses, took her in his arms as if she were a baby and opened the door.

"What an enormous bed! It was like the long boat. Where did the people get it from?"

She blushed crimson.

"Of course, she had understood from his letter that they would stay at the hotel together."

"Well, and so they would, in spite of his having to be back aboard for the morning watch. What did he care for the stupid morning prayers!"

"How could he say such a thing!"

"Hadn't they better have some coffee and a fire? The sheets felt damp! What a sensible little rogue she was to provide for his staying, too! Who would have thought that she had so much sense? Where did she get it from?"

"She didn't get it from anywhere!"

"No? Well, he might have known! He might have known everything!"

"Oh! But he was so stupid!"

"Indeed, he was stupid, was he?"

And he slipped his arm round her waist.

"But he ought to behave himself!"

"Behave himself? It was easy to talk!"

"The girl was coming with the wood!"

When it struck two, and sea and Skerries were flaming in the east, they were sitting at the open window.

"They were lovers still, weren't they? And now he must go. But he would be back at ten, for breakfast, and after that they would go for a sail."

He made some coffee on her spirit lamp, and they drank it while the sun was rising and the seagulls screamed. The gunboat was lying far out at sea and every now and then he saw the cutlasses of the watch glinting in the sunlight. It was hard to part, but the certainty of meeting again in a few hours' time helped them to bear it. He kissed her for the last time, buckled on his sword and left her.

When he arrived at the bridge and shouted: "boat ahoy!" she hid herself behind the window curtains as if she were ashamed to be seen. He blew kisses to her until the sailors came with the gig. Then a last: "Sleep well and dream of me" and the gig put off. He watched her through his glasses, and for a long time he could distinguish a little figure with black hair. The sunbeams fell on her nightdress and bare throat and made her look like a mermaid.

The reveille went. The long-drawn bugle notes rolled out between the green islands over the shining water and returned from behind the pine woods. The whole crew assembled on deck and the Lord's Prayer and "Jesus, at the day's beginning" were read. The little church tower of Dalarö answered with a faint ringing of bells, for it was Sunday. Cutters came up in the morning breeze: flags were flying, shots resounded, light summer dresses gleamed on the bridge, the steamer, leaving a crimson track behind her, steamed up, the fishers hauled in their nets, and the sun shone on the blue, billowy water and the green islands.

At ten o'clock six pairs rowed the gig ashore from the gunboat. They were together again. And as they sat at breakfast in the large dining room, the hotel guests watched and whispered: "Is she his wife?" He talked to her in an undertone like a lover, and she cast down her eyes and smiled; or hit his fingers with her dinner napkin.

The boat lay alongside the bridge; she sat at the helm, he looked after the foresail. But he could not take his eyes off her finely shaped figure in the light summer dress, her determined little face and proud eyes, as she sat looking to windward, while her little hand in its strong leather glove held the mainsheet. He wanted to talk to her and was purposely clumsy in tacking; then she scolded him as if he were a cabin boy, which amused him immensely.

"Why didn't you bring the baby with you?" he asked her teasingly.

"Where should I have put it to sleep?"

"In the long boat, of course?"

She smiled at him in a way which filled his heart with happiness.

"Well, and what did the proprietress say this morning?"

"What should she say?"

"Did she sleep well last night?"

"Why shouldn't she sleep well?"

"I don't know; she might have been kept awake by rats, or perhaps by the rattling of a window; who can tell what might not disturb the gentle sleep of an old maid!"

"If you don't stop talking nonsense, I shall make the sheet fast and sail you to the bottom of the sea."

They landed at a small island and ate their luncheon which they had brought with them in a little basket. After lunch they shot at a target with a revolver. Then they pretended to fish with rods, but they caught nothing and sailed out again into the open sea where the eidergeese were, through a strait where they watched the carp playing about the rushes. He never tired of looking at her, talking to her, kissing her.

In this manner they met for six summers, and always they were just as young, just as mad and just as happy as before. They spent the winter in Stockholm in their little cabins. He amused himself by rigging boats for his little boys or telling them stories of his adventures in China and the South Sea Islands, while his wife sat by him, listening and laughing at his funny tales. It was a charming room, that could not be equaled in the whole world. It was crammed full of Japanese sunshades and armor, miniature pagodas from India, bows and lances from Australia, nigger drums and dried flying fish, sugar cane and opium pipes. Papa, whose hair was growing thin at the top, did not feel very happy outside his own four walls. Occasionally he played at drafts with his friend, the auditor, and sometimes they had a game at Boston and drank a glass of grog. At first his wife had joined in the game, but now that she had four children, she was too busy; nevertheless, she liked to sit with the players for a little and look at their cards, and whenever she passed Papa's chair he caught her round the waist and asked her whether she thought he ought to be pleased with his hand.

This time the corvette was to be away for six months. The captain did not feel easy about it, for the children were growing up and the responsibility of the big establishment was too much for Mama. The captain himself was not quite so young and vigorous as he had been, but — it could not be helped and so he left.

Directly he arrived at Kronborg he posted a letter to her.

"My darling Topmast," it began.

"Wind moderate, S.S.E. by E. + 10° C. 6 bells, watch below. I cannot express in words what I feel on this voyage during which I shall not see you. When we kedged out (at 6 p.m. while a strong gale blew from N.E. by N.) I felt as if a belaying pin were suddenly being driven into my chest and I actually had a sensation as if a chain had been drawn through the hawsepipes of my ears. They say that sailors can feel the approach of misfortune. I don't know whether this is true, but I shall not feel easy until I have had a letter from you. Nothing has happened on board, simply because nothing must happen. How are you all at home? Has Bob had his new boots, and do they fit? I am a wretched correspondent as you know, so 111 stop now. With a big kiss right on this x.

"Your old Pal.

"P.S. You ought to find a friend (female, of course) and don't forget to ask the proprietress at Dalaro to take care of the long boat until my return. The wind is getting up; it will blow from the North tonight."

Off Portsmouth the captain received the following letter from his wife:

"Dear old Pal,

"It's horrible here without you, believe me. I have had a lot of worry, too, for little Alice has got a new tooth. The doctor said it was unusually early, which was a sign of (but I'm not going to tell you that). Bob's boots fit him very well and he is very proud of them.

"You say in your letter that I ought to find a friend of my own sex. Well, I have found one, or, rather, she has found me. Her name is Ottilia Sandegren, and she was educated at the seminary. She is rather grave and takes life very seriously, therefore you need not be afraid, Pal, that your Topmast will be led astray. Moreover, she is religious. We really ought to take religion a little more seriously, both of us. She is a splendid woman. She has just arrived and sends you her kind regards.

"Your Gurli"

The captain was not overpleased with this letter. It was too short and not half as bright as her letters generally were. Seminary, religion, grave, Ottilia: Ottilia twice! And then Gurli! Why not Gulla as before? H'm!

A week later he received a second letter from Bordeaux, a letter which was accompanied by a book, sent under separate cover.

"Dear William!" — "H'm! William! No longer Pal!" — "Life is a struggle" — "What the deuce does she mean? What has that to do with us?" — "from beginning to end. Gently as a river in Kedron" — "Kedron! she's quoting the Bible!" — "our life has glided along. Like sleepwalkers we have been walking on the edge of precipices without being aware of them" — "The seminary, oh! the seminary!" — "Suddenly we find ourselves face to face with the ethical" — "The ethical? Ablative!" — "asserting itself in its higher potencies!" — "Potencies?" — "Now that I am awake from my long sleep and ask myself: has our marriage been a marriage in the true sense of the word? I must admit with shame and remorse that this has not been the case. For love is of divine origin. (St. Matthew xi. 22, 24.)"

The captain had to mix himself a glass of rum and water before he felt able to continue his reading. — "How earthly, how material our love has been! Have our souls lived in that harmony of which Plato speaks? (Phaidon, Book vi. Chap. ii. Par. 9). Our answer is bound to be in the negative. What have I been to you? A housekeeper and, oh! The disgrace!

your mistress! Have our souls understood one another? Again we are bound to answer 'No.'" – "To Hell with all Ottilias and seminaries! Has she been my housekeeper? She has been my wife and the mother of my children!" – "Read the book I have sent you! It will answer all your questions. It voices that which for centuries has lain hidden in the hearts of all women! Read it, and then tell me if you think that our union has been a true marriage. Your Gurli."

His presentiment of evil had not deceived him. The captain was beside himself; he could not understand what had happened to his wife. It was worse than religious hypocrisy.

He tore off the wrapper and read on the title page of a book in a paper cover: *Et Dukkehjem af Henrik Ibsen.* A Doll's House? Well, and – ? His home had been a charming doll's house; his wife had been his little doll and he had been her big doll. They had danced along the stony path of life and had been happy. What more did they want? What was wrong? He must read the book at once and find out.

He finished it in three hours. His brain reeled. How did it concern him and his wife? Had they forged bills? No! Hadn't they loved one another? Of course they had!

He locked himself into his cabin and read the book a second time; he underlined passages in red and blue, and when the dawn broke, he took "A well-meant little ablative on the play *A Doll's House,* written by the old Pal on board the Vanadis in the Atlantic off Bordeaux. (Lat. 45° Long. 16°.)

"1. She married him because he was in love with her and that was a deuced clever thing to do. For if she had waited until she had fallen in love with someone, it might have happened that *he* would not have fallen in love with her, and then there would have been the devil to pay. For it happens very rarely that both parties are equally in love."
"2. She forges a bill. That was foolish, but it is not true that it was done for the husband's sake only, for she has never loved him; it would have been the truth if she had said that she had done it for him, herself and the children. Is that clear?"
"3. That he wants to embrace her after the ball is only a proof of his love for her, and there is no wrong in that; but it should not be done on the stage. *'Il y a des choses qui se font mais que ne se disent point,'* as the French say, Moreover, if the poet had been fair, he would also save shown an opposite case. *'La petite chienne veut, mais le grand chien ne veut pas,'* says Ollendorf. (Vide the long boat at Dalarö.)"

"4. That she, when she discovers that her husband is a fool (and that he is when he offers to condone her offence because it has not leaked out) decides to leave her children 'not considering herself worthy of bringing them up,' is a not very clever trick of coquetry. If they have both been fools (and surely they don't teach at the seminary that it is right to forge bills) they should pull well together in future in double harness."

"Least of all is she justified in leaving her children's education in the hands of the father whom she despises."

"5. Nora has consequently every reason for staying with her children when she discovers what an imbecile her husband is."

"6. The husband cannot be blamed for not sufficiently appreciating her, for she doesn't reveal her true character until after the row."

"7. Nora has undoubtedly been a fool; she herself does not deny it."

"8. There is every guarantee of their pulling together more happily in future; he has repented and promised to turn over a new leaf. So has she. Very well! Here's my hand, let's begin again at the beginning. Birds of a feather flock together. There's nothing lost, we've both been fools! You, little Nora, were badly brought up. I, old rascal, didn't know any better. We are both to be pitied. Pelt our teachers with rotten eggs, but don't hit me alone on the head. I, though a man, am every bit as innocent as you are! Perhaps even a little more so, for I married for love, you for a home. Let us be friends, therefore, and together teach our children the valuable lesson we have learnt in the school of life."

"Is that clear? All right then!

"This was written by Captain Pal with his stiff fingers and slow brain!

"And now, my darling dolly, I have read your book and given you my opinion. But what have we to do with it? Didn't we love one another? Haven't we educated one another and helped one another to rub off our sharp corners? Surely you'll remember that we had many a little encounter in the beginning! What fads of yours are those? To hell with all Ottilias and seminaries!

"The book you sent me is a queer book. It is like a watercourse with an insufficient number of buoys, so that one might run aground at any moment. But I pricked the chart and found calm waters. Only, I couldn't do it again. The devil may crack these nuts which are rotten inside when one has managed to break the shell. I wish you peace and happiness and the recovery of your sound common sense.

"How are the little ones? You forgot to mention them. Probably you were thinking too much of Nora's unfortunate kiddies, (which exist only in a play of that sort). Is my little boy crying? My nightingale singing, my dolly dancing? She must always do that if she wants to make her old pal happy. And now may God bless you and prevent evil thoughts from rising between us. My heart is sadder than I can tell. And I am expected to sit down and write a critique on a play. God bless you and the babies; kiss their rosy cheeks for your faithful old Pal."

When the captain had sent off his letter, he went into the officers' mess and drank a glass of punch. The doctor was there, too.

"Have you noticed a smell of old black breeches?" he asked. "I should like to hoist myself up to the cat block and let a good old N.W. by N. blow right through me."

But the doctor did not understand what he was driving at.

"Ottilia, Ottilia!. . . What she wants is a taste of the handspike. Send the witch to the quarterdeck and let the second mess loose on her behind closed hatches. One knows what is good for an old maid."

"What's the matter with you, old chap?" asked the doctor.

"Plato! Plato! To the devil with Plato! To be six months at sea makes one sick of Plato. That teaches one ethics! Ethics? I bet a marlinspike to a large rifle: if Ottilia were married she would cease talking of Plato."

"What on earth *is* the matter?"

"Nothing. Do you hear? You're a doctor. What's the matter with those women? Isn't it bad for them to remain unmarried? Doesn't it make them. . .? What?"

The doctor gave him his candid opinion and added that he was sorry that there were not enough men to go round.

"In a state of nature the male is mostly polygamous; in most cases there is no obstacle to this, as there is plenty of food for the young ones (beasts of prey excepted): abnormalities like unmated females do not exist in nature. But in civilized countries, where a man is lucky if he earns enough bread, it is a common occurrence, especially as the females are in preponderance. One ought to treat unmarried women with kindness, for their lot is a melancholy one."

"With kindness! That's all very well; but supposing they are anything but kind themselves!"

And he told the doctor the whole story, even confessing that he had written a critique on a play.

"Oh! well, no end of nonsense is written," said the doctor, putting his hand on the lid of the jug which contained the punch. "In the end science decides all great questions! Science, and nothing else."

When the six months were over and the captain, who had been in constant, but not very pleasant, correspondence with his wife, (she had sharply criticized his critique), at last landed at Dalarö, he was received by his wife, all the children, two servants and Ottilia. His wife was affectionate, but not cordial. She held up her brow to be kissed. Ottilia was as tall as a stay, and wore her hair short; seen from the back she looked like a swab. The supper was dull and they drank only tea. The long boat took in a cargo of children and the captain was lodged in one of the attics.

What a change! Poor old Pal looked old and felt puzzled.

"To be married and yet not have a wife," he thought, "it's intolerable!"

On the following morning he wanted to take his wife for a sail. But the sea did not agree with Ottilia. She had been ill on the steamer. And, moreover, it was Sunday. Sunday? That was it! Well, they would go for a walk. They had a lot to talk about. Of course, they had a lot to say to each other. But Ottilia was not to come with them!

They went out together, arm in arm. But they did not talk much; and what they said were words uttered for the sake of concealing their thoughts more than for the sake of exchanging ideas.

They passed the little cholera cemetery and took the road leading to the Swiss Valley. A faint breeze rustled through the pine trees and glimpses of the blue sea flashed through the dark branches.

They sat down on a stone. He threw himself on the turf at her feet. Now the storm is going to burst, he thought, and it did.

"Have you thought at all about our marriage?" she began.

"No," he replied, with every appearance of having fully considered the matter, "I have merely felt about it. In my opinion love is a matter of sentiment; one steers by landmarks and makes port; take compass and chart and you are sure to founder."

"Yes, but our home has been nothing but a doll's house."

"Excuse me, but this is not quite true. You have never forged a bill; you have never shown your ankles to a syphilitic doctor of whom you wanted to borrow money against security *in natura*; you have never been so romantically silly as to expect your husband to give himself up for a crime which his wife had committed from ignorance, and which was not a crime because there was no plaintiff; and you have never lied to me. I have treated you every bit as honestly as Helmer treated his wife when he took her into his full confidence and allowed her to have a voice in the banking business; tolerated her interference with the appointment of an employee. We have therefore been husband and wife according to all conceptions, old and new-fashioned."

"Yes, but I have been your housekeeper!"

"Pardon me, you are wrong. You have never had a meal in the kitchen, you have never received wages, you have never had to account for money spent. I have never scolded you because one thing or the other was not to my liking. And do you consider my work: to reckon and to brace, to ease off and call out 'Present arms,' count herrings and measure rum, weigh peas and examine flour, more honorable than yours: to look after the servants, cater for the house and bring up the children?"

"No, but you are paid for your work! You are your own master! You are a man!"

"My dear child, do you want me to give you wages? Do you want to be my housekeeper in real earnest? That I was born a man is an accident. I might almost say a pity, for it's very nearly a crime to be a man nowadays, but it isn't my fault. The devil take him who has stirred up the two halves of humanity, one against the other! He has much to answer for. Am I the master? Don't we both rule? Have I ever decided any important matter without asking for your advice? What? But you — you bring up the children exactly as you like! Don't you remember that I wanted you to stop rocking them to sleep because I said it produced a sort of intoxication? But you had your own way! Another time I had mine, and then it was your turn again. There was no compromise possible, because there was no middle course to steer between rocking and not rocking. We got on very well until now. But you have thrown me over for Ottilia's sake!"

"Ottilia! always Ottilia! Didn't you yourself send her to me?"

"No, not her personally! But there can be no doubt that it is she who rules now."

"You want to separate me from all I care for!"

"Is Ottilia all you care for? It almost looks like it!"

"But I can't send her away now that I have engaged her to teach the girls pedagogics and Latin."

"Latin! Great Scott! Are the girls to be ruined?"

"They are to know everything a man knows, so that when the time comes, their marriage will be a true marriage."

"But, my love, all husbands don't know Latin! I don't know more than one single word, and that is 'ablative.' And we have been happy in spite of it. Moreover, there is a movement to strike off Latin from the plan of instruction for boys, as a superfluous accomplishment. Doesn't this teach you a lot? Isn't it enough that the men are ruined, are the women to be ruined, too? Ottilia, Ottilia, what have I done to you, that you should treat me like this!"

"Supposing we dropped that matter. – Our love, William, has not been what it should be. It has been sensual!"

"But, my darling, how could we have had children, if it hadn't? And it has not been sensual only."

"Can a thing be both black and white? Tell me that!"

"Of course, it can. There's your sunshade for instance, it is black outside and white inside."

"Sophist!"

"Listen to me, sweetheart, tell me in your own way the thoughts which are in your heart; don't talk like Ottilia's books. Don't let your head run away with you; be yourself again, my sweet, darling little wife."

"Yours, your property, bought with your labor."

"Just as I am your property, your husband, at whom no other woman is allowed to look if she wants to keep her eyes in her head; your husband, who made a present of himself to you, or rather, gave himself to you in exchange. Are we not quits?"

"But we have trifled away our lives! Have we ever had any higher interests, William?"

"Yes, the very highest, Gurli; we have not always been playing, we have had grave hours, too. Have we not called into being generations to come? Have we not both bravely worked and striven for the little ones, who are to grow up into men and women? Have you not faced death four times for their sakes? Have you not robbed yourself of your nights' rest in order to rock their cradle, and of your days' pleasures, in order to attend to them? Couldn't we now have a large six-roomed flat in the main street, and a footman to open the door, if it were not for the children? Wouldn't you be able to wear silk dresses and pearls? And I, your old Pal, wouldn't have *crows' nests* in my knees, if it hadn't been for the kiddies. Are we really no better than dolls? Are we as selfish as old maids say? Old maids, rejected by men as no good. Why are so many girls unmarried? They all boast of proposals and yet they pose as martyrs! Higher interests! Latin! To dress in low neck dresses for charitable purposes and leave the children at home, neglected! I believe that my interests are higher than Ottilia's, when I want strong and healthy children, who will succeed where we have failed. But Latin won't help them! Good-bye, Gurli! I have to go back on board. Are you coming?"

But she remained sitting on the stone and made no answer. He went with heavy footsteps, very heavy footsteps. And the blue sea grew dark and the sun ceased shining.

"Pal, Pal, where is this to lead to?" he sighed, as he stepped over the fence of the cemetery. "I wish I lay there, with a wooden cross to mark my place, among the roots of the trees. But I am sure I couldn't rest, if I were there without her! Oh! Gurli! Gurli!

"Everything has gone wrong, now, mother," said the captain on a chilly autumn day to his mother-in-law, to whom he was paying a visit.

"What's the matter, Willy, dear?"

"Yesterday they met at our house. On the day before yesterday at the Princess's. Little Alice was suddenly taken ill. It was unfortunate, of course, but I didn't dare to send for Gurli, for fear she might think that it was done on purpose to annoy her! Oh! when once one has lost faith. . . . I asked a friend at the Admiralty yesterday whether it was legal in Sweden to kill one's wife's friends with tobacco smoke. I was told it wasn't, and that even if it were it was better not to do it, for fear of doing more harm than good. If only it happened to be an admirer! I should take him by the neck and throw him out of the window. What am I to do?"

"It's a difficult matter, Willy, dear, but we shall be able to think of a way out of it. You can't go on living like a bachelor."

"No, of course, I can't."

"I spoke very plainly to her, a day or two ago. I told her that she would lose you if she didn't mend her ways."

"And what did she say?"

"She said you had a right to do as you liked with your body."

"Indeed! And she, too? A fine theory! My hair is fast turning grey, mother!"

"It's a good old scheme to make a wife jealous. It's generally kill or cure, for if there is any love left, it brings it out."

"There is, I know, there is!"

"Of course, there is. Love doesn't die suddenly; it gets used up in the course of the years, perhaps. Have a flirtation with Ottilia, and we shall see!"

"Flirt with Ottilia? With Ottilia?"

"Try it. Aren't you up in any of the subjects which interest her?"

"Well, yes! They are deep in statistics, now. Fallen women, infectious diseases. If I could lead the conversation to mathematics! I am well up in that!"

"There you are! Begin with mathematics — by and by put her shawl round her shoulders and button her overshoes. Take her home in the evening. Drink her health and kiss her when Gurli is sure to see it. If necessary, be a little officious. She won't be angry, believe me. And give her a big dose of mathematics, so big that Gurli has no option but to sit and listen to it quietly. Come again in a week's time and tell me the result."

The captain went home, read the latest pamphlets on immorality and at once started to carry out his scheme.

A week later he called on his mother-in-law, serene and smiling, and greatly enjoying a glass of good sherry. He was in high spirits.

"Now tell me all about it," said the old woman, pushing her spectacles up on her forehead.

"It was difficult work at first," he began, "for she distrusted me. She thought I was making fun of her. Then I mentioned the effect which the computation of probabilities had had on the statistics of morality in America. I told her that it had simply been epoch-making. She knew nothing about it, but the subject attracted her. I gave her examples and proved in figures that it was possible to calculate with a certain amount of probability the percentage of women who are bound to fall. She was amazed. I saw that her curiosity was aroused and that she was eager to provide herself with a trump-card for the next meeting. Gurli was pleased to see that Ottilia and I were making friends, and did everything to further my scheme. She pushed her into my room and closed the door; and there we sat all afternoon, making calculations. The old witch was happy, for she felt that she was making use of me, and after three hours' work we were fast friends. At supper my wife found that such old friends as Ottilia and I ought to call one another by their Christian names. I brought out my good old sherry to celebrate the occasion. And then I kissed her on the lips, may God forgive me for my sins! Gurli looked a little startled, but did not seem to mind. She was radiant with happiness. The sherry was strong and Ottilia was weak. I wrapped her in her cloak and took her home. I gently squeezed her arm and told her the names of the stars. She became enthusiastic! She had always loved the stars, but had never been able to remember their names. The poor women were not allowed to acquire any knowledge. Her enthusiasm grew and we parted as the very best of friends who had been kept apart through misunderstanding each other for such a long, long time.

"On the next day more mathematics. We worked until supper time. Gurli came in once or twice and gave us an encouraging nod. At supper we talked of nothing but stars and mathematics, and Gurli sat there, silently, listening to us. Again I took her home. On my way back I met a friend. We went to the Grand Hotel and drank a glass of punch. It was one o'clock when I came home. Gurli was still up waiting for me.

"'Where have you been all this time, William?' she asked.

"Then the devil entered into my soul and I replied:

"'We had such a lot to talk about that I forgot all about the time.'

"*That* blow struck home.

"'I don't think it's nice to run about half the night with a young woman,' she said.

"I pretended to be embarrassed and stammered:

"'If one has so much to say to one another, one forgets sometimes what is nice and what is not.'

"'What on earth did you talk about?' asked Gurli, pouting.

"'I really can't remember.'

"You managed very well, my boy," said the old woman. "Go on!"

"On the third day," continued the captain, "Gurli came in with her needlework and remained in the room until the lesson in mathematics was over. Supper was not quite as merry as usual, but on the other hand, very astronomical. I assisted the old witch with her overshoes, a fact which made a great impression on Gurli. When Ottilia said good-night, she only offered her cheek to be kissed. On the way home I pressed her arm and talked of the sympathy of souls and of the stars as the home of the souls. I went to the Grand Hotel, had some punch and arrived home at two o'clock. Gurli was still up; I saw it, but I went straight to my room, like the bachelor I was, and Gurli did not like to follow me and ply me with questions.

"On the following day I gave Ottilia a lesson in astronomy. Gurli declared that she was much interested and would like to be present; but Ottilia said we were already too far advanced and she would instruct her in the rudiments later on. This annoyed Gurli and she went away. We had a great deal of sherry for supper. When Ottilia thanked me for a jolly evening, I put my arm round her waist and kissed her. Gurli grew pale. When I buttoned her overshoes, I . . . I. . . ."

"Never mind me," said the old lady, "I am an old woman."

He laughed. "All the same, mother, she's not so bad, really she isn't. But when I was going to put on my overcoat, I found to my astonishment the maid waiting in the hall, ready to accompany Ottilia home. Gurli made excuses for me; she said I had caught a cold on the previous evening, and that she was afraid the night air might do me harm. Ottilia looked self-conscious and left without kissing Gurli.

"I had promised to show Ottilia some astronomical instruments at the College at twelve o'clock on the following day. She kept her appointment, but she was much depressed. She had been to see Gurli, who had treated her very unkindly, so she said. She could not imagine why. When I came home to dinner I found a great change in Gurli. She was cold and mute as a fish. I could see that she was suffering. Now was the time to apply the knife.

"'What did you say to Ottilia?' I commenced. 'She was so unhappy.'

"'What did I say to her? Well, I said to her that she was a flirt. That's what I said.'

"'How could you say such a thing?' I replied. 'Surely, you're not jealous!'

"'I! Jealous of her!' she burst out.

"'Yes, that's what puzzles me, for I am sure an intelligent and sensible person like Ottilia could never have designs on another woman's husband!'

"'No,' (she was coming to the point) 'but another woman's husband might have designs on her.'

"'Huhuhu!' she went for me tooth and nail. I took Ottilia's part; Gurli called her an old maid; I continued to champion her. On this afternoon Ottilia did not turn up. She wrote a chilly letter, making excuses and winding up by saying she could see that she was not wanted. I protested and suggested that I should go and fetch her. That made Gurli wild! She was sure that I was in love with Ottilia and cared no more for herself. She knew that she was only a silly girl, who didn't know anything, was no good at anything, and — huhuhu! — could never understand mathematics. I sent for a sleigh and we went for a ride. In a hotel, overlooking the sea, we drank mulled wine and had an excellent little supper. It was just as if we were having our wedding day over again, and then we drove home."

"And then — ?" asked the old woman, looking at him over her spectacles.

"And then? H'm! May God forgive me for my sins! I seduced my own little wife. What do you say now, granny?"

"I say that you did very well, my boy! And then?"

"And then? Since then everything has been all right, and now we discuss the education of the children and the emancipation of women from superstition and old-maidishness, from sentimentality and the devil and his ablative, but we talk when we are alone together and that is the best way of avoiding misunderstandings. Don't you think so, old lady?"

"Yes, Willy, dear, and now I shall come and pay you a call."

"Do come! And you will see the dolls dance and the larks and the woodpeckers sing and chirrup; you will see a home filled with happiness up to the roof, for there is no one there waiting for miracles which only happen in fairy tales. You will see a real doll's house."

Phoenix

*T*he wild strawberries were getting ripe when he met her for the first time at the vicarage. He had met many girls before, but when he saw *her* he knew; this was she! But he did not dare to tell her so, and she only teased him for he was still at school.

He was an undergraduate when he met her for the second time. And as he put his arms round her and kissed her, he saw showers of rockets, heard the ringing of bells and bugle calls, and felt the earth trembling under his feet.

She was a woman at the age of fourteen. Her young bosom seemed to be waiting for hungry little mouths and eager baby fists. With her firm and elastic step, her round and swelling hips, she looked fit to bear at any moment a baby under her heart. Her hair was of a pale gold, like clarified honey, and surrounded her face like an aureole; her eyes were two flames and her skin was as soft as a glove.

They were engaged to be married and billed and cooed in the wood like the birds in the garden under the lime trees; life lay before them like a sunny meadow which the scythe had not yet touched. But he had to pass his examinations in mining first, and that would take him, — including the journey abroad — ten years. Ten years!

He returned to the University. In the summer he came back to the vicarage and found her every bit as beautiful. Three summers he came — and the fourth time she was pale. There were tiny red lines in the corners of her nose and her shoulders drooped a little. When the summer returned for the sixth time, she was taking iron. In the seventh she went to a watering-place. In the eighth she suffered from tooth-ache and her nerves were out of order. Her hair had lost its gloss, her voice had grown shrill, her nose was covered with little black specks; she had lost her figure, dragged her feet, and her cheeks were hollow. In the winter she had an attack of nervous fever, and her hair had to be cut off. When it grew again, it was a dull brown. He had fallen in love with a golden-haired girl of fourteen — brunettes did not attract him — and he married a woman of twenty-four, with dull brown hair, who refused to wear her dresses open at the throat.

But in spite of all this he loved her. His love was less passionate than it had been; it had become calm and steadfast. And there was nothing in the little mining-town which could disturb their happiness.

She bore him two boys, but he was always wishing for a girl. And at last a fair-haired baby girl arrived.

She was the apple of his eye, and as she grew up she resembled her mother more and more. When she was eight years old, she was just what her mother had been. And the father devoted all his spare time to his little daughter.

The housework had coarsened the mother's hands. Her nose had lost its shape and her temples had fallen in. Constant stooping over the kitchen range had made her a little round-shouldered. Father and mother met only at meals and at night. They did not complain, but things had changed.

But the daughter was the father's delight. It was almost as if he were in love with her. He saw in her the re-incarnation of her mother, his first impression of her, as beautiful as it had been fleeting. He was almost self-conscious in her company and never went into her room when she was dressing. He worshipped her.

But one morning the child remained in bed and refused to get up. Mama put it down to laziness, but papa sent for the doctor. The shadow of the angel of death lay over the house: the child was suffering from diphtheria. Either father or mother must take the other children away. He refused. The mother took them to a little house in one of the suburbs and the father remained at home to nurse the invalid. There she lay! The house was disinfected with sulfur which turned the gilded picture frames black and tarnished the silver on the dressing-table. He walked through the empty rooms in silent anguish, and at night, alone in his big bed, he felt like a widower. He bought toys for the little girl, and she smiled at him as he sat on the edge of the bed trying to amuse her with a Punch and Judy show, and asked after mama and her little brothers. And the father had to go and stand in the street before the house in the suburbs, and nod to his wife who was looking at him from the window, and blow kisses to the children. And his wife signaled to him with sheets of blue and red paper.

But a day came when the little girl took no more pleasure in Punch and Judy, and ceased smiling; and ceased talking too, for Death had stretched out his long bony arm and suffocated her. It had been a hard struggle.

Then the mother returned, full of remorse because she had deserted her little daughter. There was great misery in the home, and great wretchedness. When the doctor wanted to make a post mortem examination, the father objected. No knife should touch her, for she was not dead to him; but his resistance was overborne. Then he flew into a passion and tried to kick and bite the doctor.

When they had bedded her into the earth, he built a monument over her grave, and for a whole year he visited it every day. In the second year he did not go quite so often. His work was heavy and he had little spare time. He began to feel the burden of the years; his step was less elastic; his wound was healing. Sometimes he felt ashamed when he realized that he was mourning less and less for his child as time went by; and finally he forgot all about it.

Two more girls were born to him, but it was not the same thing; the void left by the one who had passed away could never be filled.

Life was a hard struggle. The young wife who had once been like — like no other woman on earth, had gradually lost her glamour; the gilding had worn off the home which had once been so bright and beautiful. The children had bruised and dented their mother's wedding presents, spoiled the beds and kicked the legs of the furniture. The stuffing of the sofa was plainly visible here and there, and the piano had not been opened for years. The noise made by the children had drowned the music and the voices had become harsh. The words of endearment had been cast off with the baby clothes, caresses had deteriorated into a sort of massage. They were growing old and weary. Papa was no longer on his knees before mama, he sat in his shabby armchair and asked her for a match when he wanted to light his pipe. Yes, they were growing old.

When papa had reached his fiftieth year, mama died. Then the past awoke and knocked at his heart. When her broken body, which the last agony had robbed of its few remaining charms, had been laid in its grave, the picture of his fourteen-year-old sweetheart arose in his memory. It was for her, whom he had lost so long ago that he mourned now, and with his yearning for her came remorse. But he had never been unkind to the old mama; he had been faithful to the fourteen-year-old vicar's daughter whom he had worshipped on his knees but had never led to the altar, for he had married an anaemic young woman of twenty-four. If he were to be quite candid, he would have to confess that it was she for whom he mourned; it was true, he also missed the good cooking and unremitting care of the old mama, but that was a different thing.

He was on more intimate terms with his children, now; some of them had left the old nest, but others were still at home.

When he had bored his friends for a whole year with anecdotes of the deceased, an extraordinary coincidence happened. He met a young girl of eighteen, with fair hair, and a striking resemblance to his late wife, as she had been at fourteen. He saw in this coincidence the finger of a bountiful providence, willing to bestow on him at last the first one, the well-beloved. He fell in love with her because she resembled the first one. And he married her. He had got her at last.

But his children, especially the girls, resented his second marriage. They found the relationship between their father and step-mother improper; in their opinion he had been unfaithful to their mother. And they left his house and went out into the world.

He was happy! And his pride in his young wife exceeded even his happiness.

"Only the aftermath!" said his old friends.

When a year had gone by, the young wife presented him with a baby. Papa, of course, was no longer used to a baby's crying, and wanted his night's rest. He insisted on a separate bedroom for himself, heedless of his wife's tears; really, women were a nuisance sometimes. And, moreover, she was jealous of his first wife. He had been fool enough to tell her of the extraordinary likeness which existed between the two and had let her read his first wife's love-letters. She brooded over these facts now that he neglected her. She realized that she had inherited all the first one's pet names, that she was only her understudy, as it were. It irritated her and the attempt to win him for herself led her into all sorts of mischief. But she only succeeded in boring him, and in silently comparing the two women, his verdict was entirely in favor of the first one. She had been so much more gentle than the second who exasperated him. The longing for his children, whom he had driven from their home increased his regret, and his sleep was disturbed by bad dreams for he was haunted by the idea that he had been unfaithful to his first wife.

His home was no longer a happy one. He had done a deed, which he would much better have left undone.

He began to spend a good deal of time at his club. But now his wife was furious. He had deceived her. He was an old man and he had better look out! An old man who left his young wife so much alone ran a certain risk. He might regret it some day!

"Old? She called him old? He would show her that he was not old!"

They shared the same room again. But now matters were seven times worse. He did not want to be bothered with the baby at night. The proper place for babies was the nursery. No! he hadn't thought so in the case of the first wife.

He had to submit to the torture.

Twice he had believed in the miracle of Phoenix rising from the ashes of his fourteen year old love, first in his daughter, then in his second wife. But in his memory lived the first one only, the little one from the vicarage, whom he had met when the wild strawberries were ripe, and kissed under the lime trees in the wood, but whom he had never married.

But now, as his sun was setting and his days grew short, he saw in his dark hours only the picture of the old mama, who had been kind to him and his children, who had never scolded, who was plain, who cooked the meals and patched the little boys' knickers and the skirts of the little girls. His flush of victory being over, he was able to see facts clearly. He wondered whether it was not, after all, the old mama who had been the real true Phoenix, rising, calm and beautiful, from the ashes of the fourteen year old bird of paradise, laying its eggs, plucking the feathers from its breast to line the nest for the young ones, and nourishing them with its life-blood until it died.

He wondered . . . but when at last he laid his weary head on the pillow, never again to lift it up, he was convinced that it was so.

Romeo and Julia

One evening the husband came home with a roll of music under his arm and said to his wife:

"Let us play duets after supper!"

"What have you got there?" asked his wife.

"Romeo and Julia, arranged for the piano. Do you know it?"

"Yes, of course I do," she replied, "but I don't remember ever having seen it on the stage."

"Oh! It's splendid! To me it is like a dream of my youth, but I've only heard it once, and that was about twenty years ago."

After supper, when the children had been put to bed and the house lay silent, the husband lighted the candles on the piano. He looked at the lithographed title-page and read the title: Romeo and Julia.

"This is Gounod's most beautiful composition," he said, "and I don't believe that it will be too difficult for us."

As usual his wife undertook to play the treble and they began. D major, common time, *allegro giusto.*

"It is beautiful, isn't it?" asked the husband, when they had finished the overture.

"Y — es," admitted the wife, reluctantly.

"Now the martial music," said the husband; "it is exceptionally fine. I can remember the splendid choruses at the Royal Theater."

They played a march.

"Well, wasn't I right?" asked the husband, triumphantly, as if he had composed "Romeo and Julia" himself.

"I don't know; it rather sounds like a brass band," answered the wife.

The husband's honor and good taste were involved; he looked for the Moonshine Aria in the fourth act. After a little searching he came across an aria for soprano. That must be it.

And he began again.

Tram-tramtram, tram-tramtram, went the bass; it was very easy to play.

"Do you know," said his wife, when it was over, "I don't think very much of it."

The husband, quite depressed, admitted that it reminded him of a barrel organ.

"I thought so all along," confessed the wife.

"And I find it antiquated, too. I am surprised that Gounod should be out of date, already," he added dejectedly. "Would you like to go on playing? Let's try the Cavatina and the Trio; I particularly remember the soprano; she was divine."

When they stopped playing, the husband looked crestfallen and put the music away, as if he wanted to shut the door on the past.

"Let's have a glass of beer," he said. They sat down at the table and had a glass of beer.

"It's extraordinary," he began, after a little while, "I never realized before that we've grown old, for we really must have vied with Romeo and Julia as to who should age faster. It's twenty years ago since I heard the opera for the first time. I was a newly fledged undergraduate then, I had many friends and the future smiled at me. I was immensely proud of the first down on my upper lip and my little college cap, and I remember as if it were today, the evening when Fritz, Phil and myself went to hear this opera. We had heard 'Faust' some years before and were great admirers of Gounod's genius. But Romeo beat all our expectations. The music roused our wildest enthusiasm. Now both my friends are dead. Fritz, who was ambitious, was a private secretary when he died, Phil a medical student; I who aspired to the position of a minister of state have to content myself with that of a regimental judge. The years have passed by quickly and imperceptibly. Of course I have noticed that the lines under my eyes have grown deeper and that my hair has turned grey at the temples, but I should never have thought that we had traveled so far on the road to the grave."

"Yes, my dear, we've grown old; our children could teach us that. And you must see it in me too, although you don't say anything."

"How can you say that!"

"Oh! I know only too well, my dear," continued the wife, sadly; "I know that I am beginning to lose my good looks, that my hair is growing thin, that I shall soon lose my front teeth. . . ."

"Just consider how quickly everything passes away" — interrupted her husband. "It seems to me that one grows old much more rapidly nowadays, than one used to do. In my father's house Haydn and Mozart were played a great deal, although they were dead long before he was born. And now — now Gounod has grown old-fashioned already! How distressing it is to meet again the ideals of one's youth under these altered circumstances! And how horrible it is to feel old age approaching!"

He got up and sat down again at the piano; he took the music and turned over the pages as if he were looking for keepsakes, locks of hair, dried flowers and ends of ribbon in the drawer of a writing-table. His eyes were riveted on the black notes which looked like little birds climbing up and down a wire fencing; but where were the spring songs, the passionate protestations, the jubilant avowals of the rosy days of first love? The notes stared back at him like strangers; as if the memory of life's spring-time were grown over with weeds.

Yes, that was it; the strings were covered with dust, the sounding board was dried up, the felt worn away.

A heavy sigh echoed through the room, heavy as if it came from a hollow chest, and then silence fell.

"But all the same, it is strange," the husband said suddenly, "that the glorious prologue is missing in this arrangement. I remember distinctly that there was a prologue with an accompaniment of harps and a chorus which went like this."

He softly hummed the tune, which bubbled up like a stream in a mountain glen; note succeeded note, his face cleared, his lips smiled, the lines disappeared, his fingers touched the keys, and drew from them melodies, powerful, caressing and full of eternal youth, while with a strong and ringing voice he sang the part of the bass.

His wife started from her melancholy reverie and listened with tears in her eyes.

"What are you singing?" she asked, full of amazement.

"Romeo and Julia! Our Romeo and our Julia!"

He jumped up from the music stool and pushed the music towards his astonished wife.

"Look! This was the Romeo of our uncles and aunts, this was — read it — Bellini! Oh! We are not old, after all!"

The wife looked at the thick, glossy hair of her husband, his smooth brow and flashing eyes, with joy.

"And you? You look like a young girl. We have allowed old Bellini to make fools of us. I felt that something was wrong."

"No, darling, I thought so first."

"Probably you did; that is because you are younger than I am."

"No, you. . . ."

And husband and wife, like a couple of children, laughingly quarrel over the question of which of them is the elder of the two, and cannot understand how they could have discovered lines and grey hairs where there are none.

Prolificacy

*H*e was a supernumerary at the Board of Trade and drew a salary of twelve hundred crowns. He had married a young girl without a penny; for love, as he himself said, to be no longer compelled to go to dances and run about the streets, as his friends maintained. But be that as it may, the life of the newly-wedded couple was happy enough to begin with.

"How cheaply married people can live," he said one day, after the wedding was a thing of the past. The same sum which had been barely enough to cover the wants of the bachelor now sufficed for husband and wife. Really, marriage was an excellent institution. One had all one's requirements within one's four walls: club, café, everything; no more bills of fare, no tips, no inquisitive porter watching one as one went out with one's wife in the morning.

Life smiled at him, his strength increased and he worked for two. Never in all his life had he felt so full of overflowing energy; he jumped out of bed as soon as he woke up in the morning, buoyantly, and in the highest spirits, he was rejuvenated.

When two months had elapsed, long before his new circumstances had begun to pall, his wife whispered a certain piece of information into his ear. New joys! New cares! But cares so pleasant to bear! It was necessary, however, to increase their income at once, so as to receive the unknown world-citizen in a manner befitting his dignity. He managed to obtain an order for a translation.

Baby-clothes lay scattered about all over the furniture, a cradle stood waiting in the hall, and at last a splendid boy arrived in this world of sorrows.

The father was delighted. And yet he could not help a vague feeling of uneasiness whenever he thought of the future. Income and expenditure did not balance. Nothing remained but to reduce his dress allowance.

His frock coat began to look threadbare at the seams; his shirt front was hidden underneath a large tie, his trousers were frayed. It was an undeniable fact that the porters at the office looked down on him on account of his shabbiness.

In addition to this he was compelled to lengthen his working day.

"It must be the first and last," he said. But how was it to be done?

He was at a loss to know.

Three months later his wife prepared him in carefully chosen words that his paternal joys would soon be doubled. It would not be true to say that he rejoiced greatly at the news. But there was no alternative now; he must travel along the road he had chosen, even if married life should prove to be anything but cheap.

"It's true," he thought, his face brightening, "the younger one will inherit the baby-clothes of his elder brother. This will save a good deal of expense, and there will be food enough for them — I shall be able to feed them just as well as others."

And the second baby was born.

"You are going it," said a friend of his, who was a married man himself, but father of one child only.

"What is a man to do?"

"Use his common-sense."

"Use his common-sense? But, my dear fellow, a man gets married in order to . . . I mean to say, not only in order to . . . but yet in order to. . . . Well, anyhow, we are married and that settles the matter."

"Not at all. Let me tell you something, my dear boy; if you are at all hoping for promotion it is absolutely necessary that you should wear clean linen, trousers which are not frayed at the bottom, and a hat which is not of a rusty brown."

And the sensible man whispered sensible words into his ear. As the result, the poor husband was put on short commons in the midst of plenty.

But now his troubles began.

To start with his nerves went to pieces, he suffered from insomnia and did his work badly. He consulted a doctor. The prescription cost him three crowns; and such a prescription! He was to stop working; he had worked too hard, his brain was overtaxed. To stop work would mean starvation for all of them, and to work spelt death, too!

He went on working.

One day, as he was sitting at his desk, stooping over endless rows of figures, he had an attack of faintness, slipped off his chair and fell to the ground.

A visit to a specialist — eighteen crowns. A new prescription; he must ask for sick leave at once, take riding exercise every morning and have steak and a glass of port for breakfast.

Riding exercise and port!

But the worst feature of the whole business was a feeling of alienation from his wife which had sprung up in his heart — he did not know whence it came. He was afraid to go near her and at the same time he longed for her presence. He loved her, loved her still, but a certain bitterness was mingled with his love.

"You are growing thin," said a friend.

"Yes, I believe I've grown thinner," said the poor husband.

"You are playing a dangerous game, old boy!"

"I don't know what you mean!"

"A married man in half mourning! Take care, my friend!"

"I really don't know what you're driving at. ."

"It's impossible to go against the wind for any length of time. Set all sails and run, old chap, and you will see that everything will come right. Believe me, I know what I'm talking about. You understand me."

He took no notice of the advice for a time, fully aware of the fact that a man's income does not increase in proportion to his family; at the same time he had no longer any doubt about the cause of his malady.

It was summer again. The family had gone into the country. On a beautiful evening husband and wife were strolling along the steep shore, in the shade of the alder trees, resplendent in their young green. They sat down on the turf, silent and depressed. He was morose and disheartened; gloomy thoughts revolved behind his aching brow. Life seemed a great chasm which had opened to engulf all he loved.

They talked of the probable loss of his appointment; his chief had been annoyed at his second application for sick leave. He complained of the conduct of his colleagues, he felt himself deserted by everyone; but the fact which hurt him more than anything else was the knowledge that she, too, had grown tired of him.

"Oh! but she hadn't! She loved him every bit as much as she did in those happy days when they were first engaged. How could he doubt it?"

"No, he didn't doubt it; but he had suffered so much, he wasn't master of his own thoughts."

He pressed his burning cheek against hers, put his arm round her and covered her eyes with passionate kisses.

The gnats danced their nuptial dance above the birch tree without a thought of the thousands of young ones which their ecstasy would call into being; the carp laid their eggs in the reed grass, careless of the millions of their kind to which they gave birth; the swallow made love in broad daylight, not in the least afraid of the consequences of their irregular liaisons.

All of a sudden he sprang to his feet and stretched himself like a sleeper awakening from a long sleep, which had been haunted by evil dreams, he drank in the balmy air in deep drafts.

"What's the matter?" whispered his wife, while a crimson blush spread over her face.

"I don't know. All I know is that I live, that I breathe again."

And radiant, with laughing face and shining eyes, he held out his arms to her, picked her up as if she were a baby and pressed his lips to her forehead. The muscles of his legs swelled until they looked like the muscles of the leg of an antique god, he held his body erect like a young tree and intoxicated with strength and happiness, he carried his beloved burden as far as the footpath where he put her down.

"You will strain yourself, sweetheart," she said, making a vain attempt to free herself from his encircling arms.

"Never, you darling! I could carry you to the end of the earth, and I shall carry you, all of you, no matter how many you are now, or how many you may yet become."

And they returned home, arm in arm, their hearts singing with gladness.

"If the worst comes to the worst, sweet love, one must admit that it is very easy to jump that abyss which separates body and soul!"

"What a thing to say!"

"If I had only realized it before, I should have been less unhappy. Oh! those idealists!"

And they entered their cottage.

The good old times had returned and had, apparently, come to stay. The husband went to work to his office as before. They lived again through love's spring time. No doctor was required and the high spirits never flagged.

After the third christening, however, he came to the conclusion that matters were serious and started playing his old game with the inevitable results: doctor, sick-leave, riding-exercise, port! But there must be an end of it, at all costs. Every time the balance-sheet showed a deficit.

But when, finally, his whole nervous system went out of joint, he let nature have her own way. Immediately expenses went up and he was beset with difficulties.

He was not a poor man, it is true, but on the other hand he was not blest with too many of this world's riches.

"To tell you the truth, old girl," he said to his wife, "it will be the same old story over again."

"I am afraid it will, my dear," replied the poor woman, who, in addition to her duties as a mother, had to do the whole work of the house now.

After the birth of her fourth child, the work grew too hard for her and a nursemaid had to be engaged.

"Now it must stop," avowed the disconsolate husband. "This must be the last."

Poverty looked in at the door. The foundations on which the house was built were tottering.

And thus, at the age of thirty, in the very prime of their life, the young husband and wife found themselves condemned to celibacy. He grew moody, his complexion became grey and his eyes lost their luster. Her rich beauty faded, her fine figure wasted away, and she suffered all the sorrows of a mother who sees her children growing up in poverty and rags.

One day, as she was standing in the kitchen, frying herrings, a neighbor called in for a friendly chat.

"How are you?" she began.

"Thank you, I'm not up to very much. How are you?"

"Oh! I'm not at all well. Married life is a misery if one has to be constantly on one's guard."

"Do you think you are the only one?"

"What do you mean?"

"Do you know what my husband said to me the other day? One ought to spare the draft cattle! And I suffer under it all, I can tell you. No, there's no happiness in marriage. Either husband or wife is bound to suffer. It's one or the other!"

"Or both!"

"But what about the men of science who grow fat at the expense of the Government?"

"They have to think of so many things, and moreover, it is improper to write about such problems; they must not be discussed openly."

"But that would be the first necessity!" And the two women fell to discussing their bitter experiences.

In the following summer they were compelled to remain in town; they were living in a basement with a view of the gutter, the smell of which was so objectionable that it was impossible to keep the windows open.

The wife did needlework in the same room in which the children were playing; the husband, who had lost his appointment on account of his extreme shabbiness, was copying a manuscript in the adjoining room, and grumbling at the children's noise. Hard words were bandied through the open door.

It was Whitsuntide. In the afternoon the husband was lying on the ragged leather sofa, gazing at a window on the other side of the street. He was watching a woman of evil reputation who was dressing for her evening stroll. A spray of lilac and two oranges were lying by the side of her looking-glass.

She was fastening her dress without taking the least notice of his inquisitive glances.

"She's not having a bad time," mused the celibate, suddenly kindled into passion. "One lives but once in this world, and one must live one's life, happen what will!"

His wife entered the room and caught sight of the object of his scrutiny. Her eyes blazed; the last feeble sparks of her dead love glowed under the ashes and revealed themselves in a temporary flash of jealousy.

"Hadn't we better take the children to the Zoo?" she asked.

"To make a public show of our misery? No, thank you!"

"But it's so hot in here. I shall have to pull down the blinds."

"You had better open a window!"

He divined his wife's thoughts and rose to do it himself. Out there, on the edge of the pavement, his four little ones were sitting, in close proximity of the waste pipes. Their feet were in the dry gutter, and they were playing with orange peels which they had found in the sweepings of the road. The sight stabbed his heart, and he felt a lump rising in his throat. But poverty had so blunted his feelings that he remained standing at the window with his arms crossed.

All at once two filthy streams gushed from the waste pipes, inundated the gutter and saturated the feet of the children who screamed, half suffocated by the stench.

"Get the children ready as quickly as you can," he called, giving way at the heart-rending scene.

The father pushed the perambulator with the baby, the other children clung to the hands and skirts of the mother.

They arrived at the cemetery with its dark-stemmed lime trees, their usual place of refuge; here the trees grew luxuriantly, as if the soil were enriched by the bodies which lay buried underneath it.

The bells were ringing for evening prayers. The inmates of the poorhouse flocked to the church and sat down in the pews left vacant by their wealthy owners, who had attended to their souls at the principal service of the day, and were now driving in their carriages to the Royal Deer Park.

The children climbed about the shallow graves, most of which were decorated with armorial bearings and inscriptions.

Husband and wife sat down on a seat and placed the perambulator, in which the baby lay sucking at its bottle, by their side. Two puppies were disporting themselves on a grave close by, half hidden by the high grass.

A young and well dressed couple, leading by the hand a little girl clothed in silk and velvet, passed the seat on which they sat. The poor copyist raised his eyes to the young dandy and recognized a former colleague from the Board of Trade who, however, did not seem to see him. A feeling of bitter envy seized him with such intensity that he felt more humiliated by this "ignoble sentiment" than by his deplorable condition. Was he angry with the other man because he filled a position which he himself had coveted? Surely not. But of a sense of justice, and his suffering was all the deeper because it was shared by the whole class of the disinherited. He was convinced that the inmates of the poorhouse, bowed down under the yoke of public charity, envied his wife; and he was quite sure that many of the aristocrats who slept all around him in their graves, under their coats of arms, would have envied him his children if it had been their lot to die without leaving an heir to their estates. Certainly, nobody under the sun enjoyed complete happiness, but why did the plums always fall to the lot of those who were already sitting in the lap of luxury? And how was it that the prizes always fell to the organizers of the great lottery? The disinherited had to be content with the mass said at evening prayers; to their share fell morality and those virtues which the others despised and of which they had no need because the gates of heaven opened readily enough to their wealth. But what about the good and just God who had distributed His gifts so unevenly? It would be better, indeed, to live one's life without this unjust God, who had, moreover, candidly admitted that the "wind blew where it listed"; had He not himself confessed, in these words, that He did not interfere in the concerns of man? But failing the church, where should we look for comfort? And yet, why ask for comfort? Wouldn't it be far better to strive to make such arrangements that no comfort was needed? Wouldn't it?

His speculations were interrupted by his eldest daughter who asked him for a leaf of the lime tree, which she wanted for a sunshade for her doll. He stepped on the seat and raised his hand to break off a little twig, when a constable appeared and rudely ordered him not to touch the trees. A fresh humiliation. At the same time the constable requested him not to allow his children to play on the graves, which was against the regulations.

"We'd better go home," said the distressed father. "How carefully they guard the interests of the dead, and how indifferent they are to the interests of the living."

And they returned home.

He sat down and began to work. He had to copy the manuscript of an academical treatise on overpopulation.

The subject interested him and he read the contents of the whole book.

The young author who belonged to what was called the ethical school, was preaching against vice.

"What vice?" mused the copyist. "That which is responsible for our existence? Which the priest orders us to indulge in at every wedding when he says: Be fruitful and multiply and fill the earth?"

The manuscript ran on: Propagation, without holy matrimony, is a destructive vice, because the fate of the children, who do not receive proper care and nursing, is a sad one. In the case of married couples, on the other hand, it becomes a sacred duty to indulge one's desires. This is proved, among other things, by the fact that the law protects even the female ovum, and it is right that it should be so.

"Consequently," thought the copyist, "there is a providence for legitimate children, but not for illegitimate ones Oh! this young philosopher! And the law which protects the female ovum! What business, then, have those microscopic things to detach themselves at every change of the moon? Those sacred objects ought to be most carefully guarded by the police!"

All these futilities he had to copy in his best handwriting.

They overflowed with morality, but contained not a single word of enlightenment.

The moral or rather the immoral gist of the whole argument was: There is a God who feeds and clothes all children born in wedlock; a God in His heaven, probably, but what about the earth? Certainly, it was said that He came to earth once and allowed himself to be crucified, after vainly trying to establish something like order in the confused affairs of mankind; He did not succeed.

The philosopher wound up by screaming himself hoarse in trying to convince his audience that the abundant supply of wheat was an irrefutable proof that the problem of overpopulation did not exist; that the doctrine of Malthus was not only false, but criminal, socially as well as morally.

And the poor father of a family who had not tasted wheaten bread for years, laid down the manuscript and urged his little ones to fill themselves with gruel made of rye flour and bluish milk, a dish which satisfied their craving, but contained no nourishment.

He was wretched, not because he considered water gruel objectionable, but because he had lost his precious sense of humor, that magician who can transform the dark rye into golden wheat; almighty love, emptying his horn of plenty over his poor home, had vanished. The children had become burdens, and the once beloved wife a secret enemy despised and despising him.

And the cause of all this unhappiness? The want of bread! And yet the large store houses of the new world were breaking down under the weight of the overabundant supply of wheat. What a world of contradictions! The manner in which bread was distributed must be at fault.

Science, which has replaced religion, has no answer to give; it merely states facts and allows the children to die of hunger and the parents of thirst.

Autumn

They had been married for ten years. Happily? Well, as happily as circumstances permitted. They had been running in double harness, like two young oxen of equal strength, each of which is conscientiously doing his own share.

During the first year of their marriage they buried many illusions and realized that marriage was not perfect bliss. In the second year the babies began to arrive, and the daily toil left them no time for brooding.

He was very domesticated, perhaps too much so; his family was his world, the center and pivot of which he was. The children were the radii. His wife attempted to be a center, too, but never in the middle of the circle, for that was exclusively occupied by him, and therefore the radii fell now on the top of one another, now far apart, and their life lacked harmony.

In the tenth year of their marriage he obtained the post of secretary to the Board of Prisons, and in that capacity he was obliged to travel about the country. This interfered seriously with his daily routine; the thought of leaving his world for a whole month upset him. He wondered whom he would miss more, his wife or his children, and he was sure he would miss them both.

On the eve of his departure he sat in the corner of the sofa and watched his portmanteau being packed. His wife was kneeling on the She brushed his black suit and folded it carefully, so that it should take up as little space as possible. He had no idea how to do these things.

She had never looked upon herself as his housekeeper, hardly as his wife, she was above all things mother: a mother to the children, a mother to him. She darned his socks without the slightest feeling of degradation, and asked for no thanks. She never even considered him indebted to her for it, for did he not give her and the children new stockings whenever they wanted them, and a great many other things into the bargain? But for him, she would have to go out and earn her own living, and the children would be left alone all day.

He sat in the sofa corner and looked at her. Now that the parting was imminent, he began to feel premature little twinges of longing. He gazed at her figure. Her shoulders were a little rounded; much bending over the cradle, ironing board and kitchen range had robbed her back of its straightness. He, too, stooped a little, the result of his toil at the writing-table, and he was obliged to wear spectacles. But at the moment he really was not thinking of himself. He noticed that her plaits were thinner than they had been and that a faint suggestion of silver lay on her hair. Had she sacrificed her beauty to him, to him alone? No, surely not to him, but to the little community which they formed; for, after all, she had also worked for herself. His hair, too, had grown thin in the struggle to provide for all of them. He might have retained his youth a little longer, if there hadn't been so many mouths to fill, if he had remained a bachelor; but he didn't regret his marriage for one second.

"It will be a good thing for you to get away for a bit," said his wife; "you have been too much at home."

"I suppose you are glad to get rid of me," he replied, not without bitterness; "but I — I shall miss you very much."

"You are like a cat, you'll miss your cozy fireside, but not me; you know you won't."

"And the kiddies?"

"Oh, yes! I daresay you'll miss them when you are away, for all your scolding when you are with them. No, no, I don't mean that you are unkind to them, but you do grumble a lot! All the same I won't be unjust, and I know that you love them."

At supper he was very tired and depressed. He didn't read the evening paper, he wanted to talk to his wife. But she was too busy to pay much attention to him; she had no time to waste; moreover, her ten years' campaign in kitchen and nursery had taught her self-control.

He felt more sentimental than he cared to show, and the topsy-turvy-dom of the room made him fidgety. Scraps of his daily life lay scattered all over chairs and chests of drawers; his black portmanteau yawned wide-open like a coffin; his white linen was carefully laid on the top of his black suit, which showed slight traces of wear and tear at the knees and elbows. It seemed to him that he himself was lying there, wearing a white shirt with a starched front. Presently they would close the coffin and carry it away.

On the following morning — it was in August — he rose early and dressed hurriedly. His nerves were unstrung. He went into the nursery and kissed the children who stared at him with sleepy eyes. Then he kissed his wife, got into a cab, and told the driver to drive him to the station.

The journey, which he made in the company of his Board, did him good; it really was a good thing for him to get out of his groove; domesticity lay behind him like a stuffy bedroom, and on the arrival of the train at Linkoping he was in high spirits.

An excellent dinner had been ordered at the best hotel and the remainder of the day was spent in eating it. They drank the health of the Lord Lieutenant; no one thought of the prisoners on whose behalf the journey had been undertaken.

Dinner over, he had to face a lonely evening in his solitary room. A bed, two chairs, a table, a washing-stand and a wax candle, which threw its dim light on bare walls. He couldn't suppress a feeling of nervousness. He missed all his little comforts, — slippers, dressing gown, pipe rack and writing table; all the little details which played an important part in his daily life. And the kiddies? And his wife? What were they doing? Were they all right? He became restless and depressed. When he wanted to wind up his watch, he found that he had left his watch-key at home. It was hanging on the watch-stand which his wife had given him before they were married. He went to bed and lit a cigar. Then he wanted a book out of his portmanteau and he had to get up again. Everything was packed so beautifully, it was a pity to disturb it. In looking for the book, he came across his slippers. She had forgotten nothing. Then he found the book. But he couldn't read. He lay in bed and thought of the past, of his wife, as she had been ten years ago. He saw her as she had been then; the picture of her, as she now was, disappeared in the blue-grey clouds of smoke which rose in rings and wreaths to the rain-stained ceiling. An infinite yearning came over him. Every harsh word he had ever spoken to her now grated on his ears; he thought remorsefully of every hour of anguish he had caused her. At last he fell asleep.

The following day brought much work and another banquet with a toast to the Prison-Governor — the prisoners were still unremembered. In the evening solitude, emptiness, coldness. He felt a pressing need to talk to her. He fetched some notepaper and sat down to write. But at the very outset he was confronted by a difficulty. How was he to address her? Whenever he had sent her a few lines to say that he would not be home for dinner, he had always called her "Dear Mother." But now he was not going to write to the mother, but to his fiancée, to his beloved one. At last he made up his mind and commenced his letter with "My Darling Lily," as he had done in the old days. At first he wrote slowly and with difficulty, for so many beautiful words and phrases seemed to have disappeared from the clumsy, dry language of everyday life; but as he warmed to his work, they awakened in his memory like forgotten melodies, valse tunes, fragments of poems, elder-blossoms, and swallows, sunsets on a mirrorlike sea. All his memories of the springtime of life came dancing along in clouds of gossamer and enveloped her. He drew a cross at the bottom of the page, as lovers do, and by the side of it he wrote the words: "Kiss here."

When the letter was finished and he read it through, his cheeks burned and he became self-conscious. He couldn't account for the reason.

But somehow he felt that he had shown his naked soul to a stranger.

In spite of this feeling he posted the letter.

A few days elapsed before he received a reply. While he was waiting for it, he was a prey to an almost childish bashfulness and embarrassment.

At last the answer came. He had struck the right note, and from the din and clamor of the nursery, and the fumes and smell of the kitchen, a song arose, clear and beautiful, tender and pure, like first love.

Now an exchange of love-letters began. He wrote to her every night, and sometimes he sent her a postcard as well during the day. His colleagues didn't know what to think of him. He was so fastidious about his dress and personal appearance, that they suspected him of a love affair. And he was in love — in love again. He sent her his photograph, without the spectacles, and she sent him a lock of her hair.

Their language was simple like a child's, and he wrote on colored paper ornamented with little doves. Why shouldn't they? They were a long way off forty yet, even though the struggle for an existence had made them feel that they were getting old. He had neglected her during the last twelvemonth, not so much from indifference as from respect — he always saw in her the mother of his children.

The tour of inspection was approaching its end. He was conscious of a certain feeling of apprehension when he thought of their meeting. He had corresponded with his sweetheart; should he find her in the mother and housewife? He dreaded a disappointment. He shrank at the thought of finding her with a kitchen towel in her hand, or the children clinging to her skirts. Their first meeting must be somewhere else, and they must meet alone. Should he ask her to join him at Waxholm, in the Stockholm Archipelago, at the hotel where they had spent so many happy hours during the period of their engagement? Splendid idea! There they could, for two whole days, re-live in memory the first beautiful spring days of their lives, which had flown, never to return again.

He sat down and made the suggestion in an impassioned love-letter. She answered by return agreeing to his proposal, happy that the same idea had occurred to both of them.

*T*wo days later he arrived at Waxholm and engaged rooms at the hotel. It was a beautiful September day. He dined alone, in the great dining room, drank a glass of wine and felt young again. Everything was so bright and beautiful. There was the blue sea outside; only the birch trees on the shore had changed their tints. In the garden the dahlias were still in full splendor, and the perfume of the mignonette rose from the borders of the flower beds. A few bees still visited the dying calyces but returned disappointed to their hives. The fishing boats sailed up the Sound before a faint breeze, and in tacking the sails fluttered and the sheets shook; the startled seagulls rose into the air screaming, and circled round the fishermen who were fishing from their boats for small herring.

He drank his coffee on the verandah, and began to look out for the steamer which was due at six o'clock.

Restlessly, apprehensively, he paced the verandah, anxiously watching fiord and Sound on the side where Stockholm lay, so as to sight the steamer as soon as she came into view.

At last a little cloud of smoke showed like a dark patch on the horizon. His heart thumped against his ribs and he drank a liqueur. Then he went down to the shore.

Now he could see the funnel right in the center of the Sound, and soon after he noticed the flag on the fore-topmast. . . . Was she really on the steamer, or had she been prevented from keeping the tryst? It was only necessary for one of the children to be ill, and she wouldn't be there, and he would have to spend a solitary night at the hotel. The children, who during the last few weeks had receded into the background, now stepped between her and him. They had hardly mentioned them in their last letters, just as if they had been anxious to be rid of all eyewitnesses and spoil-sports.

He stamped on the creaking landing-stage and then remained standing motionless near a bollard staring straight at the steamer which increased in size as she approached, followed in her wake by a river of molten gold that spread over the blue, faintly rippled expanse. Now he could distinguish people on the upper deck, a moving crowd, and sailors busy with the ropes, now a fluttering speck of white near the wheelhouse. There was no one besides him on the landing-stage, the moving white speck could only be meant for him, and no one would wave to him but her. He pulled out his handkerchief and answered her greeting, and in doing so he noticed that his handkerchief was not a white one; he had been using colored ones for years for the sake of economy.

The steamer whistled, signaled, the engines stopped, she came alongside, and now he recognized her. Their eyes met in greeting; the distance was still too great for words. Now he could see her being pushed slowly by the crowd across the little bridge. It was she, and yet it wasn't.

Ten years stretched between her and the picture of her which he had had in his mind. Fashion had changed, the cut of the clothes was different. Ten years ago her delicate face with its olive complexion was framed by the cap which was then worn, and which left the forehead free; now her forehead was hidden by a wicked imitation of a bowler hat. Ten years ago the beautiful lines of her figure were clearly definable under the artistic draperies of her cloak which playfully now hid, now emphasized the curve of her shoulders and the movement of her arms; now her figure was completely disguised by a long driving coat which followed the lines of her dress but completely concealed her figure. As she stepped off the landing-bridge, he caught sight of her little foot with which he had fallen in love, when it was encased in a buttoned boot, shaped on natural lines; the shoe which she was now wearing resembled a pointed Chinese slipper, and did not allow her foot to move in those dancing rhythms which had bewitched him.

It was she and yet it was not she! He embraced and kissed her. She enquired after his health and he asked after the children. Then they walked up the strand.

Words came slowly and sounded dry and forced. How strange! They were almost shy in each other's presence, and neither of them mentioned the letters.

In the end he took heart of grace and asked:

"Would you like to go for a walk before sunset?"

"I should love to," she replied, taking his arm.

They went along the high-road in the direction of the little town. The shutters of all the summer residences were closed; the gardens plundered. Here and there an apple, hidden among the foliage, might still be found hanging on the trees, but there wasn't a single flower in the flower beds. The verandahs, stripped of their sunblinds, looked like skeletons; where there had been bright eyes and gay laughter, silence reigned.

"How autumnal!" she said.

"Yes, the forsaken villas look horrible."

They walked on.

"Let us go and look at the house where we used to live."

"Oh, yes! It will be fun."

They passed the bathing vans.

Over there, squeezed in between the pilot's and the gardener's cottages, stood the little house with its red fence, its verandah and its little garden.

Memories of past days awoke. There was the bedroom where their first baby had been born. What rejoicing! What laughter! Oh! youth and gaiety! The rose tree which they had planted was still there. And the strawberry-bed which they had made — no, it existed no longer, grass had grown over it. In the little plantation traces of the swing which they had put up were still visible, but the swing itself had disappeared.

"Thank you so much for your beautiful letters," she said, gently pressing his arm.

He blushed and made no reply.

Then they returned to the hotel, and he told her anecdotes, in connection with his tour.

He had ordered dinner to be served in the large dining room at the table where they used to sit. They sat down without saying grace.

It was a tête-à-tête dinner. He took the bread-basket and offered her the bread. She smiled. It was a long time since he had been so attentive. But dinner at a seaside hotel was a pleasant change and soon they were engaged in a lively conversation. It was a duet in which one of them extolled the days that had gone, and the other revived memories of "once upon a time." They were re-living the past. Their eyes shone and the little lines in their faces disappeared. Oh! golden days! Oh! time of roses which comes but once, if it comes at all, and which is denied to so many of us — so many of us.

At dessert he whispered a few words into the ear of the waitress; she disappeared and returned a few seconds later with a bottle of champagne.

"My dear Axel, what are you thinking of?"

"I am thinking of the spring that has past, but will return again."

But he wasn't thinking of it exclusively, for at his wife's reproachful words there glided through the room, catlike, a dim vision of the nursery and the porridge bowl.

However — the atmosphere cleared again; the golden wine stirred their memories, and again they lost themselves in the intoxicating rapture of the past.

He leaned his elbow on the table and shaded his eyes with his hand, as if he were determined to shut out the present — this very present which, — after all, had been of his own seeking.

The hours passed. They left the dining room and went into the drawing room which boasted a piano, ordering their coffee to be brought there.

"I wonder how the kiddies are?" said she, awakening to the hard facts of real life.

"Sit down and sing to me," he answered, opening the instrument.

"What would you like me to sing? You know I haven't sung a note for many days."

He was well aware of it, but he *did* want a song.

She sat down before the piano and began to play. It was a squeaking instrument that reminded one of the rattling of loose teeth.

"What shall I sing?" she asked, turning round on the music-stool.

"You know, darling," he replied, not daring to meet her eyes.

"Your song! Very well, if I can remember it." And she sang: "Where is the blessed country where my beloved dwells?"

But alas! Her voice was thin and shrill and emotion made her sing out of tune. At times it sounded like a cry from the bottom of a soul which feels that noon is past and evening approaching. The fingers which had done hard work strayed on the wrong keys. The instrument, too, had seen its best days; the cloth on the hammers had worn away; it sounded as if the springs touched the bare wood.

When she had finished her song, she sat for a while without turning round, as if she expected him to come and speak to her. But he didn't move; not a sound broke the deep silence. When she turned round at last, she saw him sitting on the sofa, his cheeks wet with tears. She felt a strong impulse to jump up, take his head between her hands and kiss him as she had done in days gone by, but she remained where she was, immovable, with downcast eyes.

He held a cigar between his thumb and first finger. When the song was finished, he bit off the end and struck a match.

"Thank you, Lily," he said, puffing at his cigar, "will you have your coffee now?"

They drank their coffee, talked of summer holidays in general and suggested two or three places where they might go next summer. But their conversation languished and they repeated themselves.

At last he yawned openly and said: "I'm off to bed."

"I'm going, too," she said, getting up. "But I'll get a breath of fresh air first, on the balcony."

He went into the bedroom. She lingered for a few moments in the dining room, and then talked to the landlady for about half an hour of spring-onions and woolen underwear.

When the landlady had left her she went into the bedroom and stood for a few minutes at the door, listening. No sound came from within. His boots stood in the corridor. She opened the door gently and went in. He was asleep.

He was asleep!

*A*t breakfast on the following morning he had a headache, and she fidgeted.

"What horrible coffee," he said, with a grimace.

"Brazilian," she said, shortly.

"What shall we do today?" he asked, looking at his watch.

"Hadn't you better eat some bread and butter, instead of grumbling at the coffee?" she said.

"Perhaps you're right," he answered, "and I'll have a liqueur at the same time. That champagne last night, ugh!"

He asked for bread and butter and a liqueur and his temper improved.

"Let's go to the Pilot's Hill and look at the view."

They rose from the breakfast table and went out.

The weather was splendid and the walk did them good. But they walked slowly; she panted, and his knees were stiff; they drew no more parallels with the past.

They walked across the fields. The grass had been cut long ago, there wasn't a single flower anywhere. They sat down on some large stones.

He talked of the Board of Prisons and his office. She talked of the children.

Then they walked on in silence. He looked at his watch.

"Three hours yet till dinner time," he said. And he wondered how they could kill time on the next day.

They returned to the hotel. He asked for the papers. She sat down by the side of him with a smile on her lips.

They talked little during dinner. After dinner she mentioned the servants.

"For heaven's sake, leave the servants alone!" he exclaimed.

"Surely we haven't come here to quarrel!"

"Am I quarreling?"

"Well, I'm not!"

An awkward pause followed. He wished somebody would come. The children! Yes! This tête-à-tête embarrassed him, but he felt a pain in his heart when he thought of the bright hours of yesterday.

"Let's go to Oak Hill," she said, "and gather wild strawberries."

"There are no wild strawberries at this time of the year, it's autumn."

"Let's go all the same."

And they went. But conversation was difficult. His eyes searched for some object on the roadside which would serve for a peg on which to hang a remark, but there was nothing. There was no subject which they hadn't discussed. She knew all his views on everything and disagreed with most of them. She longed to go home, to the children, to her own fireside. She found it absurd to make a spectacle of herself in this place and be on the verge of a quarrel with her husband all the time.

After a while they stopped, for they were tired. He sat down and began to write in the sand with his walking stick. He hoped she would provoke a scene.

"What are you thinking of?" she asked at last.

"I?" he replied, feeling as if a burden were falling off his shoulders, "I am thinking that we are getting old, mother: our innings are over, and we have to be content with what has been. If you are of the same mind, we'll go home by the night boat."

"I have thought so all along, old man, but I wanted to please you."

"Then come along, we'll go home. It's no longer summer, autumn is here."

They returned to the hotel, much relieved.

He was a little embarrassed on account of the prosaic ending of the adventure, and felt an irresistible longing to justify it from a philosophical standpoint.

"You see, mother," he said, "my lo — h'm" (the word was too strong) "my affection for you has undergone a change in the course of time. It has developed, broadened; at first it was centered on the individual, but later on, on the family as a whole. It is not now you, personally, that I love, nor is it the children, but it is the whole. . . ."

"Yes, as my uncle used to say, children are lightning conductors!"

After his philosophical explanation he became his old self again. It was pleasant to take off his frock coat; he felt, as if he were getting into his dressing gown.

When they entered the hotel, she began at once to pack, and there she was in her element.

They went downstairs into the saloon as soon as they got on board. For appearance sake, however, he asked her whether she would like to watch the sunset; but she declined.

At supper he helped himself first, and she asked the waitress the price of black bread.

When he had finished his supper, he remained sitting at the table, lingering over a glass of porter. A thought which had amused him for some time, would no longer be suppressed.

"Old fool, what?" he said, lifting his glass and smiling at his wife who happened to look at him at the moment.

She did not return his smile but her eyes, which had flashed for a second, assumed so withering an expression of dignity that he felt crushed.

The spell was broken, the last trace of his old love had vanished; he was sitting opposite the mother of his children; he felt small.

"No need to look down upon me because I have made a fool of myself for a moment," she said gravely. "But in a man's love there is always a good deal of contempt; it is strange."

"And in the love of a woman?"

"Even more, it is true! But then, she has every cause."

"It's the same thing — with a difference. Probably both of them are wrong. That which one values too highly, because it is difficult of attainment, is easily underrated when one has obtained it."

"Why does one value it too highly?"

"Why is it so difficult of attainment?"

The steam whistle above their heads interrupted their conversation. They landed.

When they had arrived home, and he saw her again among her children, he realized that his affection for her had undergone a change, and that her affection for him had been transferred to and divided amongst all these little screamers. Perhaps her love for him had only been a means to an end. His part had been a short one, and he felt deposed. If he had not been required to earn bread and butter, he would probably have been cast off long ago.

He went into his study, put on his dressing gown and slippers, lighted his pipe and felt at home.

Outside the wind lashed the rain against the windowpanes, and whistled in the chimney.

When the children had been put to bed, his wife came and sat by him.

"No weather to gather wild strawberries," she said.

"No, my dear, the summer is over and autumn is here."

"Yes, it is autumn," she replied, "but it is not yet winter, there is comfort in that."

"Very poor comfort if we consider that we live but once."

"Twice when one has children; three times if one lives to see one's grandchildren."

"And after that, the end."

"Unless there is a life after death."

"We cannot be sure of that! Who knows? I believe it, but my faith is no proof."

"But it is good to believe it. Let us have faith! Let us believe that spring will come again! Let us believe it!"

"Yes, let us believe it," he said, gathering her to his breast.

Compulsory Marriage

*H*is father died early and from that time forth he was in the hands of a mother, two sisters and several aunts. He had no brother. They lived on an estate in the Swedish province, Soedermanland, and had no neighbors with whom they *could be* on friendly terms. When he was seven years old, a governess was engaged to teach him and his sisters, and about the same time a girl cousin came to live with them.

He shared his sisters' bedroom, played their games and went bathing with them; nobody looked upon him as a member of the other sex. Before long his sisters took him in hand and became his schoolmasters and tyrants.

He was a strong boy to start with, but left to the mercy of so many doting women, he gradually became a helpless molly-coddle.

Once he made an attempt to emancipate himself and went to play with the boys of the cottagers. They spent the day in the woods, climbed the trees, robbed the birds' nests and threw stones at the squirrels. Frithiof was as happy as a released prisoner, and did not come home to dinner. The boys gathered whortle-berries, and bathed in the lake. It was the first really enjoyable day of his life.

When he came home in the evening, he found the whole house in great commotion. His mother though anxious and upset, did not conceal her joy at his return; Aunt Agatha, however, a spinster, and his mother's eldest sister, who ruled the house, was furious. She maintained that it would be a positive crime not to punish him. Frithiof could not understand why it should be a crime, but his aunt told him that disobedience was a sin. He protested that he had never been forbidden to play with the children of the cottagers. She admitted it but said that, of course, there could never have been two questions about it. And she remained firm, and regardless of his mother's pleading eyes, took him away to give him a whipping in her own room. He was eight years old and fairly big for his age.

When the aunt touched his waist-belt to unbutton his knickers, a cold shiver ran down his back; he gasped and his heart thumped against his ribs. He made no sound, but stared, horror-struck, at the old woman who asked him, almost caressingly, to be obedient and not to offer any resistance. But when she laid hands on his shirt, he grew hot with shame and fury. He sprang from the sofa on which she had pushed him, hitting out right and left. Something unclean, something dark and repulsive, seemed to emanate from this woman, and the shame of his sex rose up in him as against an assailant.

But the aunt, mad with passion, seized him, threw him on a chair and beat him. He screamed with rage, pain he did not feel, and with convulsive kicks tried to release himself; but all of a sudden he lay still and was silent.

When the old woman let him go, he remained where he was, motionless.

"Get up!" she said, in a broken voice.

He stood up and looked at her. One of her cheeks was pale, the other crimson. Her eyes glowed strangely and she trembled all over. He looked at her curiously, as one might examine a wild beast, and all of a sudden a supercilious smile raised his upper lip; it seemed to him as if his contempt gave him an advantage over her. "She-devil!" He flung the word, newly acquired from the children of the cottagers, into her face, defiantly and scornfully, seized his clothes and flew downstairs to his mother, who was sitting in the dining room, weeping.

He wanted to open his heart to her and complain of his aunt's treatment, but she had not the courage to comfort him. So he went into the kitchen where the maids consoled him with a handful of currants.

From this day on he was no longer allowed to sleep in the nursery with his sisters, but his mother had his bed removed to her own bedroom. He found his mother's room stuffy and the new arrangement dull; she frequently disturbed his sleep by getting up and coming to his bed in the night to see whether he was covered up; then he flew into a rage and answered her questions peevishly.

He was never allowed to go out without being carefully wrapped up by someone, and he had so many mufflers that he never knew which one to put on. Whenever he tried to steal out of the house, someone was sure to see him from the window and call him back to put on an overcoat.

By and by his sisters' games began to bore him. His strong arms no longer wanted to play battledore and shuttlecock, they longed to throw stones. The squabbles over a petty game of croquet, which demanded neither muscle nor brain, irritated him.

The governess was another one of his trials. She always spoke to him in French and he invariably answered her in Swedish. A vague disgust with his whole life and surroundings began to stir in him.

The free and easy manner in which everybody behaved in his presence offended him, and he retaliated by heartily loathing all with whom he came in contact. His mother was the only one who considered his feelings to a certain extent: she had a big screen put round his bed.

Ultimately the kitchen and the servants' hall became his refuge; there everything he did was approved of. Occasionally, of course, matters were discussed there which might have aroused a boy's curiosity, but for him there were no secrets. On one occasion, for instance, he had accidentally come to the maids' bathing-place. The governess, who was with him, screamed, he could not understand why, but he stopped and talked to the girls who were standing or lying about in the water. Their nudity made no impression upon him.

He grew up into a youth. An inspector was engaged to teach him farming for he was, of course, to take over the management of the estate in due time. They chose an old man who held the orthodox faith. The old man's society was not exactly calculated to stimulate a young man's brain, but it was an improvement on the old conditions. It opened new points of view to him and roused him to activity. But the inspector received daily and hourly so many instructions from the ladies, that he ended by being nothing but their mouth-piece.

At the age of fifteen Frithiof was confirmed, received a present of a gold watch and was allowed to go out on horseback; he was not permitted, however, to realize his greatest ambition, namely to go shooting. True, there was no longer any fear of a whipping from his arch-enemy, but he dreaded his mother's tears. He always remained a child, and never managed to throw off the habit of giving way to the judgment of other people.

The years passed; he had attained his twentieth year. One day he was standing in the kitchen watching the cook, who was busy scaling a perch. She was a pretty young woman with a delicate complexion. He was teasing her and finally put his hand down her back.

"Do behave yourself, now, Mr. Frithiof," said the girl.

"But I am behaving myself," he replied, becoming more and more familiar.

"If mistress should see you!"

"Well supposing she did?"

At this moment his mother passed the open kitchen door; she instantly turned away and walked across the yard.

Frithiof found the situation awkward and slunk away to his bedroom.

A new gardener entered their service. In their wisdom, anxious to avoid trouble with the maids, the ladies had chosen a married man. But, as misfortune would have it, the gardener had been married long enough to be the father of an exceedingly pretty young daughter.

Frithiof quickly discovered the sweet blossom among the other roses in the garden, and poured out all the good-will which lay stored up in his heart for *that* half of humanity to which he did not belong, on this young girl, who was rather well developed and not without education.

He spent a good deal of his time in the garden and stopped to talk to her whenever he found her working at one of the flower-beds or cutting flowers. She did not respond to his advances, but this only had the effect of stimulating his passion.

One day he was riding through the wood, haunted, as usual, by visions of her loveliness which, in his opinion, reached the very pinnacle of perfection. He was sick with longing to meet her alone, freed from all fear of incurring some watcher's displeasure. In his heated imagination the desire of being near her had assumed such enormous proportions, that he felt that life without her would be impossible.

He held the reins loosely in his hand, and the horse picked his way leisurely while its rider sat on its back wrapped in deep thought. All of a sudden something light appeared between the trees and the gardener's daughter emerged from the underwood and stepped out on the footpath.

Frithiof dismounted and took off his hat. They walked on, side by side, talking, while he dragged his horse behind him. He spoke in vague words of his love for her; but she rejected all his advances.

"Why should we talk of the impossible?" she asked.

"What is impossible?" he exclaimed.

"That a wealthy gentleman like you should marry a poor girl like me."

There was no denying the aptitude of her remark, and Frithiof felt that he was worsted. His love for her was boundless, but he could see no possibility of bringing his doe safely through the pack which guarded house and home; they would tear her to pieces.

After this conversation he gave himself up to mute despair.

In the autumn the gardener gave notice and left the estate without giving a reason. For six weeks Frithiof was inconsolable, for he had lost his first and only love; he would never love again.

In this way the autumn slowly passed and winter stood before the door. At Christmas a new officer of health came into the neighborhood. He had grown-up children, and as the aunts were always ill, friendly relations were soon established between the two families. Among the doctor's children was a young girl and before long Frithiof was head over ears in love with her. He was at first ashamed of his infidelity to his first love, but he soon came to the conclusion that love was something impersonal, because it was possible to change the object of one's tenderness; it was almost like a power of attorney made out on the holder.

As soon as his guardians got wind of this new attachment, the mother asked her son for a private interview.

"You have now arrived at that age," she began, "when a man begins to look out for a wife."

"I have already done that, my dear mother," he replied.

"I'm afraid you've been too hasty," she said. "The girl of whom, I suppose, you are thinking, doesn't possess the moral principles which an educated man should demand."

"What? Amy's moral principles! Who has anything to say against them?"

"I won't say a word against the girl herself, but her father, as you know, is a freethinker."

"I shall be proud to be related to a man who can think freely, without considering his material interests."

"Well, let's leave him out of the question; you are forgetting, my dear Frithiof, that you are already bound elsewhere."

"What? Do you mean. . . ."

"Yes; you have played with Louisa's heart."

"Are you talking of cousin Louisa?"

"I am. Haven't you looked upon yourselves as fiancés since your earliest childhood? Don't you realize that she has put all her faith and trust in you?"

"It's you who have played with us, driven us together, not I!" answered the son.

"Think of your old mother, think of your sisters, Frithiof. Do you want to bring a stranger into this house which has always been our home, a stranger who will have the right to order us about?"

"Oh! I see; Louisa is the chosen mistress!"

"There's no chosen mistress, but a mother always has a right to choose the future wife of her son; nobody is so well fitted to undertake such a task. Do you doubt my good faith? Can you possibly suspect me, your mother, of a wish to injure you?" "No, no! but I – I don't love Louisa; I like her as a sister, but. . . ."

"Love? Nothing in all the world is so inconstant as love! It's folly to rely on it, it passes away like a breath; but friendship, conformity of views and habits, similar interests and a long acquaintanceship, these are the surest guarantees of a happy marriage. Louisa is a capable girl, domesticated and methodical, she will make your home as happy as you could wish."

Frithiof's only way of escape was to beg his mother for time to consider the matter.

Meanwhile all the ladies of the household had recovered their health, so that the doctor was no longer required. Still he called one day, but he was treated like a burglar who had come to spy out the land. He was a sharp man and saw at once how matters stood. Frithiof returned his call but was received coldly. This was the end of their friendly relations.

Frithiof came of age.

Frantic attempts were now made to carry the fortress by storm. The aunts cringed before the new master and tried to prove to him that they could not be dispensed with, by treating him as if he were a child. His sisters mothered him more than ever, and Louisa began to devote a great deal of attention to her dress. She laced herself tightly and curled her hair. She was by no means a plain girl, but she had cold eyes and a sharp tongue.

Frithiof remained indifferent; as far as he was concerned she was sexless; he had never looked at her with the eyes of a man. But now, after the conversation with his mother, he could not help a certain feeling of embarrassment in her presence, especially as she seemed to seek his society. He met her everywhere; on the stairs, in the garden, in the stables even. One morning, when he was still in bed, she came into his room to ask him for a pin; she was wearing a dressing-jacket and pretended to be very shy.

He took a dislike to her, but nevertheless she was always in his mind.

In the meantime the mother had one conversation after another with her son, and aunt and sisters never ceased hinting at the anticipated wedding.

Life was made a burden to him. He saw no way of escape from the net in which he had been caught. Louisa was no longer his sister and friend, though he did not like her any the better for it; his constant dwelling on the thought of marrying her had had the result of making him realize that she was a woman, an unsympathetic woman, it was true, but still a woman. His marriage would mean a change in his position, and, perhaps, delivery from bondage. There were no other girls in the neighborhood, and, after all, she was probably as good as any other young woman.

And so he went one day to his mother and told her that he had made up his mind. He would marry Louisa on condition that he should have an establishment of his own in one of the wings of the house, and his own table. He also insisted that his mother should propose for him, for he could not bring himself to do it.

The compromise was accepted and Louisa was called in to receive Frithiof's embrace and timid kiss. They both wept for reasons which neither of them understood. They felt ashamed of themselves for the rest of the day. Afterwards everything went on as before, but the motherliness of aunts and sisters knew no bounds. They furnished the wing, arranged the rooms, settled everything; Frithiof was never consulted in the matter.

The preparations for the wedding were completed. Old friends, buried in the provinces, were hunted up and invited to be present at the ceremony.

The wedding took place.

On the morning after his wedding day Frithiof was up early. He left his bedroom as quickly as possible, pretending that his presence was necessary in the fields.

Louisa, who was still sleepy, made no objection. But as he was going out she called after him:

"You won't forget breakfast at eleven!"

It sounded like a command.

He went to his den, put on a shooting coat and waterproof boots and took his gun, which he kept concealed in his wardrobe. Then he went out into the wood.

It was a beautiful October morning. Everything was covered with hoar frost. He walked quickly as if he were afraid of being called back, or as if he were trying to escape from something. The fresh air had the effect of a bath. He felt a free man, at last, and he used his freedom to go out for a morning stroll with his gun. But this exhilarating feeling of bodily freedom soon passed. Up to now he had at least had a bedroom of his own. He had been master of his thoughts during the day and his dreams at night. That was over. The thought of that common bedroom tormented him; there was something unclean about it. Shame was cast aside like a mask, all delicacy of feeling was dispensed with, every illusion of the "high origin" of man destroyed; to come into such close contact with nothing but the beast in man had been too much for him, for he had been brought up by idealists. He was staggered by the enormity of the hypocrisy displayed in the intercourse between men and women; it was a revelation to him to find that the inmost substance of that indescribable womanliness was nothing but the fear of consequences. But supposing he had married the doctor's daughter, or the gardener's little girl? Then to be alone with her would be bliss, while to be alone with his wife was depressing and unlovely; then the coarse desire to satisfy a curiosity and a want would be transformed into an ecstasy more spiritual than carnal.

He wandered through the wood without a purpose, without an idea of what he wanted to shoot; be only felt a vague desire to hear a shot and to kill something; but nothing came before his gun. The birds had already migrated. Only a squirrel was climbing about the branches of a pine tree, staring at him with brilliant eyes. He raised the gun and pulled the trigger; but the nimble little beast was already on the other side of the trunk when the shot hit the tree. But the sound impressed his nerves pleasantly.

He left the footpath and went through the undergrowth. He stamped on every fungus that grew on his way. He was in a destructive mood. He looked for a snake so as to trample on it or kill it with a shot.

Suddenly he remembered that he ought to go home and that it was the morning after his wedding day. The mere thought of the curious glances to which he would be exposed had the effect of making him feel like a criminal, about to be unmasked and shown up for having committed a crime against good manners and, what was worse, against nature. Oh! that he could have left this world behind him! But how was he to do that?

His thoughts grew tired at last of revolving round and round the same problem and he felt a craving for food.

He decided to return home and have some breakfast.

On entering the gate which led to the courtyard, he saw the whole house-party standing before the entrance hall. As soon as they caught sight of him they began to cheer. He crossed the yard with uncertain footsteps and listened with ill-concealed irritation to the sly questions after his health. Then he turned away and went into the house, never noticing his wife, who was standing amongst the group waiting for him to go up to her and kiss her.

At the breakfast table he suffered tortures; tortures which he knew would be burned into his memory for all times. The insinuations of his guests offended him and his wife's caresses stung him. His day of rejoicing was the most miserable day of his life.

In the course of a few months the young wife, with the assistance of aunts and sisters, had established her overrule in the house. Frithiof remained, what he had always been, the youngest and dullest member of the household. His advice was sometimes asked for, but never acted upon; he was looked after as if he were still a child. His wife soon found it unbearable to dine with him alone, for he kept an obstinate silence during the meal. Louisa could not stand it; she must have a lightning conductor; one of the sisters removed into the wing.

Frithiof made more than one attempt to emancipate himself, but his attempts were always frustrated by the enemy; they were too many for him, and they talked and preached until he fled into the wood.

The evenings held terror for him. He hated the bedroom, and went to it as to a place of execution. He became morose and avoided everybody.

They had been married for a year now, and still there was no promise of a child; his mother took him aside one day to have a talk to him.

"Wouldn't you like to have a son?" she asked.

"Of course, I would," he replied.

"You aren't treating your wife very kindly," said the mother as gently as possible.

He lost his temper.

"What? What do you say? Are you finding fault with me? Do you want me to toil all day long? H'm! You don't know Louisa! But whose business is it but mine? Bring your charge against me in such a way that I can answer it!"

But the mother was not disposed to do that.

Lonely and miserable, he made friends with the inspector, a young man, addicted to wine and cards. He sought his company and spent the evenings in his room; he went to bed late, as late as possible.

On coming home one night, he found his wife still awake and waiting for him.

"Where have you been?" she asked sharply.

"That's my business," he replied.

"To be married and have no husband is anything but pleasant," she rejoined. "If we had a child, at least!"

"It isn't my fault that we haven't!"

"It isn't mine!"

A quarrel arose as to whose fault it was, and the quarrel lasted for two years.

As both of them were too obstinate to take medical advice, the usual thing happened. The husband cut a ridiculous figure, and the wife a tragic one. He was told that a childless woman was sacred because, for some reason or other, "God's" curse rested on her. That "God" could also stoop to curse a man was beyond the women's comprehension.

But Frithiof had no doubt that a curse rested on him for his life was dreary and unhealthy. Nature has created two sexes, which are now friends, now enemies. He had met the enemy, an overwhelming enemy.

"What is a capon?" he was asked by one of his sisters one day. She was busy with her needlework and asked the question à propos of nothing.

He looked at her suspiciously. No, she did not know the meaning of the word; she had probably listened to a conversation and her curiosity was aroused.

But the iron had entered his soul. He was being laughed at. He grew suspicious. Everything he heard and saw he connected with that charge. Beside himself with rage, he seduced one of the maids.

His act had the desired result. In due time he was a father.

Now Louisa was looked upon as a martyr and he as a blackguard. The abuse left him indifferent, for he had vindicated his honor — if it was an honor and not merely a lucky chance to be born without defects.

But the incident roused Louisa's jealousy and — it was a strange thing — awakened in her a sort of love for her husband. It was a love which irritated him, for it showed itself in unremitting watchfulness and nervous obtrusiveness; sometimes even in maternal tenderness and solicitude which knew no bounds. She wanted to look after his gun, see whether it was charged; she begged him on her knees to wear his overcoat when he went out. . . . She kept his home with scrupulous care, tidied and dusted all day long; every Saturday the rooms were turned inside out, the carpets beaten and his clothes aired. He had no peace and never knew when he would be turned out of his room so that it could be scrubbed.

There was not sufficient to do to occupy him during the day, for the women looked after everything. He studied agriculture and attempted to make improvements, but all his efforts were frustrated. He was not master in his own house.

Finally he lost heart. He had grown taciturn because he was always contradicted. The want of congenial company and fellows-in-misfortune gradually dulled his brain; his nerves went to pieces; he neglected his appearance and took to drink.

He was hardly ever at home now. Frequently he could be found, intoxicated, at the public house or in the cottages of the farm laborers. He drank with everybody and all day long. He stimulated his brain with alcohol for the sake of the relief he found in talking. It was difficult to decide whether he drank in order to be able to talk to somebody who did not contradict him, or whether he drank merely in order to get drunk.

He sold privileges and farm produce to the cottagers to provide himself with money, for the women held the cash. Finally he burgled his own safe and stole the contents.

There was an orthodox, church-going inspector on the premises now; the previous one had been dismissed on account of his intemperate habits. When at last, through the clergyman's influence, the proprietor of the inn lost his license Frithiof took to drinking with his own farm laborers. Scandal followed on scandal.

He developed into a heavy drinker who had epileptic fits whenever he was deprived of alcohol.

He was ultimately committed to an institution where he remained as an incurable patient.

At lucid intervals, when he was capable of surveying his life, his heart was filled with compassion for all women who are compelled to marry without love; his compassion was all the deeper because he had suffered in his own flesh the curse which lies on every violation of nature; and yet he was only a man.

He saw the cause of his unhappiness in the family — the family as a social institution, which does not permit the child to become an independent individual at the proper time.

He brought no charge against his wife, for was she not equally unhappy, a victim of the same unfortunate conditions which are honored by the sacred name of Law?

Corinna

*H*er father was a general, her mother died when she was still a baby. After her mother's death few ladies visited the house; the callers were mostly men. And her father took her education into his own hands.

She went out riding with him, was present at the maneuvers, took an interest in gymnastics and attended the musters of the reserves.

Since her father occupied the highest rank in their circle of friends, everybody treated him with an amount of respect which is rarely shown to equals, and as she was the general's daughter, she was treated in the same way. She held the rank of a general and she knew it.

There was always an orderly sitting in the hall who rose with much clanking and clashing of steel and stood at attention whenever she went in or out. At the balls none but the majors dared to ask her for a dance; she looked upon a captain as a representative of an inferior race, and a lieutenant as a naughty boy.

She fell into the habit of appreciating people entirely according to their rank. She called all civilians "fishes," poorly-clad people "rascals," and the very poor "the mob."

The ladies, however, were altogether outside this scale. Her father, who occupied a position above all men, and who was saluted respectfully wherever he went, always stood up before a lady, regardless of her age, kissed the hands of those he knew, and was at the beck and call of every pretty woman. The result of this was that very early in life she became very firmly convinced of the superiority of her own sex, and accustomed herself to look upon a man as a lower being.

Whenever she went out on horseback, a groom invariably rode behind her. When she stopped to admire the landscape, he stopped too. He was her shadow. But she had no idea what he looked like, or whether he was young or old. If she had been asked about his sex, she would not have known how to reply; it had never occurred to her that the shadow could have a sex; when, in mounting, she placed her little riding-boot in his hand, she remained quite indifferent, and even occasionally raised her habit a little as if nobody were present.

These inbred conceptions of the surpassing importance of rank influenced her whole life. She found it impossible to make friends with the daughters of a major or a captain, because their fathers were her father's social inferiors. Once a lieutenant asked her for a dance. To punish him for his impudence, she refused to talk to him in the intervals. But when she heard later on that her partner had been one of the royal princes, she was inconsolable. She who knew every order and title, and the rank of every officer, had failed to recognize a prince! It was too terrible!

She was beautiful, but pride gave her features a certain rigidity which scared her admirers away. The thought of marriage had never occurred to her. The young men were not fully qualified, and those to whose social position there was no objection, were too old. If she, the daughter of a general, had married a captain, then a major's wife would have taken precedence of her. Such a degradation would have killed her. Moreover, she had no wish to be a man's chattel, or an ornament for his drawing room. She was accustomed to command, accustomed to be obeyed; she could obey no man. The freedom and independence of a man's life appealed to her; it had fostered in her a loathing for all womanly occupations.

Her sexual instinct awoke late. As she belonged to an old family which on her father's side, had squandered its strength in a soulless militarism, drink and dissipation, and on her mother's had suppressed fertility to prevent the splitting up of property, Nature seemed to have hesitated about her sex at the eleventh hour; or perhaps had lacked strength to determine on the continuation of the race. Her figure possessed none of those essentially feminine characteristics, which Nature requires for her purposes, and she scorned to hide her defects by artificial means.

The few women friends she had, found her cold and indifferent towards everything connected with the sex problem. She treated it with contempt, considered the relationship between the sexes disgusting, and could not understand how a woman could give herself to a man. In her opinion Nature was unclean; to wear clean underlinen, starched petticoats and stockings without holes was to be virtuous; poor was merely another term for dirt and vice.

Every summer she spent with her father on their estate in the country.

She was no great lover of the country. Nature made her feel small; she found the woods uncanny, the lake made her shudder, there was danger hidden in the tall meadow-grass. She regarded the peasants as

cunning and rather filthy beasts. They had so many children, and she
had no doubt that both boys and girls were full of vice. Nevertheless
they were always invited to the manor house on Midsummer day and
on the general's birthday, to play the part of the chorus of grand opera,
that is to say, to cheer and dance, and look like the figures in a painting.

It was springtime. Helena, on her thoroughbred mare, had penetrated
into the depths of the country. She felt tired and dismounted; she
fastened her mare to a birch tree which grew near an enclosure. Then
she strolled along by the side of a ditch and began to gather wild orchids.
The air was soft and balmy, steam was rising from the ground. She could
hear the frogs jumping into the ditch which was half-full of water.

All at once the mare neighed and, stretching her slender neck over
the fence, drew in the air with wide-open nostrils.

"Alice!" she called out, "be quiet, old girl!"

And she continued to gather the modest flowers which so cleverly
hide their secrets behind the prettiest and neatest curtains that for all
the world look like printed calico.

But the mare neighed again. From behind the hazel bushes on the
other side of the enclosure came an answer, a second neighing, deeper
and fuller. The swampy ground of the enclosure shook, powerful hoofs
scattered the stones, to right and left and a black stallion appeared at
full gallop. The tense neck carried a magnificent head, the muscles lay
like ropes under the glossy skin. As he caught sight of the mare, his eyes
began to flash. He stopped and stretched out his neck as if he were going
to yawn, raised his upper lip and showed his teeth. Then he galloped
across the grass and approached the railings.

Helena picked up her skirt and ran to her mare; she raised her hand
to seize the bridle, but the mare broke away and took the fence. Then
the wooing began.

She stood at the fence and called, but the excited mare paid no heed.
Inside the enclosure the horses chased one another; the situation was a
critical one. The breath of the stallion came like smoke from his nostrils
and white foam flecked his shoulders.

Helena longed to escape, for the scene filled her with horror. She had
never witnessed the raging of a natural instinct in a living body. This
uncontrolled outbreak terrified her.

She wanted to run after her mare and drag her away by force, but she
was afraid of the savage stallion. She wanted to call for help, but she
was loath to attract other eyewitnesses. She turned her back to the scene
and decided to wait.

The sound of horses' hoofs came from the direction of the highroad;
a carriage appeared in sight.

There was no escape; although she was ashamed to stay where she was, it was too late now to run away, for the horses were slowing down and the carriage stopped a few yards in front of her.

"How beautiful!" exclaimed one of the occupants of the carriage, a lady, and raised her golden lorgnette so as to get a better view of the spectacle.

"But why are we stopping?" retorted the other, irritably. "Drive on!"

"Don't you think it beautiful?" asked the elder lady.

The coachman's smile was lost in his great beard, as he urged the horses on.

"You are such a prude, my dear Milly," said the first voice. "To me this kind of thing is like a thunderstorm, or a heavy sea. . . ."

Helena could hear no more. She felt crushed with vexation, shame and horror.

A farm laborer came shuffling along the highroad. Helena ran to meet him, so as to prevent him from witnessing the scene, and at the same time ask his help. But he was already too near.

"I believe it's the miller's black stallion," he said gravely. "In that case it will be better to wait until it's all over, for he won't brook interference. If the lady will leave it to me, I will bring her mare home later on."

Glad to have done with the matter, Helena hurried away.

When she arrived home, she was ill.

She refused to ride her mare again, for in her eyes the beast had become unclean.

This pretty adventure had a greater influence on Helena's psychic development than might have been expected. The brutal outbreak of a natural instinct, the undisguised exhibition of which in the community of men is punished with a term of imprisonment, haunted her as if she had been present at an execution. It distressed her during the day and disturbed her dreams at night. It increased her fear of nature and made her give up her former amazon's life. She remained at home and gave herself up to study.

The house boasted a library. But as misfortune would have it, no additions had been made since her grandfather's death. All books were therefore a generation too old, and Helena found antiquated ideals. The first book which fell into her hands was Madame de Staël's *Corinna* The way in which the volume lay on the shelf indicated that it had served a special purpose. Bound in green and gold, a little shabby at the edges, full of marginal notes and underlined passages, the work of her late mother, it became a bridge, as it were, between mother and daughter, which enabled the now grown-up daughter to make the acquaintance of the dead mother. These pencil notes were the story of a soul. Displeasure with the prose of life and the brutality of nature, had inflamed the writer's imagination and inspired it to construct a dreamworld in which the souls dwelled, disincarnate. It was essentially an aristocratic world, this dreamworld, for it required financial independence from its denizens, so that the soul might be fed with thoughts. This brain-fever, called romance, was therefore the gospel of the wealthy, and became absurd and pitiful as soon as it penetrated to the lower classes.

Corinna became Helena's ideal: the divinely inspired poetess who like the nun of the middle-ages, had vowed a vow of chastity, so that she might lead a life of purity, who was, of course, admired by a brilliant throng, rose to immeasurable heights above the heads of the petty everyday mortals. It was the old ideal all over again, transposed: salutes, standing at attention, rolling of drums, the first place everywhere. Helena was quite ignorant of the fact that Madame de Staël outlived the Corinna ideal, and did not become a real influence until she came out of her dreamworld into the world of facts.

She ceased to take an interest in everyday affairs, she communed with herself and brooded over her ego. The inheritance which her mother had left her in posthumous notes began to germinate. She identified herself with both Corinna and her mother, and spent much time in meditating on her mission in life. That nature had intended her to become a mother and do her share in the propagation of the human race, she refused to admit her mission was to explain to humanity what Madame de Staël's Corinna had thought fifty years ago; but she imagined the thoughts were her own, striving to find expression.

She began to write. One day she attempted verse. She succeeded. The lines were of equal length and the last words rhymed. A great light dawned on her: she was a poetess. One thing more remained: she wanted ideas; well she could take them from *Corinna.*

In this way quite a number of poems originated.

But they had also to be bestowed on the world, and this could not be done unless they were printed. One day she sent a poem entitled *Sappho* and signed *Corinna* to the *Illustrated Newspaper.* With a beating heart she went out to post the letter herself, and as it dropped into the pillarbox, she prayed softly to "God."

A trying fortnight ensued. She ate nothing, hardly closed her eyes, and spent her days in solitude.

When Saturday came and the paper was delivered, she trembled as if she were fever-stricken, and when she found that her verses were neither printed nor mentioned in "Letters to Correspondents," she almost broke down.

On the following Saturday, when she could count on an answer with some certainty, she slipped the paper into her pocket without unfolding it, and went into the woods. When she had arrived at a secluded spot and made sure that no one was watching her, she unfolded the paper and hastily glanced at the contents. One poem only was printed, entitled *Bellman's-day*. She turned to "Letters to Correspondents." Her first glance at the small print made her start violently. Her fingers clutched the paper, rolled it into a ball and flung it into the underwood. Then she stared, fascinated, at the ball of white, glimmering through the green undergrowth. For the first time in her life she had received an insult. She was completely unnerved. This unknown journalist had dared what nobody had dared before: he had been rude to her. She had come out from behind her trenches into the arena where high birth counts for nothing, but where victory belongs to that wonderful natural endowment which we call talent, and before which all powers bow when it can no longer be denied. But the unknown had also offended the woman in her, for he had said:

"The Corinna of 1807 would have cooked dinners and rocked cradles if she had lived after 1870. But you are no Corinna."

For the first time she had heard the voice of the enemy, the arch-enemy, man. Cook dinners and rock cradles! They should see!

She went home. She felt so crushed that her muscles hardly obeyed her relaxed nerves.

When she had gone a little way, she suddenly turned round and retraced her footsteps. Supposing anybody found that paper! It would give her away.

She returned to the spot, and breaking off a hazel switch, dragged the paper out from where it lay and carefully smoothed it. Then she raised a piece of turf, hid the paper underneath and rolled a stone on the top. It was a hope that lay buried there, and also a proof — of what? That she had committed a crime? She felt that she had. She had done a wrong, she had shown herself naked before the other sex.

From this day on a struggle went on in her heart. Ambition and fear of publicity strove within her, and she was unable to come to a decision.

In the following autumn her father died. As he had been addicted to gambling, and more often lost than won, he left debts behind him. But in smart society these things are of no account. There was no necessity for Helena to earn her living in a shop, for a hitherto unknown aunt came forward and offered her a home.

But her father's death wrought a complete change in her position. No more salutes; the officers of the regiment nodded to her in a friendly fashion, the lieutenants asked her to dance. She saw plainly that the respect shown to her had not been shown to her personally, but merely to her rank. She felt degraded and a lively sympathy for all subalterns was born in her; she even felt a sort of hatred for all those who enjoyed her former privileges. Side by side with this feeling grew up a yearning for personal appreciation, a desire to win a position surpassing all others, although it might not figure in the Army list.

She longed to distinguish herself, to win fame, and, (why not?) to rule. She possessed one talent which she had cultivated to some extent, although she had never risen above the average; she played the piano. She began to study harmony and talked of the sonata in G minor and the symphony in F major as if she had written them herself. And forthwith she began to patronize musicians.

Six months after her father's death, the post of a lady-in-waiting was offered to her. She accepted it. The rolling of drums and military salutes recommenced, and Helena gradually lost her sympathy with subalterns. But the mind is as inconstant as fortune, and fresh experiences again brought about a change of her views.

She discovered one day, and the day was not long in coming, that she was nothing but a servant. She was sitting in the Park with the Duchess. The Duchess was crocheting.

"I consider those blue stockings perfectly idiotic," said the Duchess.

Helena turned pale; she stared at her mistress.

"I don't," she replied.

"I didn't ask your opinion," replied the Duchess, letting her ball of wool roll into the dust.

Helena's knees trembled; her future, her position passed away before her eyes like a flash of lightning. She went to pick up the wool. It seemed to her that her back was breaking as she stooped, and her cheeks flamed when the Duchess took the ball without a word of thanks.

"You are not angry?" asked the Duchess, staring impertinently at her victim.

"Oh, no, Your Royal Highness," was Helena's untruthful reply.

"They say that you are a blue-stocking yourself," continued the Duchess. "Is it true?"

Helena had a feeling as if she were standing nude before her tormentor and made no reply.

For the second time the ball rolled into the dust. Helena pretended not to notice it, and bit her lips to hold back the angry tears which were welling up in her eyes. "Pick up my wool, please," said the Duchess.

Helena drew herself up, looked the autocrat full in the face and said: "I won't."

And with these words she turned and fled. The sand gritted under her feet, and little clouds of dust followed in the wake of her train. She almost ran down the stone steps and disappeared.

Her career at court was ended; but a sting remained. Helena was made to feel what it means to be in disgrace, and above all things what it means to throw up one's post. Society does not approve of changes and nobody would believe that she had voluntarily renounced the sunshine of the court. No doubt she had been sent away. Yes, it must be so, she had been sent away. Never before had she felt so humiliated, so insulted. It seemed to her that she had lost caste; her relations treated her with coldness, as if they were afraid that her disgrace might be infectious; her former friends gave her the cold shoulder when they met her, and limited their conversation to a minimum.

On the other hand, as she stooped from her former height, the middle-classes received her with open arms. It was true, at first their friendliness offended her more than the coldness of her own class, but in the end she preferred being first down below to being last up above. She joined a group of Government officials and professors who hailed her with acclamations. Animated by the superstitious awe with which the middle classes regard everybody connected with the court, they at once began to pay her homage. She became their chosen leader and hastened to form a regiment. A number of young professors enlisted at once and she arranged lectures for women. Old academic rubbish was brought out from the lumber-room, dusted and sold for new wares. In a dining room, denuded of its furniture, lectures on Plato and Aristotle were given to an audience which unfortunately held no key to this shrine of wisdom.

Helena, in conquering these pseudo-mysteries felt the intellectual superior of the ignorant aristocracy. This feeling gave her an assurance which impressed people. The men worshipped her beauty and aloofness; but she never felt in the least moved in their company. She accepted their homage as a tribute due to women and found it impossible to respect these lackeys who jumped up and stood at attention whenever she passed.

But in the long run her position as an unmarried woman failed to satisfy her, and she noted with envious eyes the freedom enjoyed by her married sisters. They were at liberty to go wherever they liked, talk to whom they liked, and always had a footman in their husband to meet them and accompany them on their way home. In addition, married women had a better social position, and a great deal more influence. With what condescension for instance, they treated the spinsters! But whenever she thought of getting married, the incident with her mare flashed into her mind and terror made her ill.

In the second year the wife of a professor from Upsala, who combined with her official position great personal charm, appeared on the scene. Helena's star paled; all her worshippers left her to worship the new sun. As she no longer possessed her former social position, and the savor of the court had vanished like the scent on a handkerchief, she was beaten in the fight. One single vassal remained faithful to her, a lecturer on ethics, who had hitherto not dared to push himself forward. His attentions were well received, for the severity of his ethics filled her with unlimited confidence. He wooed her so assiduously that people began to gossip; Helena, however, took no notice, she was above that.

One evening, after a lecture on "The Ethical Moment in Conjugal Love" or "Marriage as a Manifestation of Absolute Identity," for which the lecturer received nothing but his expenses and a grateful pressure of hands, they were sitting in the denuded dining room on their uncomfortable cane chairs, discussing the subject.

"You mean to say then," said Helena, "that marriage is a relationship of co-existence between two identical Egos?"

"I mean what I said already in my lecture, that only if there exists such a relationship between two congruous identities, *being* can conflow into *becoming* of higher potentiality."

"What do you mean by *becoming?*" asked Helena, blushing.

"The post-existence of two egos in a new ego."

"What? You mean that the continuity of the ego, which through the cohabitation of two analogous beings will necessarily incorporate itself into a becoming. . . ."

"No, my dear lady, I only meant to say that marriage, in profane parlance, can only produce a new spiritual ego, which cannot be differentiated as to sex, when there is compatibility of souls. I mean to say that the new being born under those conditions will be a conglomerate of male and female; a new creature to whom both will have yielded their personality, a unity in multiplicity, to use a well-known term, an *'hommefemme.'* The man will cease to be man, the woman will cease to be woman."

"That is the union of souls!" exclaimed Helena, glad to have successfully navigated the dangerous cliffs.

"It is the harmony of souls of which Plato speaks. It is true marriage as I have sometimes visualized it in my dreams, but which, unfortunately, I shall hardly be able to realize in actuality."

Helena stared at the ceiling and whispered:

"Why shouldn't you, one of the elect, realize this dream?"

"Because she to whom my soul is drawn with irresistible longing does not believe in — h'm — love."

"You cannot be sure of that."

"Even if she did, she would always be tormented by the suspicion that the feeling was not sincere. Moreover, there is no woman in the world who would fall in love with me, no, not one."

"Yes, there is," said Helena, gazing into his glass eye. (He had a glass eye, but it was so well made, it was impossible to detect it.)

"Are you sure?"

"Quite sure," replied Helena. "For you are different to other men. You realize what spiritual love means, the love of the souls!"

"Even if the woman did exist, I could never marry her."

"Why not?"

"Share a room with her!"

"That needn't be the case. Madame de Staël merely lived in the same house as her husband."

"Did she?"

"What interesting topic are you two discussing?" asked the professor's wife, coming out of the drawing room.

"We were talking of *Laocoön,*" answered Helena, rising, from her chair. She was offended by the note of condescension in the lady's voice. And she made up her mind.

A week later her engagement to the lecturer was publicly announced. They decided to be married in the autumn and take up their abode at Upsala.

A brilliant banquet, in celebration of the close of his bachelor life, was given to the lecturer on ethics. A great deal of wine had been consumed and the only artist the town boasted, the professor of drawing at the Cathedral School, had depicted in bold outlines the victim's career up to date. It was the great feature of the whole entertainment. Ethics was a subject of teaching and a milch cow, like many others, and need not necessarily influence either the life of the community, or the life of the individual. The lecturer had not been a saint, but had had his adventures like everybody else; these were public property, for he had had no reason to keep them dark. With a careless smile he watched his career, pictured in chalk and colors, accompanied by witty verses, unfolding itself before his eyes, but when at last his approaching bliss was portrayed in simple but powerful sketches, he became deeply embarrassed, and the thought "If Helena were to see that!" flashed like lightning through his brain.

After the banquet, at which according to an old, time-honored custom, he had drunk eight glasses of brandy, he was so intoxicated that he could no longer suppress his fears and apprehensions. Among his hosts was a married man and to him the victim turned for counsel and advice. Since neither of them was sober, they chose, as the most secluded spot in the whole room, two chairs right in the center, immediately under the chandelier. Consequently they were soon surrounded by an eagerly listening crowd.

"Look here! You are a married man," said the lecturer at the top of his voice, so as not to be heard by the assembly, as he fondly imagined. "You must give me a word of advice, just one, only one little word of advice, for I am extremely sensitive tonight, especially in regard to this particular point."

"I will, brother," shouted his friend, "just one word, as you say," and he put his arm round his shoulders that he might whisper to him; then he continued, screaming loudly: "Every act consists of three parts, my brother: *Progresses, culmen, regressus.* I will speak to you of the first, the second is never mentioned. Well, the initiative, so to speak, that is the man's privilege — your part! You must take the initiative, you must attack, do you understand?"

"But supposing the other party does not approve of the initiative?"

The friend stared at the novice, taken aback; then he rose and contemptuously turned his back on him.

"Fool!" he muttered.

"Thank you!" was all the grateful pupil could reply.

Now he understood.

On the following day he was on fire with all the strong drink he had consumed; he went and took a hot bath, for on the third day was to be his wedding.

The wedding guests had departed; the servant had cleared the table; they were alone.

Helena was comparatively calm, but he felt exceedingly nervous. The period of their engagement had been enhanced by conversations on serious subjects. They had never behaved liked ordinary, everyday fiancés, had never embraced or kissed. Whenever he had attempted the smallest familiarity, her cold looks had chilled his ardor. But he loved her as a man loves a woman, with body and soul.

They fidgeted about the drawing room and tried to make conversation. But an obstinate silence again and again reasserted itself. The candles in the chandelier had burned low and the wax fell in greasy drops on the carpet. The atmosphere was heavy with the smell of food and the fumes of the wines which mingled with the voluptuous perfume of carnations and heliotrope, exhaled by Helena's bridal bouquet that lay on a side-table.

At last he went up to her, held out his arms, and said in a voice which he hoped sounded natural:

"And now you are my wife!"

"What do you mean?" was Helena's brusque reply.

Completely taken aback, he allowed his arms to drop to his sides. But he pulled himself together again, almost immediately, and said with a self-conscious smile:

"I mean to say that we are husband and wife."

Helena looked at him as if she thought that he had taken leave of his senses.

"Explain your words!" she said.

That was just what he couldn't do. Philosophy and ethics failed him; he was faced by a cold and exceedingly unpleasant reality.

"It's modesty," he thought. "She's quite right, but I must attack and do my duty."

"Have you misunderstood me?" asked Helena and her voice trembled.

"No, of course not, but, my dear child, h'm — we — h'm. . . ."

"What language is that? Dear child? What do you take me for? What do you mean? Albert, Albert!" — she rushed on without waiting for a reply, which she didn't want — "Be great, be noble, and learn to see in women something more than sex. Do that, and you will be happy and great!"

Albert was beaten. Crushed with shame and furious with his false friend who had counseled him wrongly, he threw himself on his knees before her and stammered:

"Forgive me, Helena, you are nobler, purer, better than I; you are made of finer fiber and you will lift me up when I threaten to perish in coarse matter."

"Arise and be strong, Albert," said Helena, with the manner of a prophetess. "Go in peace and show to the world that love and base animal passion are two very different things. Good-night!"

Albert rose from his knees and stared irresolutely after his wife who went into her room and shut the door behind her.

Full of the noblest and purest sentiments he also went into his room. He took off his coat and lighted a cigar. His room was furnished like a bachelor's room: a bed-sofa, a writing table, some book shelves, a washstand.

When he had undressed, he dipped a towel into his ewer and rubbed himself all over. Then he lay down on his sofa and opened the evening paper. He wanted to read while he smoked his cigar. He read an article on Protection. His thoughts began to flow in a more normal channel, and he considered his position.

Was he married or was he still a bachelor? He was a bachelor as before, but there was a difference — he now had a female boarder who paid nothing for her board. The thought was anything but pleasant, but it was the truth. The cook kept house, the housemaid attended to the rooms. Where did Helena come in? She was to develop her individuality! Oh, rubbish! he thought, I am a fool! Supposing his friend had been right? Supposing women always behaved in this silly way under these circumstances? She could not very well come to him — he must go to her. If he didn't go, she would probably laugh at him tomorrow, or, worse still, be offended. Women were indeed incomprehensible. He must make the attempt.

He jumped up, put on his dressing gown and went into the drawing room. With trembling knees he listened outside Helena's door.

Not a sound. He took heart of grace, and approached a step or two. Blue flashes of lightning darted before his eyes as he knocked.

No answer. He trembled violently and beads of perspiration stood on his forehead.

He knocked again. And in a falsetto voice, proceeding from a parched throat, he said:

"It's only I."

No answer. Overwhelmed with shame, he returned to his room, puzzled and chilled.

She was in earnest, then.

He crept between the sheets and again took up the paper.

He hadn't been reading long when he heard footsteps in the street which gradually approached and then stopped. Soft music fell on his ear, deep, strong voices set in:

"*Integer vitæ sclerisque purus. . . .*"

He was touched. How beautiful it was!

Purus! He felt lifted above matter. It was in accordance with the spirit of the age then, this higher conception of marriage. The current of ethics which penetrated the epoch was flowing through the youth of the country. . . .

"*Nec venenatis. . . .*"

Supposing Helena had opened her door!

He gently beat time and felt himself as great and noble as Helena desired him to be.

"*Fusce pharetra!*"

Should he open the window and thank the undergraduates in the name of his wife?

He got out of bed.

A fourfold peal of laughter crashed against the windowpanes at the very moment he lifted his hand to draw up the blind.

There could be no doubt, they were making fun of him!

Beside himself with anger he staggered back from the window and knocked against the writing-table. He was a laughingstock. A faint hatred against the woman whom he had to thank for this humiliating scene, began to stir within him, but his love acquitted her. He was incensed against the jesters down below, and swore to bring them before the authorities.

But again and again he reverted to his unpleasant position, furious that he had allowed himself to be led by the nose. He paced his room until dawn broke in the East. Then he threw himself on his bed and fell asleep, in bitter grief over the dismal ending of his wedding-day, which ought to have been the happiest day of his life.

On the following morning he met Helena at the breakfast table. She was cold and self-possessed as usual. Albert, of course, did not mention the serenade. Helena made great plans for the future and talked volumes about the abolition of prostitution. Albert met her halfway and promised to do all in his power to assist her. Humanity must become chaste, for only the beasts were unchaste.

Breakfast over, he went to his lecture. The serenade had roused his suspicions, and as he watched his audience, he fancied that they were making signs to each other; his colleagues, too, seemed to congratulate him in a way which offended him.

A big, stout colleague, who radiated vigor and *joie de vivre,* stopped him in the corridor which led to the library, seized him by the collar and said with a colossal grin on his broad face,

"Well?"

"You ought to be ashamed of yourself," was the indignant reply with which he tore himself away and rushed downstairs.

When he arrived home, his flat was crowded with his wife's friends. Women's skirts brushed against his legs, and when he sat down in an armchair, he seemed to sink out of sight into piles and piles of women's clothes.

"I've heard rumors of a serenade last night," said the professor's wife.

Albert grew pale, but Helena took up the gauntlet.

"It was well meant, but they really might have been sober. This excessive drinking among students is terrible."

"What did they sing?" asked the professor's wife.

"Oh! the usual songs: 'My life a sea,' and so on," replied Helena.

Albert stared at her in amazement, but he couldn't help admiring her.

The day went with gossip and discussions. Albert felt tired. Been joyed spending a few hours, after the daily toil was over, in pleasant conversation with women, but this was really too much. And moreover, he had to agree to everything they said, for whenever he attempted to express a contradictory opinion, they were down on him in a minute.

Night fell; it was bedtime. Husband and wife wished one another good night and retired to their separate rooms.

Again he was attacked by doubt and restlessness. He fancied that he had seen a tender look on Helena's face, and he wasn't quite sure whether she hadn't squeezed his hand. He lit a cigar and unfolded his paper. As soon as he began to read of everyday matters, he seemed to see clearly.

"It's sheer madness," he said aloud, throwing the paper aside.

He slipped on his dressing gown and went into the drawing room.

Somebody was moving in Helena's room.

He knocked.

"Is that you, Louise?" asked a voice from inside.

"No, it's only I," he whispered, hardly able to speak.

"What's the matter? What do you want?"

"I want to speak to you, Helena," he answered, hardly knowing what he was saying.

The key turned in the lock. Albert could hardly trust his ears. The door flew open. Helena stood on the threshold, still fully dressed.

"What is it you want?" she asked. Then she noticed that he was in his dressing gown and that his eyes shone strangely.

She stretched out her hand, pushed him away and slammed the door.

He heard a thud on the floor and almost simultaneously loud sobs.

Furious, but abashed, he returned to his room. She was in earnest, then! But this was certainly anything but normal.

He lay awake all night, brooding, and on the following morning he breakfasted alone.

When he came home for lunch, Helena received him with an expression of pained resignation.

"Why do you treat me like that?" she asked.

He apologized, with as few words as possible. Then he repented his curtness and climbed down.

Thus matters stood for six months. He was tossed between doubt, rage and love, but his chain held.

His face grew pale and his eyes lost their luster. His temper had become uncertain; a sullen fury smoldered beneath his outward calm.

Helena found him changed, despotic, because he was beginning to oppose her, and often left the meetings to seek amusement elsewhere.

One day he was asked to become a candidate for a professorial chair. He refused, believing that he had no chance, but Helena gave him no peace until he complied with the conditions. He was elected. He never knew the reason why, but Helena did.

A short time after there was a by-election.

The new professor, who had never dreamed of taking an active interest in public affairs, was nonplussed when he found himself nominated. His surprise was even greater when he was elected. He intended to decline, but Helena's entreaties and her argument that life in a big city was preferable to an existence in a small provincial town induced him to accept the mandate.

They removed to Stockholm.

During these six months the newly-made professor and member of Parliament had made himself acquainted with the new ideas which came from England and purposed to recreate society and the old standards of morality. At the same time he felt that the moment was not far off when he would have to break with his "boarder." He recovered his strength and vigor in Stockholm, where fearless thinkers encouraged him to profess openly the views which he had long held in secret.

Helena, on the other hand, scented a favorable opportunity in the counter-current and threw herself into the arms of the Church Party. This was too much for Albert and he rebelled. His love had grown cold; he found compensation elsewhere. He didn't consider himself unfaithful to his wife for she had never claimed constancy in a relationship which didn't exist.

His friendly intercourse with the other sex aroused his manliness and made him realize his degradation.

His growing estrangement did not escape Helena. Their home-life became unpleasant and every moment threatened to bring a catastrophe.

The opening of Parliament was imminent. Helena became restless and seemed to have changed her tactics. Her voice was more gentle and she appeared anxious to please him. She looked after the servants and saw that the meals were served punctually.

He grew suspicious and wondered, watched her movements and prepared for coming events.

One morning, at breakfast, Helena looked embarrassed and self-conscious. She played with her dinner napkin and cleared her throat several times. Then she took her courage in both her hands and made a plunge.

"Albert," she began, "I can count on you, can't I? You will serve the Cause to which I have devoted my life?"

"What cause is that?" he asked curtly, for now he had the upper hand.

"You will do something for the oppressed women, won't you?"

"Where are the oppressed women?"

"What? Have you deserted our great cause? Are you leaving us in the lurch?"

"What cause are you talking about?"

"The Women's Cause!"

"I know nothing about it."

"You know nothing about it? Oh, come! You must admit that the position of the women of the lower classes is deplorable."

"No, I can't see that their position is any worse than the position of the men. Deliver the men from their exploiters and the women too will be free."

"But the unfortunates who have to sell themselves, and the scoundrels who —"

"The scoundrels who pay! Has ever a man taken payment for a pleasure which both enjoy?"

"That is not the question! The question is whether it is just that the law of the land should punish the one and let the other go scot-free."

"There is no injustice in that. The one has degraded herself until she has become a source of infection, and therefore the State treats her as it treats a mad dog. Whenever you find a man, degraded to that degree, well, put him under police control, too. Oh, you pure angels, who despise men and look upon them as unclean beasts!. . ."

"Well, what is it? What do you want me to do?"

He noticed that she had taken a manuscript from the sideboard and held it in her hand. Without waiting for a reply, he took it from her and began to examine it. "A bill to be introduced into Parliament! I'm to be the man of straw who introduces it! Is that moral? Strictly speaking, is it honest?"

Helena rose from her chair, threw herself on the sofa and burst into tears.

He, too, rose and went to her. He took her hand in his and felt her pulse, afraid lest her attack might be serious. She seized his hand convulsively, and pressed it against her bosom.

"Don't leave me," she sobbed, "don't go. Stay, and let me keep faith in you."

For the first time in his life he saw her giving way to her emotions. This delicate body, which he had loved and admired so much, could be warmed into life! Red, warm blood flowed in those blue veins. Blood which could distil tears. He gently stroked her brow.

"Oh!" she sighed, "why aren't you always good to me like that? Why hasn't it always been so?"

"Well," he answered, "why hasn't it? Tell me, why not?"

Helena's eyelids drooped. "Why not?" she breathed, softly.

She did not withdraw her hand and he felt a gentle warmth radiating from her velvety skin; his love for her burst into fresh flames, but this time he felt that there was hope.

At last she rose to her feet.

"Don't despise me," she said, "don't despise me, dear."

And she went into her room.

What was the matter with her? Albert wondered as he went up to town. Was she passing through a crisis of some sort? Was she only just beginning to realize that she was his wife?

He spent the whole day in town. In the evening he went to the theater. They played *Le monde où l'on s'ennuit.* As he sat and watched platonic love, the union of souls, unmasked and ridiculed, he felt as if a veil of close meshed lies were being drawn from his reason; he smiled as he saw the head of the charming beast peeping from underneath the card-board wings of the stage-angel; he almost shed tears of amusement at his long, long self-deception; he laughed at his folly. What filth and corruption lay behind this hypocritical morality, this insane desire for emancipation from healthy, natural instincts. It was the ascetic teaching of idealism and Christianity which had implanted this germ into the nineteenth century.

He felt ashamed! How could he have allowed himself to be duped all this time!

There was still light in Helena's room as he passed her door on tiptoe so as not to wake her. He heard her cough.

He went straight to bed, smoked his cigar and read his paper. He was absorbed in an article on conscription, when all of a sudden Helena's door was flung open, and footsteps and screams from the drawing room fell on his ears. He jumped up and rushed out of his room, believing that the house was on fire.

Helena was standing in the drawing room in her nightgown.

She screamed when she saw her husband and ran to her room; on the threshold she hesitated and turned her head.

"Forgive me, Albert," she stammered, "it's you. I didn't know that you were still up. I thought there were burglars in the house. Please, forgive me."

And she closed her door.

What did it all mean? Was she in love with him?

He went into his room and stood before the looking-glass. Could any woman fall in love with him? He was plain. But one loves with one's soul and many a plain man had married a beautiful woman. It was true, though, that in such cases the man had nearly always possessed wealth and influence. – Was Helena realizing that she had placed herself in a false position? Or had she become aware of his intention to leave her and was anxious to win him back?

When they met at the breakfast table on the following morning, Helena was unusually gentle, and the professor noticed that she was wearing a new morning-gown trimmed with lace, which suited her admirably.

As he was helping himself to sugar, his hand accidentally touched hers.

"I beg your pardon, dear," she said with an expression on her face which he had never seen before. She looked like a young girl.

They talked about indifferent things.

On the same day Parliament opened.

Helena's yielding mood lasted and she grew more and more affectionate.

The period allowed for the introduction of new bills drew to a close.

One evening the professor came home from his club in an unusually gay frame of mind. He went to bed with his paper and his cigar. After a while he heard Helena's door creak. Silence, lasting for a few minutes, followed. Then there came a knock at his door.

"Who is there?" he shouted.

"It's I, Albert, do dress and come into the drawing room, I want to speak to you."

He dressed and went into the drawing room.

Helena had lighted the chandelier and was sitting on the sofa, dressed in her lace morning-gown.

"Do forgive me," she said, "but I can't sleep. My head feels so strange. Come here and talk to me."

"You are all unstrung, little girl," said Albert, taking her hand in his own. "You ought to take some wine."

He went into the dining room and returned with a decanter and two glasses.

"Your health, darling," he said.

Helena drank and her cheeks caught fire.

"What's wrong?" he asked, putting his arm round her waist.

"I'm not happy," she replied.

He was conscious that the words sounded dry and artificial, but his passion was roused and he didn't care.

"Do you know why you are unhappy?" he asked.

"No. I only know one thing, and that is that I love you."

Albert caught her in his arms and kissed her face.

"Are you my wife, or aren't you?" he whispered hoarsely.

"I am your wife," breathed Helena, collapsing, as if every nerve in her body had snapped.

"Altogether?" he whispered paralyzing her with his kisses.

"Altogether," she moaned, moving convulsively, like a sleeper struggling with the horrors of a nightmare.

When Albert awoke, he felt refreshed, his head was clear and he was fully conscious of what had happened in the night. He could think vigorously and logically like a man after a deep and restful sleep. The whole scene stood vividly before his mind. He saw the full significance of it, unvarnished, undisguised, in the sober light of the morning.

She had sold herself!

At three o'clock in the morning, intoxicated with love, blind to everything, half insane, he had promised to introduce her bill.

And the price! She had given herself to him calmly, coldly, unmoved.

Who was the first woman who found out that she could sell her favor? And who was the woman who discovered that man is a buyer? Whoever she was, she was the founder of marriage and prostitution. And they say that marriages are made in heaven!

He realized his degradation and hers. She wanted to triumph over her friends, to be the first woman who had taken an active share in the making of her country's laws; for the sake of this triumph she had sold herself.

Well, he would tear the mask from her face. He would show her what she really was. He would tell her that prostitution could never be abolished while women found an advantage in selling themselves.

With his mind firmly made up, he got out of bed and dressed.

He had to wait a little for her in the dining room. He rehearsed the scene which would follow and pulled himself together to meet her.

She came in calm, smiling, triumphant, but more beautiful than he had ever seen her before. A somber fire burned in her eyes, and he, who had expected that she would meet him with blushes and down-cast eyes, was crushed. She was the triumphant seducer, and he the bashful victim.

The words he had meant to say refused to come. Disarmed and humble he went to meet her and kissed her hand.

She talked as usual without the slightest indication that a new factor had entered her life.

He went to the House, fuming, with her bill in his pocket, and only the vision of the bliss in store for him, calmed his excited nerves.

But when, in the evening, he knocked quite boldly at her door, it remained closed.

It remained closed for three weeks. He cringed before her like a dog, obeyed every hint, fulfilled all her wishes — it was all in vain.

Then his indignation got the better of him and he overwhelmed her with a flood of angry words. She answered him sharply. But when she realized that she had gone too far, that his chain was wearing thin, she gave herself to him.

And he wore his chain. He bit it, strained every nerve to break it, but it held.

She soon learned how far she could go, and whenever he became restive, she yielded.

He was seized with a fanatical longing to make her a mother. He thought it might make a woman of her, bring out all that was good and wholesome in her. But the future seemed to hold no promise on that score.

Had ambition, the selfish passion of the individual, destroyed the source of life? He wondered. . . .

One morning she informed him that she was going away for a few days to stay with her friends.

When he came home on the evening of the day of her departure and found the house empty, his soul was tormented by a cruel feeling of loss and longing. All of a sudden it became clear to him that he loved her with every fiber of his being. The house seemed desolate; it was just as if a funeral had taken place. When dinner was served he stared at her vacant chair and hardly touched his food.

After supper he lit the chandelier in the drawing room. He sat down in her corner of the sofa. He fingered her needlework which she had left behind — it was a tiny jacket for a stranger's baby in a newly-founded crèche. There was the needle, still sticking in the calico, just as she had left it. He pricked his finger with it as if to find solace in the ecstasy of pain.

Presently he lighted a candle and went into her bedroom. As he stood on the threshold, he shaded the flame with his hand and looked round like a man who is about to commit a crime. The room did not betray the slightest trace of femininity. A narrow bed without curtains; a writing-table, bookshelves, a smaller table by the side of her bed, a sofa. Just like his own room. There was no dressing-table, but a little mirror hung on the wall.

Her dress was hanging on a nail. The lines of her body were clearly defined on the thick, heavy serge. He caressed the material and hid his face in the lace which trimmed the neck; he put his arm round the waist, but the dress collapsed like a phantom. "They say the soul is a spirit," he mused, "but then, it ought to be a tangible spirit, at least." He approached the bed as if he expected to see an apparition. He touched everything, took everything in his hand.

At last, as if he were looking for something, something which should help him to solve the problem, he began to tug at the handles which ornamented the drawers of her writing-table; all the drawers were locked. As if by accident he opened the drawer of the little table by her bedside, and hastily closed it again, but not before he had read the title on the paper-cover of a small book and caught sight of a few strange-looking objects, the purpose of which he could guess.

That was it then! *Facultative Sterility!* What was intended for a remedy for the lower classes, who have been robbed of the means of existence, had become an instrument in the service of selfishness, the last consequence of idealism. Were the upper classes so degenerate that they refused to reproduce their species, or were they morally corrupt? They must be both, for they considered it immoral to bring illegitimate children into the world, and degrading to bear children in wedlock.

But he wanted children! He could afford to have them, and he considered it a duty as well as a glorious privilege to pour his individuality into a new being. It was Nature's way from a true and healthy egoism towards altruism. But she traveled on another road and made jackets for the babies of strangers. Was that a better, a nobler thing to do? It stood for so much, and yet was nothing but fear of the burden of motherhood, and it was cheaper and less fatiguing to sit in the corner of a comfortable sofa and make little jackets than to bear the toil and broil of a nursery. It was looked upon as a disgrace to be a woman, to have a sex, to become a mother.

That was it. They called it working for Heaven, for higher interests, for humanity, but it was merely a pandering to vanity, to selfishness, to a desire for fame or notoriety.

And he had pitied her, he had suffered remorse because her sterility had made him angry. She had told him once that he deserved "the contempt of all good and honest men" because he had failed to speak of sterile women with the respect due to misfortune; she had told him that they were sacred, because their sorrow was the bitterest sorrow a woman could have to bear.

What, after all, was this woman working for? For progress? For the salvation of humanity? No, she was working against progress, against freedom and enlightenment. Hadn't she recently brought forward a motion to limit religious liberty? Wasn't she the author of a pamphlet on the intractability of servants? Wasn't she advocating greater severity in the administration of the military laws? Was she not a supporter of the party which strives to ruin our girls by giving them the same miserable education which our boys receive?

He hated her soul, for he hated her ideas. And yet he loved her? What was it then that he loved?

Probably, he reflected, compelled to take refuge in philosophy, probably the germ of a new being, which she carries in her womb, but which she is bent on killing.

What else could it be?

But what did she love in him? His title, his position, his influence?

How could these old and worn-out men and women rebuild society?

He meant to tell her all this when she returned home; but in his inmost soul he knew all the time that the words would never be said. He knew that he would grovel before her and whine for her favor; that he would remain her slave and sell her his soul again and again, just as she sold him her body. He knew that that was what he would do, for he was head over ears in love with her.

Unmarried and Married

*T*he young barrister was strolling on a lovely spring evening through the old Stockholm Hop-Garden. Snatches of song and music came from the pavilion; light streamed through the large windows and lit up the shadows cast by the great lime trees which were just bursting into leaf.

He went in, sat down at a vacant table near the platform and asked for a glass of punch.

A young comedian was singing a pathetic ballad of a *Dead Rat.* Then a young girl, dressed in pink, appeared and sang the Danish song: *There is nothing so charming as a moonshine ride.* She was comparatively innocent looking and she addressed her song to our innocent barrister. He felt flattered by this mark of distinction, and at once started negotiations which began with a bottle of wine and ended in a furnished flat, containing two rooms, a kitchen and all the usual conveniences.

It is not within the scope of this little story to analyze the feelings of the young man, or give a description of the furniture and the other conveniences. It must suffice if I say that they were very good friends.

But, imbued with the socialistic tendencies of our time, and desirous of having his lady-love always under his eyes, the young man decided to live in the flat himself and make his little friend his house keeper. She was delighted at the suggestion.

But the young man had a family, that is to say, his family looked upon him as one of its members, and since in their opinion he was committing an offence against morality, and casting a slur on their good name, he was summoned to appear before the assembled parents, brothers and sisters in order to be censured. He considered that he was too old for such treatment and the family tie was ruptured.

This made him all the more fond of his own little home, and he developed into a very domesticated husband, excuse me, lover. They were happy, for they loved one another, and no fetters bound them. They lived in the happy dread of losing one another and therefore they did their utmost to keep each other's love. They were indeed one.

But there was one thing which they lacked: they had no friends. Society displayed no wish to know them, and the young man was not asked to the houses of the "Upper Ten."

It was Christmas Eve, a day of sadness for all those who once had a family. As he was sitting at breakfast, he received a letter. It was from his sister, who implored him to spend Christmas at home, with his parents. The letter touched upon the strings of old feelings and put him in a bad temper. Was he to leave his little friend alone on Christmas Eve? Certainly not! Should his place in the house of his parents remain vacant for the first time on a Christmas Eve? H'm! This was the position of affairs when he went to the Law Courts.

During the interval for lunch a colleague came up to him and asked him as discreetly as possible:

"Are you going to spend Christmas Eve with your family?"

He flared up at once. Was his friend aware of his position? Or what did he mean?

The other man saw that he had stepped on a corn, and added hastily, without waiting for a reply:

"Because if you are not, you might spend it with us. You know, perhaps, that I have a little friend, a dear little soul."

It sounded all right and he accepted the invitation on condition that they should both be invited. Well, but of course, what else did he think? And this settled the problem of friends and Christmas Eve.

They met at six o'clock at the friend's flat, and while the two "old men" had a glass of punch, the women went into the kitchen.

All four helped to lay the table. The two "old men" knelt on the floor and tried to lengthen the table by means of boards and wedges. The women were on the best of terms at once, for they felt bound together by that very obvious tie which bears the great name of "public opinion." They respected one another and saved one another's feelings. They avoided those innuendoes in which husbands and wives are so fond of indulging when their children are not listening, just as if they wanted to say: "We have a right to say these things now we are married."

When they had eaten the pudding, the barrister made a speech praising the delights of one's own fireside, that refuge from the world and from all men: that harbor where one spends one's happiest hours in the company of one's real friends.

Mary-Louisa began to cry, and when he urged her to tell him the cause of her distress, and the reason of her unhappiness, she told him in a voice broken by sobs that she could see that he was missing his mother and sisters.

He replied that he did not miss them in the least, and that he should wish them far away if they happened to turn up now.

"But why couldn't he marry her?"

"Weren't they as good as married?"

"No, they weren't married properly."

"By a clergyman? In his opinion a clergyman was nothing but a student who had passed his examinations, and his incantations were pure mythology."

"That was beyond her, but she knew that something was wrong, and the other people in the house pointed their fingers at her."

"Let them point!"

Sophy joined in the conversation. She said she knew that they were not good enough for his relations; but she didn't mind. Let everybody keep his own place and be content.

Anyhow, they had friends now, and lived together in harmony, which is more than could be said of many properly constituted families. The tie which held them together remained intact, but they were otherwise unfettered. They continued being lovers without contracting any bad matrimonial habits, as, for example, the habit of being rude to one another.

After a year or two their union was blest with a son. The mistress had thereby risen to the rank of a mother, and everything else was forgotten. The pangs which she had endured at the birth of the baby, and her care for the newly born infant, had purged her of her old selfish claims to all the good things of the earth, including the monopoly of her husband's love.

In her new role as mother she gave herself superior little airs with her friend, and showed a little more assurance in her intercourse with her lover.

One day the latter came home with a great piece of news. He had met his eldest sister in the street and had found her well informed on all their private affairs. She was very anxious to see her little nephew and had promised to pay them a call.

Mary-Louisa was surprised, and at once began to sweep and dust the flat; in addition she insisted on a new dress for the occasion. And then she waited for a whole week. The curtains were sent to the laundry, the brass knobs on the doors of the stoves were made to shine, the furniture was polished. The sister should see that her brother was living with a decent person.

And then she made coffee, one morning at eleven o'clock, the time when the sister would call.

She came, straight as if she had swallowed a poker, and gave Mary-Louisa a hand which was as stiff as a batting staff. She examined the bedroom furniture, but refused to drink coffee, and never once looked her sister-in-law in the face. But she showed a faint, though genuine, interest in the baby. Then she went away again.

Mary-Louisa in the meantime had carefully examined her coat, priced the material of her dress and conceived a new idea of doing her hair. She had not expected any great display of cordiality. As a start, the fact of the visit was quite sufficient in itself, and she soon let the house know that her sister-in-law had called.

The boy grew up and by and by a baby sister arrived. Now Mary-Louisa began to show the most tender solicitude for the future of the children, and not a day passed but she tried to convince their father that nothing but a legal marriage with her would safeguard their interests.

In addition to this his sister gave him a very plain hint to the effect that a reconciliation with his parents was within the scope of possibility, if he would but legalize his liaison.

After having fought against it day and night for two years, he consented at last, and resolved that for the children's sake the mythological ceremony should be allowed to take place.

But whom should they ask to the wedding? Mary-Louisa insisted on being married in church. In this case Sophy could not be invited. That was an impossibility. A girl like her! Mary-Louisa had already learnt to pronounce the word "girl" with a decidedly moral accent. He reminded her that Sophy had been a good friend to her, and that ingratitude was not a very fine quality. Mary-Louisa, however, pointed out that parents must be prepared to sacrifice private sympathies at the altar of their children's prospects; and she carried the day.

The wedding took place.

The wedding was over. No invitation arrived from his parents, but a furious letter from Sophy which resulted in a complete rupture.

Mary-Louisa was a wedded wife, now. But she was more lonely than she had been before. Embittered by her disappointment, sure of her husband who was now legally tied to her, she began to take all those liberties which married people look upon as their right. What she had once regarded in the light of a voluntary gift, she now considered a tribute due to her. She entrenched herself behind the honorable title of "the mother of his children," and from there she made her sallies.

Simple-minded, as all duped husbands are, he could never grasp what constituted the sacredness in the fact that she was the mother of *his* children. Why his children should be different from other children, and from himself, was a riddle to him.

But, with an easy conscience, because his children had a legal mother now, he commenced to take again an interest in the world which he had to a certain extent forgotten in the first ecstasy of his love-dream, and which later on he had neglected because he hated to leave his wife and children alone.

These liberties displeased his wife, and since there was no necessity for her to mince matters now, and she was of an outspoken disposition, she made no secrets of her thoughts.

But he had all the lawyer's tricks at his fingers' ends, and was never at a loss for a reply.

"Do you think it right," she asked, "to leave the mother of your children alone at home with them, while you spend your time at a public house?"

"I don't believe you missed me," he answered by way of a preliminary.

"Missed you? If the husband spends the housekeeping money on drink, the wife will miss a great many things in the house."

"To start with I don't drink, for I merely have a mouthful of food and drink a cup of coffee; secondly, I don't spend the housekeeping money on drink, for you keep it locked up: I have other funds which I spend 'on drink.'"

Unfortunately women cannot stand satire, and the noose, made in fun, was at once thrown round his neck.

"You do admit, then, that you drink?"

"No, I don't, I used your expression in fun."

"In fun? You are making fun of your wife? You never used to do that!"

"You wanted the marriage ceremony. Why are things so different now?"

"Because we are married, of course."

"Partly because of that, and partly because intoxication has the quality of passing off."

"It was only intoxication in your case, then?"

"Not only in my case; in your case, too, and in all others as well. It passes off more or less quickly."

"And so love is nothing but intoxication as far as a man is concerned!"

"As far as a woman is concerned too!"

"Nothing but intoxication!"

"Quite so! But there is no reason why one shouldn't remain friends."

"One need not get married for that!"

"No; and that's exactly what I meant to point out."

"You? Wasn't it you who insisted on our marriage?"

"Only because you worried me about it day and night three long years."

"But it was your wish, too!"

"Only because you wished it. Be grateful to me now that you've got it!"

"Shall I be grateful because you leave the mother of your children alone with them while you spend your time at the public-house?"

"No, not for that, but because I married you!" "You really think I ought to be grateful for that?"

"Yes, like all decent people who have got their way!"

"Well, there is no happiness in a marriage like ours. Your family doesn't acknowledge me!"

"What have you got to do with my family? I haven't married yours?"

"Because you didn't think it good enough!"

"But mine was good enough for you. If they had been shoemakers, you wouldn't mind so much."

"You talk of shoemakers as if they were beneath your notice. Aren't they human beings like everybody else?"

"Of course they are, but I don't think you would have run after them."

"All right! Have your own way."

But it was not all right, and it was never again all right. Was it due to the fact of their being married, or was it due to something else? Mary-Louisa could not help admitting in her heart that the old times had been better times; they had been "jollier" she said.

He did not think that it was only owing to the fact that their marriage had been legalized for he had observed that other marriages, too, were not happy. And the worst of it all was this: when one day he went to see his old friend and Sophy, as he sometimes did, behind his wife's back, he was told that there was an end to that matter. And they had not been married. So it could not have been marriage which was to blame.

A Duel

She was plain and therefore the coarse young men who don't know how to appreciate a beautiful soul in an ugly body took no notice of her. But she was wealthy, and she knew that men run after women for the sake of their wealth; whether they do it because all wealth has been created by men and they therefore claim the capital for their sex, or on other grounds, was not quite clear to her. As she was a rich woman, she learned a good many things, and as she distrusted and despised men, she was considered an intellectual young woman.

She had reached the age of twenty. Her mother was still alive, but she had no intention to wait for another five years before she became her own mistress. Therefore she quite suddenly surprised her friends with an announcement of her engagement.

"She is marrying because she wants a husband," said some.

"She is marrying because she wants a footman and her liberty," said others.

"How stupid of her to get married," said the third; "she doesn't know that she will be even less her own mistress than she is now."

"Don't be afraid," said the fourth, "she'll hold her own in spite of her marriage."

What was he like? Who was he? Where had she found him?

He was a young lawyer, rather effeminate in appearance, with broad hips and a shy manner. He was an only son, brought up by his mother and aunt. He had always been very much afraid of girls, and he detested the officers on account of their assurance, and because they were the favorites at all entertainments. That is what he was like.

They were staying at a watering place and met at a dance. He had come late and all the girls' programs were full. A laughing, triumphant "No!" was flung into his face wherever he asked for a dance, and a movement of the program brushed him away as if he were a buzzing fly.

Offended and humiliated he left the ballroom and sat down on the verandah to smoke a cigar. The moon threw her light on the lime trees in the Park and the perfume of the mignonette rose from the flower beds.

He watched the dancing couples through the windows with the impotent yearning of the cripple; the voluptuous rhythm of the waltz thrilled him through and through.

"All alone and lost in dreams?" said a voice suddenly. "Why aren't you dancing?"

"Why aren't you?" he replied, looking up.

"Because I am plain and nobody asked me to," she answered.

He looked at her. They had known each other for some time, but he had never studied her features. She was exquisitely dressed, and in her eyes lay an expression of infinite pain, the pain of despair and vain revolt against the injustice of nature; he felt a lively sympathy for her.

"I, too, am scorned by everybody," he said. "All the rights belong to the officers. Whenever it is a question of natural selection, right is on the side of the strong and the beautiful. Look at their shoulders and epaulettes. . . ."

"How can you talk like that!"

"I beg your pardon! To have to play a losing game makes a man bitter! Will you give me a dance?"

"For pity's sake?"

"Yes! Out of compassion for me!"

He threw away his cigar.

"Have you ever known what it means to be marked by the hand of fate, and rejected? To be always the last?" he began again, passionately.

"I have known all that! But the last do not always remain the last," she added, emphatically. "There are other qualities, besides beauty, which count."

"What quality do you appreciate most in a man?"

"Kindness," she exclaimed, without the slightest hesitation. "For this is a quality very rarely found in a man."

"Kindness and weakness usually go hand in hand; women admire strength."

"What sort of women are you talking about? Rude strength has had its day; our civilization has reached a sufficiently high standard to make us value muscles and rude strength no more highly than a kind heart."

"It ought to have! And yet — watch the dancing couples!"

"To my mind true manliness is shown in loftiness of sentiment and intelligence of the heart."

"Consequently a man whom the whole world calls weak and cow-
ardly. . . ."

"What do I care for the world and its opinion!"

"Do you know that you are a very remarkable woman?" said the young
lawyer, feeling more and more interested.

"Not in the least remarkable! But you men are accustomed to regard
women as dolls. . . ."

"What sort of men do you mean? I, dear lady, have from my childhood looked up to woman as a higher manifestation of the species man,
and from the day on which I fell in love with a woman, and she returned
my love, I should be her slave."

Adeline looked at him long and searchingly.

"You are a remarkable man," she said, after a pause.

After each of the two had declared the other to be a remarkable
specimen of the species man, and made a good many remarks on the
futility of dancing, they began to talk of the melancholy influence of
the moon. Then they returned to the ballroom and took their place in
a set of quadrilles.

Adeline was a perfect dancer and the lawyer won her heart completely
because he "danced like an innocent girl."

When the set was over, they went out again on the verandah and sat
down.

"What is love?" asked Adeline, looking at the moon as if she expected
an answer from heaven.

"The sympathy of the souls," he replied, and his voice sounded like
the whispering breeze.

"But sympathy may turn to antipathy; it has happened frequently,"
objected Adeline.

"Then it wasn't genuine! There are materialists who say that there
would be no such thing as love if there weren't two sexes, and they dare
to maintain that sensual love is more lasting than the love of the soul.
Don't you think it low and bestial to see nothing but sex in the beloved
woman?"

"Don't speak of the materialists!"

"Yes, I must, so that you may realize the loftiness of my feelings for
a woman, if ever I fell in love. She need not be beautiful; beauty soon
fades. I should look upon her as a dear friend, a chum. I should never
feel shy in her company, as with any ordinary girl. I should approach
her without fear, as I am approaching you, and I should say: 'Will you
be my friend for life?' I should be able to speak to her without the
slightest tremor of that nervousness which a lover is supposed to feel

when he proposes to the object of his tenderness, because his thoughts are not pure."

Adeline looked at the young man, who had taken her hand in his, with enraptured eyes.

"You are an idealist," she said, "and I agree with you from the very bottom of my heart. You are asking for my friendship, if I understand you rightly. It shall be yours, but I must put you to the test first. Will you prove to me that you can pocket your pride for the sake of a friend?"

"Speak and I shall obey!"

Adeline took off a golden chain with a locket which she had been wearing round her neck.

"Wear this as a symbol of our friendship."

"I will wear it," he said, in an uncertain voice; "but it might make the people think that we are engaged."

"And do you object?"

"No, not if you don't! Will you be my wife?"

"Yes, Axel! I will! For the world looks askance at friendship between man and woman; the world is so base that it refuses to believe in the possibility of such a thing."

And he wore the chain.

The world, which is very materialistic at heart, repeated the verdict of her friends:

"She marries him in order to be married; he marries her because he wants a wife."

The world made nasty remarks, too. It said that he was marrying her for the sake of her money; for hadn't he himself declared that anything so degrading as love did not exist between them? There was no need for friends to live together like married couples.

The wedding took place. The world had received a hint that they would live together like brother and sister, and the world awaited with a malicious grin the result of the great reform which should put matrimony on another basis altogether.

The newly married couple went abroad.

When they returned, the young wife was pale and ill-tempered. She began at once to take riding-lessons. The world scented mischief and waited. The man looked as if he were guilty of a base act and was ashamed of himself. It all came out at last.

"They have *not* been living like brother and sister," said the world.

"What? Without loving one another? But that is — well, what is it?"

"A forbidden relationship!" said the materialists.

"It is a spiritual marriage!"

"Or incest," suggested an anarchist.

Facts remained facts, but the sympathy was on the wane. Real life, stripped of All make-believe, confronted them and began to take revenge.

The lawyer practiced his profession, but the wife's profession was practiced by a maid and a nurse. Therefore she had no occupation. The want of occupation encouraged brooding, and she brooded a great deal over her position. She found it unsatisfactory. Was it right that an intellectual woman like her should spend her days in idleness? Once her husband had ventured to remark that no one compelled her to live in idleness. He never did it again.

"She had no profession."

"True; to be idle was no profession. Why didn't she nurse the baby?"

"Nurse the baby? She wanted a profession which brought in money."

"Was she such a miser, then? She had already more than she knew how to spend; why should she want to earn money?"

"To be on an equal footing with him."

"That could never be, for she would always be in a position to which he could never hope to attain. It was nature's will that the woman was to be the mother, not the man."

"A very stupid arrangement!"

"Very likely! The opposite might have been the case, but that would have been equally stupid."

"Yes; but her life was unbearable. It didn't satisfy her to live for the family only, she wanted to live for others as well."

"Hadn't she better begin with the family? There was plenty of time to think of the others."

The conversation might have continued through all eternity; as it was it only lasted an hour.

The lawyer was, of course, away almost all day long, and even when he was at home he had his consulting hours. It drove Adeline nearly mad. He was always locked in his consulting-room with other women who confided information to him which he was bound to keep secret. These secrets formed a barrier between them, and made her feel that he was more than a match for her.

It roused a sullen hatred in her heart; she resented the injustice of their mutual relationship; she sought for a means to drag him down. Come down he must, so that they should be on the same level.

One day she proposed the foundation of a sanatorium. He said all he could against it, for he was very busy with his practice. But on further consideration he thought that occupation of some sort might be the saving of her; perhaps it would help her to settle down.

The sanatorium was founded; he was one of the directors.

She was on the Committee and ruled. When she had ruled for six months, she imagined herself so well up in the art of healing that she interviewed patients and gave them advice.

"It's easy enough," she said.

Then it happened that the house-surgeon made a mistake, and she straightway lost all confidence in him. It further happened that one day, in the full consciousness of her superior wisdom, she prescribed for a patient herself, in the doctor's absence. The patient had the prescription made up, took it and died.

This necessitated a removal to another center of activity. But it disturbed the equilibrium. A second child, which was born about the same time, disturbed it still more and, to make matters worse, a rumor of the fatal accident was spreading through the town.

The relations between husband and wife were unlovely and sad, for there had never been any love between them. The healthy, powerful natural instinct, which does not reflect, was absent; what remained was an unpleasant liaison founded on the uncertain calculations of a selfish friendship.

She never voiced the thoughts hatched behind her burning brow after she had discovered that she was mistaken in believing that she had a higher mission, but she made her husband suffer for it.

Her health failed; she lost her appetite and refused to go out. She grew thin and seemed to be suffering from a chronic cough. The husband made her repeatedly undergo medical examinations, but the doctors were unable to discover the cause of her malady. In the end he became so accustomed to her constant complaints that he paid no more attention to them.

"I know it's unpleasant to have an invalid wife," she said.

He admitted in his heart that it was anything but pleasant; had he loved her, he would neither have felt nor admitted it.

Her emaciation became so alarming, that he could not shut his eyes to it any longer, and had to consent to her suggestion that she should consult a famous professor.

Adeline was examined by the celebrity. "How long have you been ill?" he asked.

"I have never been very strong since I left the country," she replied. "I was born in the country."

"Then you don't feel well in town?"

"Well? Who cares whether I feel well or not?" And her face assumed an expression which left no room for doubt: she was a martyr.

"Do you think that country air would do you good?" continued the professor.

"Candidly, I believe that it is the only thing which could save my life."

"Then why don't you live in the country?"

"My husband couldn't give up his profession for my sake."

"He has a wealthy wife and we have plenty of lawyers."

"You think, then, that we ought to live in the country?"

"Certainly, if you believe that it would do you good. You are not suffering from any organic disease, but your nerves are unstrung; country air would no doubt benefit you."

Adeline returned home to her husband very depressed.

"Well?"

"The professor had sentenced her to death if she remained in town."

The lawyer was much upset. But since the fact that his distress was mainly caused by the thought of giving up his practice was very apparent, she held that she had absolute proof that the question of her health was a matter of no importance to him.

"What? He didn't believe that it was a matter of life and death? Didn't he think the professor knew better than he? Was he going to let her die?"

He was not going to let her die. He bought an estate in the country and engaged an inspector to look after it.

As a sheriff and a district-judge were living on the spot, the lawyer had no occupation. The days seemed to him as endless as they were unpleasant. Since his income had stopped with his practice, he was compelled to live on his wife's money. In the first six months he read a great deal and played "Fortuna." In the second six months he gave up reading, as it served no object. In the third he amused himself by doing needle-work.

His wife, on the other hand, devoted herself to the farm, pinned up her skirts to the knees and went into the stables. She came into the house dirty, and smelling of the cow-shed. She felt well and ordered the laborers about that it was a pleasure to hear her, for she had grown up in the country and knew what she was about.

When her husband complained of having nothing to do, she laughed at him.

"Find some occupation in the house. No one need ever be idle in a house like this."

He would have liked to suggest some outside occupation, but he had not the courage.

He ate, slept, and went for walks. If he happened to enter the barn or the stables, he was sure to be in the way and be scolded by his wife.

One day, when he had grumbled more than usual, while the children had been running about, neglected by the nurse, she said:

"Why don't you look after the children? That would give you something to do."

He stared at her. Did she really mean it?

"Well, why shouldn't he look after the children? Was there anything strange in her suggestion?"

He thought the matter over and found nothing strange in it. Henceforth he took the children for a walk every day.

One morning, when he was ready to go out, the children were not dressed. The lawyer felt angry and went grumbling to his wife; of the servants he was afraid.

"Why aren't the children dressed?" he asked.

"Because Mary is busy with other things. Why don't you dress them? You've nothing else to do. Do you consider it degrading to dress your own children?"

He considered the matter for a while, but could see nothing degrading in it. He dressed them.

One day he felt inclined to take his gun and go out by himself, although he never shot anything.

His wife met him on his return.

"Why didn't you take the children for a walk this morning?" she asked sharply and reproachfully.

"Because I didn't feel inclined to do so." "You didn't feel inclined? Do you think I want to work all day long in stable and barn? One ought to do *something* useful during the day, even if it does go against one's inclination."

"So as to pay for one's dinner, you mean?"

"If you like to put it that way! If I were a big man like you, I should be ashamed to be lying all day long on a sofa, doing nothing."

He really felt ashamed, and henceforth he established himself the children's nurse. He never failed in his duties. He saw no disgrace in it, yet he was unhappy. Something was wrong, somewhere, he thought, but his wife always managed to carry her point.

She sat in the office and interviewed inspector and overseer; she stood in the store-room and weighed out stores for the cottagers. Everybody who came on the estate asked for the mistress, nobody ever wanted to see the master.

One day he took the children past a field in which cattle were grazing. He wanted to show them the cows and cautiously took them up to the grazing herd. All at once a black head, raised above the backs of the other animals, stared at the visitors, bellowing softly.

The lawyer picked up the children and ran back to the fence as hard as he could. He threw them over and tried to jump it himself, but was caught on the top. Noticing some women on the other side, he shouted: "The bull! the bull!"

But the women merely laughed, and went to pull the children, whose clothes were covered with mud, out of the ditch.

"Don't you see the bull?" he screamed.

"It's no bull, sir," replied the eldest of the women, "the bull was killed a fortnight ago."

He came home, angry and ashamed and complained of the women to his wife. But she only laughed.

In the afternoon, as husband and wife were together in the drawing room, there was a knock at the door.

"Come in!" she called out.

One of the women who had witnessed the adventure with the bull came in, holding in her hand the lawyer's gold chain.

"I believe this belongs to you, M'm," she said hesitatingly.

Adeline looked first at the woman and then at her husband, who stared at the chain with wide-open eyes.

"No, it belongs to your master," she said, taking the proffered chain. "Thank you! Your master will give you something for finding it."

He was sitting there, pale and motionless.

"I have no money, ask my wife to give you something," he said, taking the necklet.

Adeline took a crown out of her big purse and handed it to the woman, who went away, apparently without understanding the scene.

"You might have spared me this humiliation!" he said, and his voice plainly betrayed the pain he felt.

"Are you not man enough to take the responsibility for your words and actions on your own shoulders? Are you ashamed to wear a present I gave you, while you expect me to wear yours? You're a coward! And you imagine yourself to be a man!"

Henceforth the poor lawyer had no peace. Wherever he went, he met grinning faces, and farm-laborers and maid-servants from the safe retreat of sheltered nooks, shouted "the bull! the bull!" whenever he went past.

Adeline had resolved to attend an auction and stay away for a week. She asked her husband to look after the servants in her absence.

On the first day the cook came and asked him for money for sugar and coffee. He gave it to her. Three days later she came again and asked him for the same thing. He expressed surprise at her having already spent what he had given her.

"I don't want it all for myself," she replied, "and mistress doesn't mind."

He gave her the money. But, wondering whether he had made a mistake, he opened his wife's account book and began to add up the columns.

He arrived at a strange result. When he had added up all the pounds for a month, he found it came to a lispound.

He continued checking her figures, and the result was everywhere the same. He took the principal ledger and found that, leaving the high figures out of the question, very stupid mistakes in the additions had been made. Evidently his wife knew nothing of denominate quantities or decimal fractions. This unheard of cheating of the servants must certainly lead to ruin.

His wife came home. After having listened to a detailed account of the auction, he cleared his throat, intending to tell his tale, but his wife anticipated his report:

"Well, and how did you get on with the servants?"

"Oh! very well, but I am certain that they cheat you."

"Cheat me!"

"Yes; for instance the amount spent on coffee and sugar is too large."

"How do you know?"

"I saw it in your account book."

"Indeed! You poked your nose into my books?"

"Poked my nose into your books? No, but I took it upon me to check your. . . ."

"What business was it of yours?"

"And I found that you keep books without having the slightest knowledge of denominate quantities or decimal fractions."

"What? You think I don't know?"

"No, you don't! And therefore the foundations of the establishment are shaky. Your book-keeping is all humbug, old girl!"

"My book-keeping concerns no one but myself."

"Incorrect book-keeping is an offence punishable by law; if you are not liable, then I am."

"The law? I care a fig for the law!"

"I daresay! But we shall get into its clutches, if not you, then most certainly I! And therefore I am going to be book-keeper in the future."

"We can engage a man to do it."

"No, that's not necessary! I have nothing else to do."

And that settled the matter.

But once the husband occupied the chair at the desk and the people came to see *him,* the wife lost all interest in farming and cattle-breeding.

A violent reaction set in; she no longer attended to the cows and calves, but remained in the house. There she sat, hatching fresh plots.

But the husband had regained a fresh hold on life. He took an eager interest in the estate and woke up the people. Now he held the reins; managed everything, gave orders and paid the bills.

One day his wife came into the office and asked him for a thousand crowns to buy a piano.

"What are you thinking of?" said the husband. "Just when we are going to re-build the stables! We haven't the means to buy a piano."

"What do you mean?" she replied. "Why haven't we got the means? Isn't my money sufficient?"

"Your money?"

"Yes, my money, my dowry."

"That has now become the property of the family."

"That is to say yours?"

"No, the family's. The family is a small community, the only one which possesses common property which, as a rule, is administered by the husband."

"Why should he administer it and not the wife?"

"Because he has more time to give to it, since he does not bear children."

"Why couldn't they administer it jointly?"

"For the same reason that a joint stock company has only one managing director. If the wife administered as well, the children would claim the same right, for it is their property, too."

"This is mere hair-splitting. I think it's hard that I should have to ask your permission to buy a piano out of my own money."

"It's no longer your money."

"But yours?"

"No, not mine either, but the family's. And you are wrong when you say that you 'have to ask for my permission'; it's merely wise that you should consult with the administrator as to whether the position of affairs warrants your spending such a large sum on a luxury."

"Do you call a piano a luxury?"

"A new piano, when there is an old one, must be termed a luxury. The position of our affairs is anything but satisfactory, and therefore it doesn't permit you to buy a new piano at present, but I, personally, can or will have nothing to say against it."

"An expenditure of a thousand crowns doesn't mean ruin."

"To incur a debt of a thousand crowns at the wrong time may be the first step towards ruin."

"All this means that you refuse to buy me a new piano?"

"No, I won't say that. The uncertain position of affairs. . . ."

"When, oh! when will the day dawn on which the wife will manage her own affairs and have no need to go begging to her husband?"

"When she works herself. A man, your father, has earned your money. The men have gained all the wealth there is in the world; therefore it is but just that a sister should inherit less than her brother, especially as the brother is born with the duty to provide for a woman, while the sister need not provide for a man. Do you understand?"

"And you call that justice? Can you honestly maintain that it is? Ought we not all to share and share alike?"

"No, not always. One ought to share according to circumstances and merit. The idler who lies in the grass and watches the mason building a house, should have a smaller share than the mason."

"Do you mean to insinuate that I am lazy?"

"H'm! I'd rather not say anything about that. But when I used to lie on the sofa, reading, you considered me a loafer, and I well remember that you said something to that effect in very plain language."

"But what am I to do?"

"Take the children out for walks."

"I'm not constituted to look after the children."

"But there was a time when I had to do it. Let me tell you that a woman who says that she is not constituted to look after children, isn't a woman. But that fact doesn't make a man of her, by any means. What is she, then?"

"Shame on you that you should speak like that of the mother of your children!"

"What does the world call a man who will have nothing to do with women? Isn't it something very ugly?"

"I won't hear another word!"

And she left him and locked herself into her room.

She fell ill. The doctor, the almighty man, who took over the care of the body when the priest lost the care of the soul, pronounced country air and solitude to be harmful.

They were obliged to return to town so that the wife could have proper medical treatment.

Town had a splendid effect on her health; the air of the slums gave color to her cheeks.

The lawyer practiced his profession and so husband and wife had found safety-valves for their temperaments which refused to blend.

His Servant

OR, DEBIT AND CREDIT

Mr. Blackwood was a wharfinger at Brooklyn and had married Miss Dankward, who brought him a dowry of modern ideas. To avoid seeing his beloved wife playing the part of his servant, Mr. Blackwood had taken rooms in a boarding house.

The wife, who had nothing whatever to do, spent the day in playing billiards and practicing the piano, and half the night in discussing Women's Rights and drinking whiskies and sodas.

The husband had a salary of five thousand dollars. He handed over his money regularly to his wife who took charge of it. She had, moreover, a dress allowance of five hundred dollars with which she did as she liked.

Then a baby arrived. A nurse was engaged who, for a hundred dollars, took upon her shoulders the sacred duties of the mother.

Two more children were born.

They grew up and the two eldest went to school. But Mrs. Blackwood was bored and had nothing with which to occupy her mind.

One morning she appeared at the breakfast table, slightly intoxicated.

The husband ventured to tell her that her behavior was unseemly.

She had hysterics and went to bed, and all the other ladies in the house called on her and brought her flowers.

"Why do you drink so much whisky?" asked her husband, as kindly as possible. "Is there anything which troubles you?"

"How could I be happy when my whole life is wasted!"

"What do you mean by wasted? You are the mother of three children and you might spend your time in educating them."

"I can't be bothered with children."

"Then you ought to be bothered with them! You would be benefiting the whole community and have a splendid object in life, a far more honorable one, for instance, than that of being a wharfinger."

"Yes, if I were free!"

"You are freer than I am. I am under your rule. You decide how my earnings are to be spent. You have five hundred dollars pin money to spend as you like; but I have no pin money. I have to make an application to the cash-box, in other words, to you, whenever I want to buy tobacco. Don't you think that you are freer than I am?"

She made no reply; she tried to think the question out.

The upshot of it was that they decided to have a home of their own. And they set up house-keeping.

"My dear friend," Mrs. Blackwood wrote a little later on to a friend of hers, "I am ill and tired to death. But I must go on suffering, for there is no solace for an unhappy woman who has no object in life. I will show the world that I am not the sort of woman who is content to live on her husband's bounty, and therefore I shall work myself to death. . . ."

On the first day she rose at nine o'clock and turned out her husband's room. Then she dismissed the cook and at eleven o'clock she went out to do the catering for the day.

When the husband came home at one o'clock, lunch was not ready. It was the maid's fault.

Mrs. Blackwood was dreadfully tired and in tears. The husband could not find it in his heart to complain. He ate a burned cutlet and went back to his work.

"Don't work so hard, darling," he said, as he was leaving.

In the evening his wife was so tired that she could not finish her work and went to bed at ten o'clock.

On the following morning, as Mr. Blackwood went into his wife's room to say good morning to her, he was amazed at her healthy complexion.

"Have you slept well?" he asked.

"Why do you ask?"

"Because you are looking so well."

"I — am — looking — well?"

"Yes, a little occupation seems to agree with you."

"A little occupation? You call it little? I should like to know what you would call much."

"Never mind, I didn't mean to annoy you."

"Yes, you did. You meant to imply that I wasn't working hard enough. And yet I turned out your room yesterday, just as if I were a house-maid, and stood in the kitchen like a cook. Can you deny that I am your servant?"

In going out the husband said to the maid:

"You had better get up at seven in future and do my room. Your mistress shouldn't have to do your work."

In the evening Mr. Blackwood came home in high spirits but his wife was angry with him.

"Why am I not to do your room?" she asked.

"Because I object to your being my servant."

"Why do you object?"

"The thought of it makes me unhappy."

"But it doesn't make you unhappy to think of me cooking your dinner and attending to your children?"

This remark set him thinking.

He pondered the question during the whole of his tram journey to Brooklyn.

When he came home in the evening, he had done a good deal of thinking.

"Now, listen to me, my love," he began, "I've thought a lot about your position in the house and, of course, I am far from wishing that you should be my servant. I think the best thing to do is this: You must look upon me as your boarder and I'll pay for myself. Then you'll be mistress in the house, and I'll pay you for my dinner."

"What do you mean?" asked his wife, a little uneasy.

"What I say. Let's pretend that you keep a boarding-house and that I'm your boarder. We'll only pretend it, of course."

"Very well! And what are you going to pay me?"

"Enough to prevent me from being under an obligation to you. It will improve my position, too, for then I shall not feel that I am kept out of kindness."

"Out of kindness?"

"Yes; you give me a dinner which is only half-cooked, and then you go on repeating that you are my servant, that is to say, that you are working yourself to death for me."

"What are you driving at?"

"Is three dollars a day enough for my board? Any boarding-house will take me for two."

"Three dollars ought to be plenty."

"Very well! Let's say a thousand dollars per annum. Here's the money in advance!"

He laid a bill on the table.

It was made out as follows:

Rent $500

Nurse's wages	$100
Cook's wages	$150
Wife's maintenance	$500
Wife's pin money	$500
Nurse's maintenance	$300
Cook's maintenance	$300
Children's maintenance	$700
Children's clothes	$500
Wood, light, assistance	$500
	$4,500

"Divide this sum by two, since we share expenses equally, that leaves 2025 dollars. Deduct my thousand dollars and give me 1025 dollars. If you have got the money by you, all the better."

"Share expenses equally?" was all the wife could say. "Do you expect me to pay you, then?"

"Yes, of course, if we are to be on a footing of equality. I pay for half of your and the children's support. Or do you want me to pay the whole? Very well, that would mean that I should have to pay you 4050 dollars plus 1000 dollars for my board. But I pay separately for rent, food, light, wood and servants' wages. What do I get for my three dollars a day for board? The preparation of the food? Nothing else but that for 4050 dollars? Now, if I subtract really half of this sum, that is to say, my share of the expenses, 2025 dollars, then the preparation of my food costs me 2025 dollars. But I have already paid the cook for doing it; how, then, can I be expected to pay 2025 dollars, plus 1000 dollars for food?"

"I don't know."

"Neither do I. But I know that I owe you nothing after paying for the whole of your support, the children's support and the servants' support; the servants who do your work, which, in your opinion, is equal, or superior, to mine. But even if your work should really be worth more, you must remember that you have another five hundred dollars in addition to the household expenses, while I have nothing."

"I repeat that I don't understand your figures!"

"Neither do I. Perhaps we had better abandon the idea of the boarding-house. Let's put down the debit and credit of the establishment. Here's the account, if you'd like to see it."

To Mrs. Blackwood for assistance in the house, and to Mrs. Blackwood's cook and nursemaid:

Rent and maintenance	$1000

Clothes	$500
Amusements	$100
Pin money (by cash)	$500
Her children's maintenance	$1200
Her children's education	$600
On account of the maids who do her work	$850
	$4570

Paid M. Blackwood, *Wharfinger*

"Oh! It's too bad of you to worry your wife with bills!"

"With counter-bills! And even that one you need not pay, for I pay all bills."

The wife crumpled up the paper.

"Am I to pay for your children's education, too?"

"No, I will, and I shall, and I will also pay for your children's education. You shall not pay one single farthing for mine. Is that being on a footing of equality? But I shall deduct the sum for the maintenance of my children and servants: then you will still have 2100 dollars for the assistance you give to my servants. Do you want anymore bills?"

She wanted no more; never again.

The Breadwinner

*H*e wakes up in the morning from evil dreams of bills which have become due and copy which has not been delivered. His hair is damp with cold perspiration, and his cheeks tremble as he dresses himself. He listens to the chirruping of the children in the next room and plunges his burning face into cold water. He drinks the coffee which he has made himself, so as not to disturb the nursery maid at the early hour of eight o'clock. Then he makes his bed, brushes his clothes, and sits down to write.

The fever attacks him, the fever which is to create hallucinations of rooms he has never seen, landscapes which never existed, people whose names cannot be found in the directory. He sits at his writing table in mortal anguish. His thoughts must be clear, pregnant and picturesque, his writing legible, the story dramatic; the interest must never abate, the metaphors must be striking, the dialogue brilliant. The faces of those automata, the public, whose brains he is to wind up, are grinning at him; the critics whose good-will he must enlist, stare at him through the spectacles of envy; he is haunted by the gloomy face of the publisher, which it is his task to brighten. He sees the jurymen sitting round the black table in the center of which lies a Bible; he hears the sound of the opening of prison doors behind which free-thinkers are suffering for the crime of having thought bold thoughts for the benefit of the sluggards; he listens to the noiseless footfall of the hotel porter who is coming with the bill. . . .

And all the while the fever is raging and his pen flies, flies over the paper without a moment's delay at the vision of publisher or jurymen, leaving in its track red lines as of congealed blood which slowly turn to black.

When he rises from his chair, after a couple of hours, he has only enough strength left to stumble across the room. He sinks down on his bed and lies there as if Death held him in his clutches. It is not invigorating sleep which has closed his eyes, but a stupor, a long fainting fit during which he remains conscious, tortured by the horrible thought that his strength is gone, his nervous system shattered, his brain empty.

A ring at the bell of the private hotel! *Voilà le facteur!* The mail has arrived.

He rouses himself and staggers out of his room. A pile of letters is handed to him. Proofs which must be read at once; a book from a young author, begging for a candid criticism: a paper containing a controversial article to which he must reply without delay, a request for a contribution to an almanac, an admonishing letter from his publisher. How can an invalid cope with it all?

In the meantime the children's nurse has got up and dressed the children, drunk the coffee made for her in the hotel kitchen, and eaten the rolls spread with honey which have been sent up for her. After breakfast she takes a stroll in the park.

At one o'clock the bell rings for luncheon. All the guests are assembled in the dining room. He, too, is there, sitting at the table by himself.

"Where is your wife?" he is asked on all sides.

"I don't know," he replies.

"What a brute!" is the comment of the ladies, who are still in their morning gowns.

The entrance of his wife interrupts the progress of the meal, and the hungry guests who have been punctual are kept waiting for the second course.

The ladies enquire anxiously whether his, wife has slept well and feels refreshed? Nobody asks him how he feels. There is no need to enquire.

"He looks like a corpse," says one of the ladies.

And she is right.

"Dissipation," says another.

But that is anything but true. He takes no part in the conversation, for he has nothing to say to these women. But his wife talks for two. While he swallows his food, his ears are made to listen to rich praise of all that is base, and vile abuse of all that is noble and good.

When luncheon is over he takes his wife aside.

"I wish you would send Louisa to the tailor's with my coat; a seam has come undone and I haven't the time to sew it up myself."

She makes no reply, but instead of sending the coat by Louisa, she takes it herself and walks to the village where the tailor lives.

In the garden she meets some of her emancipated friends who ask her where she is going.

She replies, truthfully enough, that she is going to the tailor's for her husband.

"Fancy sending her to the tailor's! And she allows him to treat her like a servant!"

"While he is lying on the bed, taking an after-dinner nap! A nice husband!"

It is quite true, he is taking an after dinner nap, for he is suffering from anaemia.

At three o'clock the postman rings again; he is expected to answer a letter from Berlin in German, one from Paris in French, and one from London in English.

His wife, who has returned from the tailor's and refreshed herself with a cognac, asks him whether he feels inclined to make an excursion with the children. No, he has letters to write.

When he has finished his letters, he goes out for a stroll before dinner. He is longing for somebody to talk to. But he is alone. He goes into the garden and looks for the children.

The stout nurse is sitting on a garden seat, reading Mrs. Leffler's *True Women* which his wife has lent her. The children are bored, they want to run about or go for a walk.

"Why don't you take the children for a walk, Louisa?" he asks.

"Mistress said it was too hot."

His wife's orders!

He calls to the children and walks with them towards the high road; suddenly he notices that their hands and faces are dirty and their boots in holes.

"Why are the children allowed to wear such boots?" he asks Louisa.

"Mistress said. . . ."

His wife said!

He goes for a walk by himself.

It is seven o'clock and dinner-time. The ladies have not yet returned to the hotel. The two first courses have been served when they arrive with flushed faces, talking and laughing loudly.

His wife and her friend are in high spirits and smell of cognac.

"What have you been doing with yourself all day, daddy?" she asks her husband.

"I went for a walk with the children."

"Wasn't Louisa there?"

"Oh! yes, but she was otherwise engaged."

"Well, I don't think it's too much to ask of a man to keep an eye on his own children," says the friend.

"No, of course not," answers the husband. "And therefore I scolded Louisa for allowing the children to run about with dirty faces and worn-out boots."

"I never come home but I am scolded," says the wife; "You spoil every little pleasure I have with your fault-finding."

And a tiny tear moistens her reddened eyelids. The friend and all the rest of the ladies cast indignant glances at the husband.

An attack is imminent and the friend sharpens her tongue.

"Has anybody here present read Luther's views on the right of a woman?"

"What right is that?" asks his wife.

"To look out for another partner if she is dissatisfied with the one she has."

There is a pause.

"A very risky doctrine as far as a woman's interests are concerned," says the husband, "for it follows that in similar circumstances a man is justified in doing the same thing. The latter happens much more frequently than the former."

"I don't understand what you mean," says the wife.

"That's neither Luther's fault nor mine," answers the husband. "Just as it is not necessarily the husband's fault if he doesn't get on with his wife. Possibly he would get on excellently with another woman."

A dead silence follows; the diners rise from their chairs.

The husband retires to his own room. His wife and her friend leave the dining room together and sit down in the pavilion.

"What brutality!" exclaims the friend. "How can you, a sensitive, intelligent woman, consent to be the servant of that selfish brute?"

"He has never understood me," sighs the wife. Her satisfaction in being able to pronounce these damning words is so great, that it drowns the memory of a reply which her husband has given her again and again:

"Do you imagine that your thoughts are so profound that I, a man with a subtle brain, am unable to fathom them? Has it never occurred to you that it may be your shallowness which prevents you from understanding me?"

He sits down in his room, alone. He suffers from remorse, as if he had struck his mother. But she struck the first blow; she has struck him blow after blow, for many years, and never once before has he retaliated.

This coarse, heartless, cynical woman, in whose keeping he confided his whole soul with all its thoughts and emotions, was conscious of his superiority, and therefore she humiliated him, dragged him down, pulled him by the hair, covered him with abuse. Was it a crime that he struck back when she publicly taunted him? Yes — he felt as guilty as if he had murdered his dearest friend.

The twilight of the warm summer night deepens and the moon rises.

The sound of music from the drawing room floats through his window. He goes into the garden and sits down under a walnut tree. Alone! The chords of the piano blend with the words of the song:

When the veil of night was drawn
And crowded earth, mysterious sea
Became one sweet, enchanted ground
For us, until the starless dawn
Dissolved the failing moon — then we
In one long ecstasy were bound.
Now, I, alone in silence and in pain
Weep for the ache of well-remembered bliss,
For you who never can return again,
For you, my spring time, for your love, your kiss.

He strolls through the garden and looks through the window. There she sits, his living poem, which he has composed for his own delight. She sings with tears in her voice. The ladies on the sofas look at one another significantly.

But behind the laurel bushes on a garden seat two men are sitting, smoking, and chatting. He can hear what they say.

"Nothing but the effect of the cognac."

"Yes, they say that she drinks."

"And blame the husband for it."

"That's a shame! She took to drinking in Julian's studio. She was going to be an artist, you know, but she didn't succeed. When they rejected her picture at the exhibition, she threw herself at the head of this poor devil and married him to hide her defeat."

"Yes, I know, and made his life a burden until he is but the shadow of his former self. They started with a home of their own in Paris, and he kept two maids for her; still she called herself his servant. Although she was mistress over everything, she insisted that she was but his slave She neglected the house, the servants robbed them right and left, and he saw their home threatened with ruin without being able to move a finger to avert it. She opposed every suggestion he made; if he wanted black, she wanted white. In this way she broke his will and shattered, his nerves. He broke up his home and took her to a boarding-house to save her the trouble of housekeeping and enable her to devote herself entirely to her art. But she won't touch a brush and goes out all day long with her friend. She has tried to come between him and his work, too, and drive him to drink, but she has not managed it; therefore she hates him, for he is the better of the two."

"But the husband must be a fool," remarks the other man.

"He is a fool wherever his wife is concerned, but he is no exception to the rule. They have been married for twelve years and he is still in love with her. The worst of it is that he is a strong man, who commanded the respect of Parliament and Press, is breaking up. I talked to him this morning; he is ill, to say the least."

"Yes; I heard that she tried to have him locked up in a asylum, and that her friend did everything in her power to assist her."

"And he works himself to death, so that she can enjoy herself."

"Do you know why she treats him so contemptuously? Because he cannot give her all the luxury she wants. 'A man who cannot give his wife all she wants,' she said the other day at dinner, 'ce n'est pas grand' chose.' I believe that she counted on his booming her as an artist. Unfortunately his political views prevent him from being on good terms with the leading papers, and, moreover, he has no friends in artistic circles; his interests lie elsewhere."

"I see; she wanted to make use of him for her own ends; when he resisted she threw him over; but he serves his purpose as a breadwinner."

Now, I, alone in silence and in pain,
Weep for the ache of well-remembered bliss. . . .

comes her voice from the drawing room.

"Bang!" the sound came from behind the walnut tree. It was followed by a snapping of branches and a crunching of sand.

The talkers jumped to their feet.

The body of a well-dressed man lay across the road, with his head against the leg of a chair.

The song stopped abruptly. The ladies rushed into the garden. The friend poured a few drops of eau de Cologne which she held in her hand, on the face of the prostrate man.

When she realized that it was no fainting fit, she started back. "Horrible!" she exclaimed, putting her hand up to her face.

The elder of the two men, who was stooping over; the dead body, looked up.

"Be silent, woman!" he exclaimed.

"What a brute!" said the friend.

The dead man's wife fainted, but was caught in the arms of her friend and tenderly nursed by the rest of the women.

"Send for a doctor!" shouted the elder of the two men. "Run!"

Nobody took any notice; everybody was busy with the unconscious wife.

"To bring such grief on his wife! Oh! what a man! What a man!" sobbed the friend.

"Has no one a thought for the dying man? All this' fuss because a woman has fainted! Give her some brandy, that will revive her!"

"The wretched man has deserved his fate!" said the friend emphatically.

"He indeed deserved a better fate than to fall into your, hands alive. Shame on you, woman, and all honor to the breadwinner!"

He let the hand of the dead man go and rose to his, feet.

"It's all over!" he said.

0 1341 1463856 9

CPSIA information can be obtained at www.ICGtesting.com
Printed in the USA
LVOW131836210613

`39728LV00004B/557/P

9 781606 643068